D0021550

BLIND BLOODHOUND JUSTICE

Also by Virginia Lanier

A Brace of Bloodhounds
The House on Bloodhound Lane
Death in Bloodhound Red

Virginia Lanier

HarperCollins*Publishers*

Designed by Liane F. Fuji

ISBN 0-06-017547-8

For my editor, Carolyn Marino . . . for everything

Acknowledgments

I want to thank the following people for their kindness in sharing their expertise with me:

Alyce Bohannon, Mobile, Alabama, for rescuing chapter 8 from the hungry jaws of my computer; Luci Zahray, Holland, Michigan, for the Neuticles article; Kathy Kincer, Teri Holbrook, Sabrina Wylly Klausman, Celia Coker, Cynthia Houston, and the Atlanta chapter of Sisters in Crime, and a Airedale named Aggie, for making my five days in Atlanta so special; Kathy Emery and the Mid-Tennessee Chapter of Sisters in Crime, Nashville, Tennessee, for my success at the Southern Festival of Books; Rhona McGuffee, Statenville, Georgia, Adult Protection Services Investigator; and Bruce Ludemann, Lockport, New York, for sharing an O. J. story.

Special thanks to William D. Tolhurst, Lockport, New York, for writing reference books that give me fresh ideas for search and rescue. Bill is a legend in handling and training bloodhounds and has spent over twenty years as a special deputy. He has an enviable record. Every trial backed by his bloodhound testimony has resulted in a conviction. He is the inventor of the scent machine that is mentioned in this book. All references herein about the machine and its capabilities are true.

My deepest gratitude to Lori Whitwam, Elk River, Minnesota, and Alyce Bohannon, Mobile, Alabama, for combing the library stacks and researching my next book while I was writing this one.

There is a big handsome bloodhound out there somewhere who was the first bloodhound I ever touched and who gave me the inspiration to write about the breed. He was sitting in the back of a red pickup truck in Hardee's parking lot in Jasper, Florida, in late March 1993. I don't know your name, Big Guy, but I bless the day I met you!

I am deeply in debt to J. Scott Cummins, a lawyer in Santa Barbara, California, who took the first step on the long road to getting Jo Beth and the bloodhounds on the small screen, and possibly a TV series. Whether this happens or not, Scott, I'll never forget your efforts. I thank you for being a loyal and committed fan.

I also want to thank Al Rojas, my publicist with HarperCollins, and Matthew Bialer, my agent with the William Morris Agency.

From the *Dunston County Daily Times*, February 5, 1965

NO LEADS ON LOCAL MURDER AND MISSING BABY

The police have no suspects in the murder-kidnapping that occurred at the home of Calvin Newton on Baker's Mill Road on January 15, three weeks ago, according to Sheriff Ron Callis.

Velma Mae Nichols, 18, nursemaid for both the Newton and Sirmons babies, was killed by a blow to the head. Both babies were missing when Calvin Newton, 37, a local lawyer, returned home.

Patricia Ann Newton, 6 months old, was found unharmed, in a back pew of All Souls Baptist Church on Fulton Road, less than two hours after the crime was discovered.

Loretta Lynn Sirmons, 7 months old, is still missing. Bryan Sirmons, 29, the baby's father, employed on the estate as a gardener, issued a personal appeal for his baby's safe return. "Please bring her back. She's all I have. Leave her somewhere safe and call someone. I beg you."

Sheriff Callis asked the entire community to search their memories of anyone seen between 2:00 and 7:00 P.M. on the afternoon of January 15, near the Newton estate or the vicinity of All Souls Church. "No matter how harmless or trivial it appeared, it should be reported. Please call 592-5555 and help us solve this crime," he said.

1

1995

A Cold and Windy Day

January 3, Tuesday, 4:00 P.M.

Hank Cribbs was sprawled on the couch with his shoes off, reading the *Dunston County Daily Times* and making an occasional comment. I was staring out the office window at the bleak view. Dull dormant grass almost blanketed with reddish-brown pine straw, a goodly amount of fallen pine cones, and wintering robins in equal proportions with clumps of gray Spanish moss scattered here and there by the wind. The sky was the color of slate. A brown and gray day which had gotten steadily colder since daybreak.

I was debating whether to brave the cold and help feed the animals, take a nap, or just sit there. I decided to sit. I turned my gaze on the Honorable Sheriff of Dunston County, Hank Cribbs, whose long lean frame was prone on my sofa. Being sheriff, he could dress as he pleased, but he always wore the full dress uniform, warm dark brown gabardine tailored to perfection. With black hair and dark hawk-like eyes, he looked good against the contrasting background of the oatmeal-colored, rough-textured fabric of the couch. I jerked my eyes up to the area of his head, now hidden by the newspaper.

"Don't you have something to do?"

I sounded grumpy. Eyeing his bod was disconcerting. I wasn't about to start *that* again.

He lowered the paper.

"I don't see you bustling around taking care of business. Am I keeping you from some important chores?"

"I'm bored," I admitted.

"Bored? You with nothing to do? I'm amazed."

"I have plenty to do, I just don't feel like doing anything. The weather is depressing. Do you know the radio said the low would be eighteen degrees in the morning?"

"Which means a lot of frozen well pumps and busted water pipes tomorrow. Some people prepare for light freezes and think they can survive the hard freezes by ignoring them."

I didn't bother to agree with such an obvious statement. He watched me for a few moments, sat up straight, then neatly folded the paper and laid it aside.

"Say pretty please with sugar on it, and I'll tell you an interesting tale."

"If it's about who's doing who, and which partner caught them, I'm not interested."

"You *are* in a foul mood if you don't want to hear some juicy gossip. How about a double murder? Does that sound more attractive?"

"Here?" I scoffed.

"Yep."

"Recently?"

I felt a flicker of interest.

"Nope, it happened thirty years ago this month."

I groaned. "You've been reading old closed files, *again*. Don't you have enough to do with current cases? Maybe we only need a part-time sheriff if solving crime around here doesn't fill your days. I'll bring it up at the next county commissioners' meeting."

"I looked up the old file this morning, but only because I met the murderer for the first time yesterday afternoon."

He sat there looking smug.

"Aha!" I drawled in my best peach-dripping accent and smiled back at him, acknowledging that he had hooked me fair and square. I sat up straighter, turned my chair, and leaned my elbows on the desk. I was now all ears. "Is the story long and involved? Was it truly a double murder?" I sighed, and spoke before he had a chance to answer. "Wife and lover. Same ol' same ol', right?"

"Nope. Both were murdered, but he was only charged with second degree in the maid's death. They figured he shoved her when she tried to stop him. Hit her head on the concrete edge of the pool. Should have been felony manslaughter, but his lawyer didn't fight to get the charge reduced. It wouldn't have made any difference in his sentence, and he was probably sickened by the crime like everyone else. He didn't fight too hard, period. It happened during the commission of a double kidnapping. That's federal. In my estimation Samuel Debbs should have got the death penalty. He was lucky to have received life without parole."

"So why is he walking around breathing free air?"

"Medical parole. When the parole board is sure they're dying, they kick 'em loose. Heart condition. He looks like death warmed over. I bet he doesn't last a month."

"When you mentioned a maid, I smelled money. Which old family around here had all these exciting things happening thirty years ago and why haven't I ever heard any mention of these crimes?"

"Well, you were two, and I was seven. All the principals moved away soon after the trial and there wasn't any extended family. With no one around here to jog the memory, I guess everyone forgot."

"Let me guess. I bet the murderer swears he didn't do it and wants you to reopen the case and restore his good name before he kicks the bucket. Am I right?"

"The case needs a lot of time to tell, and you're only half right. He says he didn't do it, but didn't act concerned about whether I believed him or not, and he didn't mention that he wanted me to do anything about it. He was required to state his innocence, since he hasn't admitted his crime or given a judge his statement of guilt. It's the reason he had to report to my office within twenty-four hours of hitting town. His parole was conditional. He could have received an unconditional if he had given them the facts and owned up to his evil deeds."

"Are you going to do any work on it?"

"After thirty years?" He laughed. "No way. I just thought you might like to hear about it."

I held up a hand. I walked over and peered at the coffee left in the glass container. What was there had the consistency of sludge.

"I'll make a fresh pot."

I headed for the kitchen, and Bobby Lee sat up, stretched, and padded after me. In March, he'll turn two. He's a one-hundred-thirty-two-pound AKC-registered bloodhound. Twenty-nine inches to his shoulder, has a reddish-colored coat with a tiny bit of tan and white on his chest, and is an extremely handsome dog. He's also a champion mantrailer, my best canine friend, a permanent houseguest, and has been totally blind from birth.

Rudy, who was curled in a ball, raised his head to view our departure but was too lazy to get up and join us. He's a twenty-two-pound fat tomcat of indeterminate age who decided to move in a few years ago. His pelt is black as midnight and he has piercing bright green eyes. He's stubborn, spoiled, and tries to boss Bobby Lee and me around. When he doesn't get his way, he sulks. We let him get away with murder just to keep peace in the family.

In the kitchen I turned on the water and sat the Pyrex container beneath the stream. I tiptoed to the fridge, eased the door open, and stealthily slid two Chicken McNuggets from a Ziploc. Bobby Lee had kept perfect pace with me. I knew better, but it seemed he was able to sheath his toenails like Rudy. His passage was as soundless as mine. I had not bred a foolish bloodhound. He knew the treat would not materialize if Rudy appeared. He inhaled the McNuggets when I placed them under his nose. We crept back to the sink.

Bloodhounds are born hungry. They seem to crave food more often than other breeds. Now that Bobby Lee was a mature male, his weight had stabilized. He got plenty of exercise and wasn't overweight for his height and bone configuration. Rudy was. He had gained two pounds in the past year and was obese according to my vet, Harvey Gusman.

Bobby Lee and I entered the office. He went back to his place to the right of my desk chair to nap, and I made coffee. Hank was waiting patiently, hands loosely folded in his lap. I placed his coffee before him, took mine around the desk, and took a cautious sip.

Hank lit up, and I looked away from the enticing pattern of smoke curling upward toward the ceiling. I could smell the heady aroma from a distance of ten feet.

"The craving finally eased off some?"

"It's been three months, six days, five and a half hours," I answered, "but who's counting? And no, the craving hasn't eased off; I've just had a lot of practice trying to ignore it. No one who lives here smokes, which helps," I added pointedly.

"You want me to put it out?"

"Nope. Tell me about the murders."

I used up another chunk of my willpower. I couldn't avoid smokers. It would prove that I still had something to fear.

"Do you remember that big hunk of white brick out on Baker's Mill Road, the one that has the tall white fence around it? It's been boarded up for years."

"The haunted house?" I blurted. "The one where the baby cries at night?"

Damn, I could feel the color flooding my face. Hank was emitting knee-slapping laughter and I felt six years old, about the same age when I was first told the house was haunted. A playmate had scared the bejesus out of me.

"Enough already," I said with a sheepish scowl. "You brought back a childish memory. Proceed."

"It used to be known as the Newton estate," he said, suddenly sounding somber. "The owner's name was forgotten when the older kids started rumors about it being haunted. Maybe adults started the tale to keep their kids from trashing the place, who knows? We've been called out on several occasions in the past ten years that I've worked on the force when teenagers on a toot have decided to investigate. The burglar alarm is wired into the sheriff's department. We make a lot of noise on the way out there and no one is around when we arrive. We've really had very little vandalism, so in theory the ghost stories work."

I felt a cold draft on my back and shivered. "Is that where the murders took place?"

"Yep. Jo Beth, tell me, do you believe in coincidence? Yesterday afternoon, I receive a mandatory visit from a convicted murderer who served thirty years of a life sentence for two murders that occurred out there. This morning I received a phone call from a New York law firm informing me that the owner of the house is moving back next week. Coincidence? I don't think so. I want you to check it out for me. I want to know what's going on."

Hank gave me winsome smile. "Are you willing?"

2

Cold Scents Are Tough

January 3, Tuesday, 5:00 P.M.

"You lowdown conniving con man. You're setting me up! Of course the Great White Chief can't look foolish in front of his braves digging into thirty-year-old murders, no-siree! He just cons his trusty sidekick, Miss Patsy. Let her look stupid! Everyone knows she's always sticking her nose where it doesn't belong, right?"

I wasn't really angry at this point; the hyperbole was standard operating procedure. It galled me that he could predict my reaction so accurately and know I was panting for details. I would make him work for my help.

"Just remember to follow the rules," he stated. "You know you cut corners and bend the law. I want your promise you'll behave. You're not to embarrass the department or me. Do I have your word?"

His words were bad enough, but he had the audacity to shake his finger at me. Suddenly I was truly pissed.

"Follow the rules," I mimicked, "don't embarrass me. Why don't you take a flying leap at the closest wild bear!"

I propped my feet on the desk with a resounding thud, and glared at him through the vee of my athletic shoes.

He unfolded his frame and stood.

"I take it that you're not interested in reading the department's file I copied for you on the investigation? It's in my car."

"You can take your file, roll it into a tight cylinder, and insert it where the sun don't shine," I replied haughtily. "Get lost."

He made a dignified but hasty withdrawal. We go back a few years and he's learned to recognize my volatile nature. I have been known to throw things. I stared out the window at the encroaching blackness. First dark. A few minutes before all light was extinguished on the horizon and the long winter night began.

I felt the anger fading and sighed heavily. For a few weeks, almost two years ago, Hank and I were an item until we started gnawing on each another. Now we couldn't be in a room together an hour without drawing blood.

Drumming my fingers on the desk, I counted my blessings. My expansion plan was perking right along. We had seventy-three healthy dogs in the kennel undergoing various stages of training. I had a comfortable margin on advance orders to keep us in kibbles and vittles for months to come. The roof had been repaired and the bill was paid. Enough cash on hand that my heart didn't begin an erratic beat when the monthly statement arrived from the auditor. In fact, it showed we were actually making a few bucks lately. Did I want to risk the status quo by poking around in something that happened when I was two years old, wasting my time and energy on something past that I couldn't control or change?

God help me, I did. I reached for the phone.

"*Dunston County Daily Times.*"

Fred Stoker, the editor, was always there and usually answered day or night. He had been a friend of my father's, and now mine ever since I started the kennel. He insisted I call him Fred although he was approaching sixty-five.

"Hi, Fred, it's Jo Beth. How goes the war?"

"Which one? That mess in Bosnia or Miz Gertrude and Miz Thelma?"

"Are they at it again?"

"Still," he said cheerfully. "Miz Thelma insists on playing the piano at the weekly meeting of the Ladies Guild. Miz Gertrude says it knocks out her hearing aid and is now threatening to picket on the bank's parking lot. I can hardly wait until tomorrow at noon!"

"That would be worth seeing," I agreed.

"Especially since Miz Thelma swears she'll spray her with a water hose." We were both chuckling.

"Fred, I need a favor."

"Already done and waiting for you at the classified counter."

"What's waiting for me?"

"Copies of all the clips on the Newton murders. Aggie pulled them after lunch."

"Tee, hee," I responded, feeling asinine. "Who told you, as if I didn't know."

I knew, I just wanted to confirm it.

"Hank brought lunch. A rack of barbecued baby ribs and chili from Pete's Deli. He said you'd be needing them. Aggie said to keep in touch. She wants first dibs on any story."

"Tell Aggie 'for sure,' and thanks, Fred."

I swallowed my irritation. Hank had just saved me some time. I called Jasmine's extension. I had observed her return a few minutes ago.

"I have to run to town on an errand. How does chili from Pete's Deli sound?"

"Great, I'll bring sourdough rolls."

"At six."

"See ya."

I dialed Wayne Frazier's office extension. Donnie Ray Carver picked up on the first ring.

"Do you two have any plans for supper?"

"It's the first Tuesday of the month, Jo Beth. It's ladies' night at the speedway."

"How could I forget such an auspicious occasion," I remarked. "I couldn't tempt y'all with Pete's homemade chili and baby ribs?"

"We have to eat where the girls eat," Donnie Ray explained patiently. "That's when we look them over and decide who to pick up."

"How romantic," I said dryly. "Bundle up, it's cold out there. I'm curious. At what point do you mention your new truck?"

He laughed. "I start every sentence with, 'Have you seen my new truck?' Works like a charm."

"I don't doubt it. Have fun."

"Yes'em."

"Oh, did you turn on the heaters for the puppies and set the clock on the water-dish line?"

"Yes'em."

"See you in the morning."

Wayne is my kennel manager. He's been with me almost four years. He's hearing impaired. He and Donnie Ray live together in a garage apartment where Wayne and his mother, Rosie, lived before she married our fire chief and moved to a home of her own. I'm very lucky to have him.

I hired Donnie Ray right after he graduated from high school and he taught himself to be my videographer. He makes videos for my training seminars on all the different ways we school the bloodhounds. Search-and-rescue, drug searches, cadaver recovery, and suspected arson. He also records highlights of the weeklong seminars.

I know they'll both find someone one of these days, marry, and settle down. I'll do all that's possible to keep them here within my compound of fifteen fenced acres. They have become my family.

I'm fairly sure that Jasmine will remain. She had the best shot, in my humble opinion, nine months ago, to marry a wonderful person and be happy ever after. She didn't take it. Her Prince Charming finally gave up and transferred to a distant city. I stood helplessly on the sidelines and watched the dying romance. Lots of phone calls and letters, then just letters. Nothing the last three months and she never mentions him anymore.

I pulled on my heaviest jacket, a fleece-lined denim that I actually need about ten times in our short winter season, gloves, and a scarf. Picked up my purse and .32, and Bobby Lee beat me to the front door. I sometimes believe that he can read my mind. He sat alert and hopeful.

"Not tonight, Bobby Lee. It's too cold to have your window open. Be a good boy, and stay inside."

I hugged him. I knew without looking back that he would come through the cat door that was enlarged when he became a houseguest and would sit on the porch patiently waiting for my return, whether an hour, a month, or forever. A dog's devotion is unconditional and eternal.

I was nuking the chili when Jasmine arrived at six.

"In the kitchen," I called when I heard her knock. By then she was halfway through the office and I met her in the hall. I motioned her into the living room.

"Those rolls hot? Just put them on the coffee table. I lit a fire."

The living room is the least lived-in room of my house.

I have a front door that is seldom ever opened. I don't even have a drive leading to my small front stoop. Security was top priority when the house was built and still is. To my knowledge the front door has been used twice in the seven years I have lived here, and both of those times were emergencies. I only entertain in the living room when it's cold enough to build a fire. I'm very good with fireplaces. I think that's the reason I'm such a rotten cook. You just can't be perfect in everything.

I divided the quart container of chili into two dark red ceramic bowls on a tray, added a bottle of wine and a cold beer, and joined Jasmine. She had lit the candles, lowered the gas flames on the lamp sconces, and removed her coat.

We sat down on cushions with the coffee table between us. The firelight dancing in her crystal goblet caught my attention. Jasmine is a beautiful woman. I'm thirty-two, and she is five years younger, and I have an inch on her in height. Our hair is short and curly, but any similarity ends there. My hair is mousy brown, an uncontrollable riot of natural curls that frizz in high humidity, while her raven-black tresses artfully hug her scalp and compliment her long regal neck. She is African-American with skin one shade lighter than milk chocolate. I have a pale complexion. I don't tan and look like the girl next door after a bad night. It isn't her doing that I pale in comparison when we are together. I sighed. Sometimes life is not fair.

I just noticed that she was dressed to go out. She wore jeans and a sweater set in a beautiful delicate pink shade.

"Don't tell me you have a class tonight!"

"Neither rain nor . . ." She didn't finish, as she was concentrating on pouring her wine.

I popped the tab on my beer can and took a healthy swallow.

"You could shoot a cannon across the college's main parking lot tonight and not scratch a paint job," I commented. "Everyone stays home on a night like this. You're a glutton for punishment."

"First class of the new semester. I want to get a good seat."

"You'll have a lot of choices," I said with a smile.

We finished supper and she was on her second glass of wine.

I started to pour more wine in Jasmine's glass. She covered it quickly with her hand.

"If I drink another drop I'll end up dancing on the top of the professor's desk."

"To see that I would pay admission."

We carried everything back to the kitchen. I rinsed the dishes while Jasmine moved the coffee table. I told her the story that Hank had told me this morning.

"Thirty years ago," she marveled. "Now who's a glutton for punishment?"

I pointed to the folder of newspaper clippings and the other folder holding the copies of the police files.

"So how did you end up with the police files?"

"That skunk Hank tippytoed back onto the porch and left them by the office doorway. I tripped over them when I left to pick up the clippings and the chili."

"He just saved you a trip and the embarrassment of having to ask for them," she said, defending Hank.

In Jasmine's estimation, Hank can do no wrong. He rescued her from the streets eight years ago, and she idolizes him.

We gazed into the cozy flames licking over the seasoned oak that Wayne and Donnie Ray had cut at the end of last summer. I start with slivers of fat lighter, then pine, and add oak when it's drawing well. Now I added a handful of cedar chips and repositioned the screen. I never try to burn cypress; it brings bad luck. I have enough bad luck without tempting fate.

"Where are you going to start your investigation, by visiting the haunted house?" Jasmine asked. "If so, I hope you don't plan on asking me to tag along. I can't bear to watch scary movies. I turn my head when the music alerts me to coming horrors."

"I honestly don't know if there is anyplace to start. I'll read the files tonight. If I don't spot anything, maybe you'd take a crack at them. You might see something I miss."

Jasmine rose gracefully to her feet. "If I don't start moving I'll be too content to leave."

"Ditto," I added, pulling the glass doors together and closing off the fire. "If I read in here I'd wake up at midnight with a crick in my neck."

Bobby Lee and I followed her to the door.

I blew out the candles, checked the animal water dishes, and took the files to my desk. I started with the newspaper clippings. When the alarm at the gate alerted me to Jasmine's return I was well into the sheriff department's reports. I yawned, checked the doors and windows, reset the alarms, and went to bed.

3

Taking Care of Business

January 4, Wednesday, 7:45 A.M.

I stepped into the grooming room, holding the door momentarily for Bobby Lee. He was tethered to my side on his short lead. He and Rudy had returned just minutes ago from their early run. The cold morning was bracing and welcome to him, but made me feel like crawling back into bed and snuggling under the quilts. The warmth eased my shivers, which I'd acquired from the short stroll from the office across fifty feet of tarmac to reach this heated haven.

From March through October I bitch about the hot weather, copious flows of sweat, heat rash, and insects. From November through February, our short winter season, I bitch about the cold. The weather gauge on the back porch was dead bang on 18 degrees when I attached Bobby Lee to my side. Another record low would be broken. My Deep South blood was thin enough for me to live in the Mojave Desert, but most assuredly, I'd bitch about the temperature if I tried.

No one was in sight. Wayne and Donnie Ray were probably in Wayne's office, which was on the other side of the common room. I heard a low murmur and tracked the sound to the weighing room. Harvey Gusman, my veterinarian, was having a one-sided conversation with O'Henry, our resident patriarch.

Harvey was leaning over, talking to the prone bloodhound on the examination table.

"All of us get it eventually, old boy, some sooner than others."

"What's wrong with O'Henry?" I asked.

Anxiety made my voice rise. Harvey jumped like he had been shot.

"God, Jo Beth! You shouldn't sneak up on people," he said, whirling to face me.

"Sorry. Is he sick?"

He turned back to the table, working a hind leg back and forth on his patient.

"His arthritis pains him on cold days like this. It's to be expected, he's ten years old. I gave him a shot of cortisone."

"Does it ease the pain?"

"He gets aspirin for pain and cortisone for flexibility and to relieve the swelling. He's ten, Jo Beth."

"He's the first bloodhound I bought," I said, "and the second dog I ever owned."

I walked over and rubbed O'Henry's flank, caressing his ear. His tail thumped against the table.

"He sired most of my champions. He's been retired two years now, and looks great. What's the answer?"

His silence alarmed me.

"According to you, we should start taking our old people with arthritis and other pains and put them to sleep, too? Some live twenty years with pain and have productive lives!"

"People can tell us where and how much they hurt and have the right to make choices about their treatment. Dogs can't." He sounded sad.

He was standing beside me. I did a very strange thing. I took a step and placed my head against his chest. He put his arms around me and just held me.

Harvey is 5'9", just two inches taller than I am, so my head fit nicely. He's thirty-eight, single, and came down from New York when I had an opening for a veterinarian.

I own the small animal clinic and land where he practices. It faces Highway 301 and is only a few hundred feet away from my kennel as the crow flies. Going out my curving driveway and turning right, it's a longer commute. He pays rent on the building, equipment, and the small cottage, which is fifty feet behind where he works. He bills me for taking care of my animals' medical needs and I credit the amount against his rental payments. About half the time, I owe him money.

We haven't been close at all. He doesn't socialize with us here at the kennel and I know very little about him. He is very good with the animals, but neither of us has harbored any thoughts of romance, I'm sure. I pulled away slowly.

"Forgive me, I was upset. This isn't like me."

"Everyone needs the warmth of physical contact in their lives. How long has it been for you?"

"Ten months and change," I said.

"You have me beat by three months," he admitted with a small grimace. "We're too picky, awfully unlucky with love, or don't take the time to look in the right places, or maybe all of the above."

"Thanks for the hug," I replied briefly, backing away. "You will tell me when it's time?" I was looking at O'Henry.

"I'll tell you," he replied.

I felt awkward. I beat a hasty retreat.

Wayne and Donnie Ray were in Wayne's office when I opened the door from the common room. They were both intent on what they were doing and didn't notice my approach. Wayne could not hear my approach. He's deaf and doesn't speak. He couldn't see me because his head was behind his computer screen. He was romping on the keys doing what I dreaded the most, entering data into the maws of the computer from hell. He's very fast and efficient.

My computer in my office and I are barely on speaking terms. I finally mastered the basics several months after he switched all our hand-kept records, but I'm still far from an expert. After four years of fiddling with its nonsense, at least once a month I'm embarrassed when Wayne has to come over and correct some blunder. Any object that has an electrical plug or requires batteries is automatically cursed when I touch it. Gremlins pop up from out of nowhere.

Wayne is a clean-cut youth, now twenty-one, with a large open face loaded with freckles. He has brown hair and intelligence shines out of his dark brown eyes. He went on search-and-rescues with me for almost a year until I found out that he could not pull the trigger on the gun I had trained him to shoot, even if his life depended on it. I made him my kennel manager. He's worth twice what I pay him.

Donnie Ray has thin blond hair and pale green eyes. He's tough, feisty, and always striving for snappy comebacks. I call him Spielberg, just to bring him down a peg. Right now he was editing the trainee's film that he shot of the last seminar. He was bending over the splicing machine and had the sound wide open on the television, even though he was using earphones.

I walked to the audio dial and turned it down to a more acceptable level and waved a hand over the computer to catch Wayne's eye.

"What's cooking?" I signed to Wayne and told Donnie Ray, "Hi."

"All dogs including the puppies are fed. We boiled enough eggs for two days. Now we're waiting 'till it warms up a little more before we start training with the six-month group. They're too frisky to pay attention and concentrate when they're jumping around trying to stay warm," Wayne signed.

His moving hands were almost a blur. I can speak and sign different messages at the same time, but much slower than doing them separately. Try quickly patting your head with your left hand while rubbing your stomach in a circular motion with the right, and you'll get my drift.

"I'm editing my epic of last week," Donnie Ray said, completely serious. "It's the best I've ever done!"

"You say that every time," I told him wryly, and signed to Wayne. "Want some help in transferring the adults to the exercise area?"

"Nah, Donnie and I can take two at a time. Be done in no time."

This was music to my ears. I had no desire to restrain frisky bloodhounds, most of them weighing over 100 pounds in 18-degree temperatures. I didn't need that much exercise this morning.

"You could peel the sixteen dozen eggs," Donnie Ray suggested hopefully.

"Oh, I couldn't, Donnie Ray," I answered sweetly. "That would leave you nothing to do between exercising the adults and feeding the puppies their second meal."

I signed the same message so Wayne could know what I said. Wayne makes only two distinct sounds. One is his laugh, which sounds like a crow cawing, and the other is a one-syllable grunt. He was laughing when I closed the door behind me.

Donnie Ray wasn't kidding when he mentioned peeling sixteen dozen eggs. It's a two-day supply. Bloodhounds can't digest raw eggs properly. We boil, shuck, and mix them into the dogs' meals with a dozen other nutritious additives. We use more eggs than the city of Atlanta. I bet I've peeled a trillion or so, but not today.

Walking through the common room, I heard the first gate alarm. I hesitated at the doorway until I recognized the car and occupants. It was Windell Grantham and Cora Simmons, two of the day trainers. A couple of months ago they began arriving together in his car. Windell is sixty-eight, a retired druggist, and Cora is fifty-seven. She worked at the post office for years and finally quit, citing varicose veins, but the real reason was bad dreams. She confided in me when I expressed doubts of her ability to work with large animals.

Her dreams had scared her. Usually she was nude, and squirting her boring customers with a water pistol. When the toy in her dreams turned into a real gun, she decided to get out before she started stacking up bodies at her stamp window.

Jasmine and I had spent some time speculating if they were indulging in hanky-panky between the sheets. Cora was shorter than Windell, but she outweighed him by twenty pounds. They both were healthy and tanned from working outdoors with the animals. We decided they were. We also knew that it was none of our business and wished them well. I waved and called a good morning to them on my trip across the courtyard.

In the office I hung up my coat, poured my fourth cup of coffee, and stood over the air duct to warm my keister.

What to do first? I decided to pay the convicted but unrepentant murderer-kidnapper, Samuel Debbs, a visit. The search-and-rescue van had my name, the kennel's address, and a large black outlined silhouette of a bloodhound. It also had a gold-colored replica of the Sheriff's Department of Dunston County's seal, plus their name in large black letters.

I didn't want their name, flashers, or siren on my trucks, but the county commissioners had put a stipulation in the contract I signed, so I was stuck with them. Today they might come in handy. Debbs would think twice about refusing to talk to me. I glanced down at Bobby Lee, who was sitting quietly enjoying the warm air caressing his ears. I decided to take an extra incentive with me. People are reluctant to argue with someone who has a bloodhound attached to her belt.

"You wanna go, sport?"

Bobby Lee did his jiggle dance without his paws leaving the floor while I phoned Jasmine to tell her where I was going, and to buzz if she needed me. Out at the van, I watched him load up and felt a little sad.

His impulsive puppy rashness of leaping into space on blind faith alone had disappeared. After I opened the door and positioned him, I gave the order to load up. He felt the dimensions with his nose, then planted his feet in the opening, and only then sprang lightly up. He scoped out the seat with his nose before sitting and getting comfortable. He was an adult now, and moved accordingly. I really didn't believe he was growing afraid.

I think he has matured and knows that jumping into space when you're blind can sometimes be hazardous to your health. I hooked his harness to the bolt on the floor, and slipped his shoulder strap over his chest and under his belly. I left it loose enough he could lean against the door panel.

"The window will remain closed," I told him firmly.

4

To Believe or Not to Believe

January 4, Wednesday, 9:00 A.M.

On the way to Miz Charlotte's rooming house I stopped at Dunkin' Donuts and had a large thermos filled with coffee and chose six assorted pastries. The temperature was rising quickly. The white cover of frost was disappearing from the high ground where the sun shone. Thin skims of ice on shallow water would soon be gone, but the deeper ditches in shade would remain frozen all day.

I parked in front of a large house with a wide front porch holding eight wicker rocking chairs. The building was less than six feet from the sidewalk. A thick hedge of holly, neatly trimmed to below porch level, glowed with bright red berries and dark green waxy sharp-pointed leaves. The white clapboards were five years past due for two coats of enamel, but the wide front steps gleamed with fresh paint.

The town banker had built this house in 1870. Miz Charlotte's grandfather. Her father gambled away the proceeds of the bank and took early retirement. The story goes that Miz Charlotte, being an only child and a dutiful daughter, turned down a score of suitors and had cared for her father until his death. At that time, she was a thirty-year-old spinster with a mortgage and no income. She took in boarders. Now, fifty years later, she still ran her rooming house, was active in the United Daughters of the Confederacy, and looked to me like what I thought Barbie's great-grandmother should resemble.

I hooked Bobby Lee to my belt and rang the doorbell. It didn't seem possible that with only eight boarders she would net enough to pay the taxes on this establishment, much less show a profit. I knew there were eight boarders because of the eight rocking chairs on the porch. Miz Charlotte was precise in everything she did.

I also knew I didn't know the whole story because of my lawyer, Wade Bennett's, response when I once mentioned that she might be in need—maybe we should try to help. He had laughed, then quickly tried to cover the gaffe—he was also *her* lawyer—with nonsense about her frugality and Southern pride. I sensed a mystery, but I behaved myself and hadn't tried to pry. Maybe she and her housekeeper, Gloria, had a small pot patch in the backyard, where her flowers and kitchen garden were nestled among the trees and shrubs. Nah . . . maybe not.

Gloria, a fat black woman of indeterminate age, opened the door, grinned at me, and suddenly saw Bobby Lee.

"Lord, Miz Jo Beth, you can't be bringing that monster dog in this house!" Her eyes were wide with fright.

"Who is it, Gloria?" I heard Miz Charlotte's light voice clearly.

"Miz Jo Beth with a great big dog! She can't be wanting him to come in!"

Gloria sounded indignant now, along with being scared. She was holding the door, barring my entrance.

"Nonsense! Open the door at once, Gloria. The dog is quite harmless." Miz Charlotte's words were crisp and bounced with a perky snap.

Gloria continued to grumble, but the message was inaudible. She reluctantly moved backward, keeping the door between her and Bobby Lee.

"Come in, my dear Jo Beth, come in! My, the wind is cold today! What a lovely dog! Is he the one you brought to the nursing home when I was recovering from my foolish fall?"

She didn't mention that her foolish fall had been a major stroke that paralyzed her left side and almost took her to Glory and that it was five years in the past. Her only concession to the event was a cane, which she used gracefully, trying to conceal a slight limp. O'Henry had been the visiting bloodhound at the convalescent home. She had been delighted with meeting him and was now acting as if it had occurred yesterday.

"No, ma'am. I'd like to introduce Bobby Lee."

As she gracefully bent to shake, I gently squeezed Bobby Lee's right shoulder. He sat, and placed his right paw out in space. She caressed the paw with a delighted laugh and ran her hand over his head and down his ears.

"Such a beautiful dog. Am I correct in assuming he was named after our illustrious General Lee?"

"Yes, ma'am."

"Come along to the parlor, chile, we have much to talk about. Gloria, mind your manners! Quit hiding behind the door and bring coffee and some of those cinnamon buns you baked this morning."

I inwardly groaned. It was too early for a social call, but I hadn't stated my business soon enough. Miz Charlotte assumed I had come to visit and to tell her different would only embarrass her. I followed her meekly into the parlor.

Gloria brought in a silver coffee service on a tray loaded with buns and frosted lemon drop cake squares. I drank coffee and sampled the goodies. If I refrained from nourishment for the rest of the day I could offset my caloric intake.

We chatted for several minutes until I thought I could work Debbs into the conversation. "Miz Charlotte, I understand you have a new boarder, Samuel Debbs?"

"Yes, dear, I know how news travels in this town of ours, but I'm surprised you know about him so soon. I phoned Sheriff Cribbs and he confirmed that Mr. Debbs had served his time and was out on parole. I know he committed a terrible, terrible crime, but I firmly believe that when one pays for one's mistakes, one should be given another chance. The poor man has had to live for thirty years with the death of two people on his conscience. I told him if he obeyed the house rules he would be welcome here. I've invited him to attend services with me on Sunday at All Souls. He's not well at all. Heart trouble, you know. Were you worried about me and Gloria living in the same house with a convicted murderer?"

"Not you, Miz Charlotte," I said honestly. "Gloria might make a wide circle to walk around him, but not you. You have Christian charity and a forgiving heart."

She beamed upon hearing my praise but started moving her head back and forth.

"Don't make me into a saint, my dear. Thirty years ago, when the crime was committed, if others had wanted to hang him, I would have furnished the rope. I find that age brings some wisdom, and time does heal most wounds."

"I want to question him," I said, being blunt. "Do you think he'll agree to talk to me?"

"May I ask why?" she said softly, her head slightly cocked toward me, her eyes on mine.

"He has always proclaimed his innocence, that he didn't murder anyone. I want to try to find out if he's telling the truth."

"I now have to ask the same question again. Why?" She smiled to remove any rancor from her request.

"Because I can't solve my own problem, I have an insatiable desire to tackle other people's dilemmas and try to find solutions. I know it sounds crazy—"

"Not at all," she said, laughing with delight. "I knew you were like me, Jo Beth. If you could have known me fifty years ago, I was so much like you! My friends said I was the nosiest busybody in town, poking in other people's secrets, always trying to get everybody together after an argument."

I nodded, smiled, and sat still. I was trying not to squirm with impatience.

"Well," she said briskly, rising to her feet. "I'll just go see if he's up and about. He was at the breakfast table this morning at seven. I didn't hear him leave, but I can't keep up with everyone. Will you wait here?"

"Yes, ma'am, and thank you."

"It's nothing," she said, waving a hand in a dismissive gesture. She walked out of the room with her spine ramrod straight.

From her blue-tinted gray curls to her tiny feet, she looked like a miniature model for fifties chic. Her sweater set of pale blue must have came from the preteen rack at Penny's. The single strand of pearls appeared to be real, along with the matching earrings. Her makeup was light, only a tinge of blush on each cheekbone, a hint of lip gloss. A dark gray A-line wool skirt, hose, and sensible black lace-up shoes.

Her face had lines and wrinkles, but if I squinted through my lashes, she could pass for fifty. If I was lucky enough to make eighty I would like to look exactly like her. Impossible. My hem would droop, my hair would kink, and I'd drool like a bloodhound.

Bobby Lee lay curled at my side. He raised his head when he heard them coming down the stairs. He turned his face toward the door. It still surprised me at times when I saw him acting exactly like a sighted dog. He straightened in a sitting position. Rump and two front paws planted on the rug, and moved a couple of inches closer to my right leg.

Apprehension? That was unusual. Maybe he felt vibes, or some smell emanated from Debbs. I was so engrossed at his strange behavior I didn't see them enter. When I glanced up they were both inside the room. Miz Charlotte was looking at me and Debbs was eyeing Bobby Lee. I stood and so did Bobby Lee.

"Jo Beth Sidden, Samuel Debbs." Her words were matter-of-fact, not a formal introduction expected from a Southern gentlewoman. I didn't offer my hand.

Debbs was a shrunken, much older version of his press description of 1965. He was gray. His hair, his skin, and his demeanor—the hunched shoulders—all a dreary gray. Thirty years in Atlanta Federal Prison. I guess he had earned his pallor, but I refused to feel sorry for him. His 5'9" at twenty-seven now looked to be my height. Could a person shrink two inches in thirty years? At fifty-seven, he looked the same age as Miz Charlotte, with Miz Charlotte winning in physical appearance comparison.

"Will you go with me and answer some questions?"

I was trying to go for an all-business approach, but it came out brusque and uncompromising. I didn't try to correct it.

He gave an indifferent shrug and remained silent. I took it as acceptance and shook Miz Charlotte's hand.

"Thank you for the coffee. You've been most helpful."

"Please come back anytime. I enjoyed visiting with you."

She walked us to the front door.

Debbs hadn't taken his eyes off Bobby Lee for a second. I didn't go into my usual patter to relieve his mind. I didn't reassure him that Bobby Lee was harmless and was not an attack-trained bloodhound. There is no such animal, but if he believed it, amen. I wanted to dominate this interview.

At the van, I turned back my seat and gave Bobby Lee the command to load up. He carefully sniffed the opening and raised his front paws, lifted his body, and landed a little clumsy, for him. I frowned. I removed his lead and hooked his harness to the center ring directly behind the two front seats. I gave him a caress and sat in the driver's seat. Only then did I turn to face Debbs while I was fastening my seat belt.

He copied my movements and struggled into the shoulder harness, looking at mine to see how to connect it. I pulled on my driving gloves and remained silent until he finished.

When he finally looked my way, I gave him a grim smile.

"You have served your time. You can't be sent back to prison for anything you reveal to me regarding the crimes of thirty years ago. Is that perfectly clear, and do you believe it, or would you rather hear it spoken by a lawyer, or see it in writing?"

"I believe it."

"The sheriff of this county is a friend of mine. I have agreed to ask some questions, poke around a little, read the trial transcripts, et cetera. I want you to know up front that there is no chance in hell that I can make a startling discovery or find the 'real killer,' or anything of that nature. I'm a plodder, not a miracle worker. I'm going into this with serious reservations about your innocence, and frankly, I couldn't care less regardless of how the ball bounces. Is this clear?"

"Yes."

He certainly wasn't chatty.

"Here comes the kicker. For the sake of hearing your story, I'm going to suspend my disbelief of your innocence and take your word as gospel. That won't mean I believe you, I just want to hear you out. But here's the bottom line. If I even get an inkling that you are lying, shining me on, even a hint of perfidy, I'm history. In fact, we both could save a lot of time and effort if you want to say a simple 'Yes, I did it.' I wouldn't ever repeat it and I can go home and train some dogs."

"What's perfidy?"

I blinked. I peered at him and tried for a neutral expression.

"Betrayal of trust, treachery."

"I read a lot in prison, but I never run across that one."

"Well?"

I looked into his dark gray eyes set deep in his gray face and thought I saw a glint of humor. I could easily be mistaken. I wasn't as discerning as I liked to think I was.

"I didn't do it."

Simple, but far from compelling. I let out the breath that I had unconsciously been holding. So be it. Let the game begin.

5

In One Ear and Out the Other

January 4, Wednesday, 10:00 A.M.

I drove to the park and stopped in front of the Main Street landing. No one was around. Misty vapors were still rising from the water being warmer than the air currents. Debbs carried the blanket. He placed it on the built-in wooden bench that ran down one side of the wooden dock. I unhooked Bobby Lee's lead and slipped it over a boat cleat.

Opening the sack from the donut shop, I poured two cups of coffee and stirred powdered cream into mine. Debbs picked up a pastry and looked at the dark water of the creek flowing past.

"Nice spot."

His voice sounded rusty with disuse. I guess he hadn't been well-liked in prison and hadn't had too many opportunities to communicate. Baby-killers are ostracized and reviled by all other prisoners. They are the lowest of the low. I was surprised that he had stayed alive for thirty years locked inside with murderers and rapists. I didn't want to think about how hard his hard time had been. If you accepted his tenet of innocence, it would seem to me unbearable.

"They give you a bad time up there?"

"The first fifteen was spent trying to survive. After that, they mostly forgot about me, and eased up. There's quite a turnover in prisoners and guards. I guess the reason for me being there got lost in the shuffle."

"If you didn't do the crime, it must have been hell to do the time. Weren't you angry?"

"I was too busy trying to stay alive. The anger faded away after seven years or so. It was unproductive. I learned to control my feelings and made the best of a bad situation."

"Admirable, I guess, but I hold a grudge when I'm misjudged. If I were you, I'd be yelling for revenge."

"Against who?" He even managed a small smile. "Or is it against whom?"

"Beats me," I said with a grin.

I took my portable tape recorder from my jacket, pulled off my right glove, and turned it on to Record. Enough chitchat. Time to go to work.

"Mind?"

"Nope."

Bobby Lee was sawing logs. His snores could only be heard sporadically over the faint rush of water flowing through the pilings under our feet. He was stretched out in the sun and I watched the rise and fall of his rib cage. The temperature had risen. It must already be 40 degrees. It was pleasant sitting here. Not too cold, and hardly any wind.

"Did you ever form a theory about who did it?"

"When I first went inside, I was almost illiterate. I quit school when I was fourteen to help Pa on the farm. I didn't attempt to read about the crime for several years. I taught myself to read and understand what I was reading on microfiche of the back issues of the *Atlanta Constitution.* I never got to read any local coverage. The stories dried up after my trial.

"By then I had decided that one man had planned to snatch the banker's baby. When he tried it, he must have been shocked to find two babies in that yard. Not knowing which was which, he took both. The nursemaid tried to stop him and was killed. Two babies were not in his plan. He left one in the church. After he read that he had kept the wrong child, he murdered it, and faded into obscurity. He'll never be found. He's probably living worry-free in Kansas or Maine."

His scenario fit most of the facts, and he had let a trace of bitterness appear in his voice when he uttered the last sentence. He was almost convincing, but it was now my turn. I decided to throw some rocks.

"You think he wasn't a local?"

"I think he was on the bum. Planned a fast snatch for ransom and loused up."

"Why do you think he set you up, burying the shirt behind the hovel where you were staying, and the body of the child twenty yards farther back in the bush?"

"I don't think he even knew who I was. I had just arrived three days before. He lived there in the Bottom. He wanted a suspect, and there was several men living there in the transit camp. He probably did it on the way to his abode after dropping off the other child at the church."

"Ah, but that doesn't make sense," I replied. "First, it's four miles from the Newton estate to the church, then three miles from the church to the Bottom. How many of the transients who lived in the Bottom had a car in 1965?"

"I didn't, but it sure didn't keep them from convicting me. It was one of my best arguments to them when they were questioning me. How could I walk four miles out there, carry two babies another four miles, leave one in the church and walk three miles with the other on the way back?"

"What was their answer?"

"They had several. One said that I had a stolen a car. Another said my accomplice had the car and took off afterwards and was long gone before I was a suspect. The sheriff said I was young and healthy and could've easily have hiked the distance. I made the mistake of laughing in his face."

"What happened?"

"I doubt if you've ever seen one, but back in 1965 they carried small, leather-wrapped billy clubs. The handle was flexible, so they could pound on your head without too much effort. The sheriff used his on me."

"What made you laugh? You knew you were a suspect in a double homicide."

"I was drunk as a skunk. I was a drunk from the time I was twenty until the day I was arrested. After Ma died, Pa kicked me out. He had put up with my drinking for her sake. I was arrested a month after the kidnapping. I had only been in town for three days. I had let down my guard, knowing that they couldn't pin it on me because I wasn't even in town when it happened."

"Couldn't you prove it?"

"I couldn't remember the name on the logging truck that I hitched a ride with from Waycross, much less where I was and what I was doing a month before that. I had been a drunk for seven years at that point. Looking through a bottle does not improve your memory."

I didn't comment on his statement. I still had points I wanted to make.

"Back to your version of events. You said the murderer wanted to point the authorities to the Bottom. If the man lived there, that would have been a stupid move. There were miles and miles of inhabitable acreage around then. Even the estate had several square miles of land. Why didn't he bury the dead child there? Or anywhere but where he lived. No, I think you're wrong about the killer residing in the Bottom, and now established in a faraway state. I believe he was a local, and if, in the interim, he hasn't died, I think he still lives here."

"Does this mean you believe me?"

I picked my words carefully.

"I formed a *preliminary* opinion about an hour after I read your files. At this point, I haven't heard anything that makes me think I'm barking up the wrong tree."

"You lost me."

He sounded a tad disappointed. Tough.

"It's still a tossup," I explained. "Uh-oh."

Debbs turned to see what was causing my concern. A city police unit was stopped directly behind my van. Two patrolmen were walking towards the dock.

"Stay seated. Don't open your mouth unless you're asked a direct question. Don't react to any insult directed at you, or me. And don't forget to say yes sir and no sir. Got it?"

"Got it," he answered quietly.

I slipped the tape recorder in my pocket and stood.

Casually I hooked Bobby Lee's lead to my belt. I was standing with my back to them, gazing out over the water, when they stopped in front of Debbs.

"Lord a mercy, gal, is this the best you can dig up to screw? Let's have your name, boy."

Patrolman Andy Carpenter had spoken. Loudmouth good ol' boy and my ex-husband Bubba's drinking buddy. The other cop, Floyd Graham, was a spitting image of his partner. Both of their waists had increased a good ten inches since high school and playing football on the same team with Bubba. They wore their gun belts pushed down low to accommodate their beer bellies.

"Samuel Debbs, sir," Debbs answered, sounding humble. He removed his knit cap and clutched it in his lap.

"Let's see some identification, boy," barked Floyd.

I knew I'd only make it worse if I opened my mouth. I bit back a retort and held onto my temper. Debbs had been rousted by felons and guards alike for the past thirty years. One more time wouldn't kill him. Then I remembered his bad heart. It might. I couldn't just stand here and take a chance that these chauvinistic pigs might mess him up because they hated my guts. I took a deep breath, turned around, and stepped in front of Debbs.

"Back off," I said sharply.

They both gaped at me. Floyd gave me a savage grin.

"You're impeding a police officer who is checking out a suspicious stranger. You may be the sheriff's snatch, but he doesn't run the police department in this here town. Now step out of the way before I am forced to move you."

Andy was grinning from ear to ear. He was looking forward to pawing me during the action he was sure would follow within the next minute. I saw movement at the edge of my vision. I couldn't chance breaking eye contact with Floyd. I could only hope whoever it was would be a solid citizen, preferably the mayor.

"How about Chief Justice Constance Dalby?" My lips curled in contempt. "Does that name ring any bells? You can't have forgotten how she took down Sheriff Carlson for me sometime back. I'll make both of you a promise. Touch me or Debbs and she'll fry your ass."

"I think you're all mouth, cunt," Floyd countered.

"Try me."

I risked a quick peek behind them. Mr. Mac, Charles Mac Donald, an ex-county commissioner and admired icon of Southern correctness, was patiently waiting just out of hearing range. He wouldn't dream of interrupting our conversation. I have always maintained that I would rather be lucky than rich. I threw up a hand to signal a genuine display of pleasure.

"Mr. Mac, please join us!"

Floyd and Andy turned their heads to check. Floyd spoke under his breath as he watched Mac Donald's dignified approach.

"You got it coming, bitch. We owe you for Bubba."

"Can't wait," I shot back.

Both of them started towards him, briefly touching their caps. I heard mumbled greetings. Then the cops left.

"Get up and go to the van," I told Debbs softly. "Nod, smile, and keep walking."

I watched him follow my orders.

"Mr. Mac, you're a sight for sore eyes! How are you?"

"I'm very glad that my morning constitutional was delayed by the cold weather. How may I help you?"

"You already have," I said, laughing. "It seems that you arrived in the nick of time, like the cavalry."

"I sensed that. My hearing is not what it used to be, but I can still read body language. They were in a very combative stance. Perhaps I should speak to Chief Ballard?"

"Thank you, but no. Please don't. The modern Southern woman prefers to fight her own battles. It makes her stronger."

"Pity. I'm old-fashioned enough that it pains me when I see women not treated with respect." He smiled. "And opening their own doors."

"You may still open doors for me. I'm not a purist."

"I see that you still follow some of the arcane Southern code. I gather that your companion couldn't be introduced?"

Bless his heart, his curiosity was just as strong as mine was.

"I didn't want to embarrass you by introducing you to a convicted baby killer and kidnapper. I thought you might have known or been friends of the Newtons."

"That was Debbs?" He glanced towards the van. "I heard he was back in town. I did know Calvin and Celeste. She died in childbirth, and he died a year later. We were acquaintances, not close friends. I might have surprised you, my dear, if you had presented Mr. Debbs."

"Oh?" Now I was curious.

"I have always held reservations about his guilt. The arrest was precipitous, and also timely. The evidence was all circumstantial."

"You're saying you *might* have shaken hands with him?"

"We'll never know now, will we?"

6

If It Walks Like a Duck . . .

January 4, Wednesday, 11:30 A.M.

Driving Debbs back to Miz Charlotte's rooming house, I took a different and more scenic route. We traveled most of the way in silence before he opened his mouth.

"Who's Bubba?"

"My ex, Buford Ray Sidden Junior. I married him when I was eighteen and fresh out of high school. I have lived to regret it. I divorced him three years later while he was in prison. First week he was released, he tried to break every bone in my body with a baseball bat. He succeeded with quite a few. Since then, his main goal in life is to catch me and finish the job. He stalks me when he's out of prison. He's been through those revolving doors several times in the past eleven years. My abiding principle is to keep breathing and stay out of his reach."

"Those two lawmen are friends of his?"

"Oh yes, they played on the same high school football team. They're also staunch drinking buddies."

"You dating the sheriff?"

I felt my ears burning. Those two sorry excuses for manhood had aired most of my dirty linen in a very short time. I felt it was none of his business, but I was digging into his past, so I guess he felt entitled to probe into mine.

"We dated for a short time. Now we're friends."

Sometimes, I amended, but didn't say so. I waited for more questions, but none were forthcoming.

I pulled to the curb.

He hesitated.

"What do I call you?"

"Jo Beth will be fine. Which do you prefer, Debbs or Samuel?"

His expression didn't change when I omitted the courtesy title of Mister.

"Sam will do."

"Right. I'll call first if I need to speak with you again."

He climbed out. I glanced in the rearview mirror. He stood on the sidewalk watching me as I pulled away.

Jasmine and I were eating lunch. She'd stopped me in the courtyard and invited me to share a beef pot pie that she had made from a leftover roast.

"Delicious. You'll have to give me your recipe," I told her while forking up the last bite.

"Whatever for? You never cook!"

"Well, when I retire, I plan to become domestic. Wayne and Donnie Ray will have wives, but you'll need someone to feed you. I'm collecting recipes towards that day."

"Sure you are," she said sardonically. "It's hard trying to picture you in an apron puttering around in a kitchen wearing bedroom slippers. It's your turn to make supper. What are we having?"

"I've been saving this treat for a special occasion. Joe down at the Deli has put in a new line of pizza. Deep dish, with five special toppings!"

"We're gonna turn into a pizza." She moaned, "We eat pizza three times a week!"

"You're just spoiled by Rosie's care packages and Miz Jansee's cooking during seminar week. You know we gain at least two pounds every time she opens the common room kitchen. Eating takeout in between her weeks of cooking is the only way to control our waistlines."

"You're strange, Jo Beth," she said, shaking her head.

We cleared the table and poured fresh coffee. I told her the events of the morning.

"Now that you've met him, do you believe him?"

"One minute I do, and the next minute I don't. Let's just say I'm straddling the fence right now, not knowing which way to jump."

Jasmine frowned. "I can't seem to line up the way it happened. Let me start, and you correct me if I'm wrong on any of it."

"I'm all ears," I said.

"Back in January of 1965, Calvin Newton was a thirty-seven-year-old lawyer. He inherited serious money from his parents, had been married to a woman in ill health who died in childbirth the previous July. She had a daughter named—"

"Patricia Ann," I said.

Jasmine had reached for the files on the table.

"Patricia Ann, who was six months old. Isn't it strange that both men had daughters so close in age, and neither had wives or any other close relatives?"

"Strange in what way?"

"You know what I mean. Everybody here in this town has oodles of brothers and sisters, aunts and uncles, and cousins galore."

"Well, think on it," I said grimacing. "Here I am, no near and dear in sight, and you were an only child and have no kin. Is that weird?"

"We're both weird and an exception to the rule. Back to the crime. Calvin Newton hired Velma Mae Nichols, a black girl of eighteen, to be a live-in nanny."

"A young African-American woman," I corrected.

"She was black and I'm black. Will you knock it off and let me continue?"

"Sorry."

"Calvin Newton employed another woman, older and white, who cleaned house, shopped, et cetera, but she wasn't working the day of the kidnapping, right?"

"Correct."

"Newton also had a live-in gardener, Bryan Sirmons, who was twenty-nine years old, lived in the estate's cottage, and had a seven-month-old daughter, Loretta Lynn. His wife ran away with her bowling buddy when the baby was six weeks old. What a name to hang on a kid, Loretta Lynn!"

"She was a rising star in Nashville in 'sixty-five. Everyone loved her," I explained.

"You're the country music fan, not me," she said. "Anyway, Bryan Sirmons was having trouble finding and keeping someone to watch his baby girl while he worked. So Calvin Newton volunteered the services of Velma Mae, his daughter's nanny, during Sirmons's working hours. They had just started this arrangement shortly before the kidnapping?"

"Yep, Velma Mae had only been taking care of both of the babies for less than a week. This fact looms large in the investigators' reports. It's the reason that they think both babies were taken," I added. "He didn't know which was which."

"Now comes the day of the kidnapping. It's sometime in the early afternoon. Velma Mae had both babies lying on a blanket in the sun near the swimming pool. Someone—obviously the kidnapper—slipped in, took the babies, and Velma Mae intervened."

"This is where they started guessing," I injected. "They couldn't prove their theory. It's all conjecture with no eyewitness, other than the babies. 'Course, they thought Debbs could tell them if he admitted he was there, which he never did."

"Somehow, Velma Mae was pushed or knocked down, striking her head on the edge of the pool apron, and the blow killed her."

"I have my own version of events. Surely the would-be kidnapper had some kind of plan. Maybe he hid behind some shrubbery a week before and checked out the nanny's routine. Possibly she sometimes went to the house for a minute, leaving the child alone. However, when she went inside this day, he ran over and discovered two babies. He didn't know which was the right one, so he grabbed up both of them. Maybe she came back too soon, or saw him through the window. She ran out and tried to help the children, and died. You can't plan on a person accidentally dying. Her death was not in the plan."

"You still think it was a local? If it was, she could easily have recognized him. Maybe that's why he killed her."

"I think he would have considered the possibility of her seeing him. He must have been wearing something to disguise his features, a hat with a scarf pulled up, or a stocking over his head. Who knows?"

"Which means you think Debbs *didn't* do it," Jasmine replied, pouncing on my answer.

"I'm leaning that way, just don't paint me into a corner on this one. I'm still not completely convinced."

"Okay, the man is now a murderer and has two babies, in a town where everybody usually knows everyone they meet on the streets, even recognizing a lot of their cars. How did he get from the mansion to the church, drop off a baby, and disappear without someone spotting him?"

"He was shot full of luck," I said. "He took an enormous chance when he carried the baby that far to leave it where it would be safe and soon be found."

"I agree," Jasmine added. "Now the poser. He made a quick decision on which child to keep, and he chose the wrong little girl. I guess he had used up all of his luck by this time. But," she said, eyes glittering, "why didn't he attempt to collect ransom on the child he had after going to so much trouble, instead of killing her?"

"He could have," I said, rubbing my temples. "Newton was willing to pay for her return. He liked Sirmons a lot. They had become friends during the three-year period that he employed him. He also felt guilty that his money had made his daughter a target and Sirmons's child was missing because of it, plus the death of the nanny. He made several public pleas to the kidnapper, promising to pay without the authorities' knowledge."

"Then why didn't the kidnapper try to collect? I know you have decided why he didn't. I'm just dying to hear what *you* think happened."

"You disagree," I uttered, finally catching on. "Let's hear what you think."

"No," she said, shaking a finger. "I want to hear yours again, so I can shoot it down. Proceed."

"I see. Well, I could be dead wrong. I believe the local was afraid to get involved again. After all, he had pulled it off with being bold and having some good luck. Now it was different. He was a murderer, plus a kidnapper. If they trapped him in his attempt to secure ransom, he could face the electric chair."

I saw she was ready to start debating, but I held up a hand for silence.

"I'm not quite finished. Also, I think the second baby died during the period between the snatch and leaving the other child at the church."

"What? Where did this come from? That's not what you said earlier, when you were giving me your capsule version of events!"

"I'm entitled to change my mind."

"You?" She sounded skeptical. "You're the last one to admit you're wrong."

"Not so," I returned with an earnest expression.

"There's something you haven't told me," she accused.

"I might have left out a related fact from this morning's events."

"I know that's right! 'Fess up!"

"When I drove Debbs home, I went back a longer, different route. You could actually say I detoured a little."

"Where?" She was impatient.

"I went on Baker's Mill Road."

"That's miles out of—"

Her mouth fell open with surprise.

"You drove him by the Newton place? Why?"

"I wanted to see his reaction. There was nothing, not a flicker of recognition. There were two trucks sitting at the gate waiting for someone to let them in. A telephone truck and a large Bekins van. It was obvious that people are moving in. He didn't bat an eyelash."

"One, he's been in prison for thirty years." Jasmine counted as she turned down one finger. "He's learned to conceal facial expressions, to show a stoic front. Two, maybe he didn't know they had moved out right after his trial."

"I don't care if he's been incarcerated for fifty years, he would have shown something by just recognizing the place. And yes, he knew the place was not lived in by the family for years. Hank told him yesterday afternoon. Debbs had requested Hank to pass on the fact for him that he was in town and would be willing to meet with the father of the dead child, if he so desired. Then to see the place and evidence that someone was moving in, well—I rest my case."

"If you're correct, and the kidnapper was local, shouldn't he have known which tyke was worth the ransom?"

"Not necessarily," I replied. "What if he was Velma Mae's boyfriend, a teenager like her? She could have had her accident before identifying the target."

"That's reaching," Jasmine returned with a frown.

"Just supposing."

"Let's leave the identity of the perp for a moment, and continue. A month passes. No sign of the child. No clues. They search everywhere and find nothing. Then an anonymous phone call comes into the sheriff's office. The mystery caller says a homeless man in the Bottom was acting strange, and had been observed burying something directly behind his shack."

"Thirty years ago," I corrected, "they were called bums or vagrants.

The homeless title came along later. This is one of the reasons that I believe the child was not abducted by Debbs. A child in a vagrants' camp would have stood out like a sore thumb then. Now whole families, including babies, are on the road."

"Whatever he was called, what did they find first, after a search for a spot that had recently been dug up?"

Jasmine was leafing through the report.

"A filthy undershirt," I supplied.

"Covered with blood?" Jasmine eyed me.

"Where would blood come from?" I was acting innocent. "The nanny hit her head and died from the trauma. There may have been some blood, but none was apparent on the dirty material. The baby was strangled. No blood there."

"Then why was it buried?" She pushed the question through clenched teeth, trying not to lose her temper.

"To implicate Debbs, and to make them continue to dig, is my read," I answered.

"Then they found the grave, near where the undershirt was buried."

"It took them three more days. The child was farther back in the woods, in a deeper hole. They spent two days grilling all the men in the Bottom."

"What made them believe it was Debbs?" Jasmine asked.

"The report doesn't spell it out. My guess is, the others could prove where they were during the period the child was kidnapped. Debbs couldn't. And after all," I added with sarcasm, "the grave was in a direct line behind his temporary shelter from the elements. They needed a killer, and he was handy."

"Your version has a lot of smoke and mirrors," she said, sounding unconvinced.

"I'll be happy to listen to yours," I replied politely.

The phone chirped.

"Saved by the bell," Jasmine said with good humor.

I suppose she was having second thoughts about her take on the situation. I know I sure was.

"Just a minute, Hank, she's right here."

Jasmine passed me the phone.

"What's up?" I inquired.

"You've got a call out, Jo Beth." Hank sounded angry. "It's a doozie. Two armed men just knocked over The Trading Post, bound and gagged Alec Salter and his wife, May Belle, and left them in the walk-in freezer."

7

Decisions, Decisions

January 4, Wednesday, 1:15 P.M.

By the time Jasmine and I arrived at The Trading Post, the EMTs were loading Mr. Alec and Miz May Belle in separate ambulances. I didn't see Hank anywhere. There were enough official vehicles in the parking lot to form a parade down Main Street.

The afternoon was balmy. I was in my airtight rescue suit, partially unzipped to let in some of the breeze. The temperature was in the fifties, and if you stayed in the sunshine, short sleeves felt good. I glanced up at the almost denuded limbs of the ancient sycamores that lined the left side of the property. A few stubborn yellow and brown leaves still clung to branches, but all the rest were blown against the sagging wire fence, or moving across the frost-nipped grass in spurts from the eight-to-ten-mile wind.

I was unloading Bobby Lee when Deputy John Stinger walked up.

"Need any help?" He briefly touched his cap in greeting.

"If I remember correctly, Deputy, the last time we met you were pretty apprehensive about Marjorie. Got over your fear of bloodhounds?"

"I was under a lot of pressure then. You were searching for my pot patch," he said with a smirk.

"Don't get sassy with me, Deputy. I trust you didn't plant this year?"

"I gave you my word, or don't you believe me?"

"Stringer, I'm standing six feet away from you, and can easily pick up the smell of stale marijuana smoke from your clothing. The sheriff doesn't smell the weed as often as I do, or maybe his nose isn't as good as mine, but you're heading for the unemployment line. I don't believe in giving a dumb ass a second chance."

"Wait a minute here," he croaked, sounding both startled and alarmed. "I promised not to plant anymore, and I haven't! I told you I couldn't promise to quit smoking it, but I told you I wouldn't smoke on duty, and I haven't. Honest! Today is my day off. I was called in for this robbery, they needed extra hands. Give me a break, Miz Jo Beth, I haven't gone back on my word."

Stringer didn't know it, but I certainly wasn't going to tell Hank that I had lied like a rug last year when he asked me to check and see if he was growing. I had covered for Stringer because Hank didn't need a dirty deputy just after he became sheriff. To admit now that I had lied would make him even more distrustful of me.

I gave a theatrical sigh. "I hope I'm not making a mistake here," I said reluctantly.

"Thanks, Miz Jo Beth. You won't regret it."

He took off looking subdued.

Jasmine approached. Bobby Lee greeted a frisky Miz Melanie by smelling both ends while she reciprocated.

"What's wrong with the deputy?" Jasmine was gazing at his retreating back.

"We were having a discussion about obedience training," I deadpanned.

"Talked to Hank yet?"

"Let's go find him," I suggested.

Hank came out of the front entrance before we reached the sidewalk. John Fray, a Georgia Bureau of Investigation agent, in charge of the Waycross office, accompanied him.

"Oh shit," I murmured.

"Behave!" Jasmine admonished me under her breath.

I arranged my face into a neutral mask.

Hank nodded at Jasmine and me. I gave Fray a small, insincere smile.

"Ladies," said Fray.

"What can you tell us?" I directed both my voice and gaze towards Hank.

Agent Fray and I did not get along. We clashed each time we met. He thought he was King-Of-All-He-Surveyed. I couldn't stand him. He strutted like a peacock, dished out orders to everyone, and generally made an ass out of himself.

"The Salters have to be thawed out, the EMTs didn't see any wounds. Both were semiconscious when we arrived, very dazed, and couldn't answer any questions. We don't know how long they were in the freezer. The two men wore ski masks. They took Miz May Belle's car. Left a car here that was stolen in Waycross last night."

"How many witnesses?" I asked.

"One," Hank replied.

"Who?" I heard his uncertainty. If he didn't like the only witness, I knew I wouldn't either.

"Miz Catherine. She walked up as Miz May Belle's car was pulling off the parking lot."

"Chatty Cathy?" I groaned. "Say it isn't so! Ol' Lady Pickett?" I was hoping I had misheard the name.

"You got it." Hank sounded defeated.

"She's obviously senile and decrepit," Fray said harshly. "She needs a keeper!"

"Watch your mouth, Fray," I said angrily. "She may be senile, but she's far from decrepit, and she has a whole town of keepers! She's *ours*. *We* can comment, *outsiders* can't!"

"Just a minute—" Fray sputtered.

Hank stepped quickly between us, grabbing my shoulder to turn me away while talking loudly to drown out Fray.

"Why don't you go inside, Jo Beth, and see if you can get any more information out of her?"

He walked me a safe distance away before he stopped.

"Way to go, pal. Just keep poking him with a sharp stick, and one of these days he's gonna strike. Mind your manners."

"He's impossible," I muttered sulkily. "What's he doing here?"

"He was in the office when the call came in and wanted to tag along. I'm stuck with him and you've just riled the hell out of him. Thanks a heap."

"Sorry. He rubs me the wrong way."

"Me too," he admitted with a brief smile, "but I can't tell him off. You gonna behave?"

"I'll try."

"Go talk to Miz Catherine."

I found her sitting in a rocking chair pulled up close to the large gas heater in the middle of the main room of The Trading Post. In trying to draw out some additional facts from her, I came up empty. She talked nonstop for twenty minutes while she played with Bobby Lee's ears. She had seen the ski masks but they hadn't rung any warning bells to her; she didn't yet realize the store had been robbed. She had called Hank because Alec and May Belle hadn't came out of the back room to wait on her, and she needed a potato for her supper.

I gave up and hugged her neck.

I glanced around the store and remembered what fun it had been, as a child, to look over the merchandise, piled higher than we could reach. The Salters had welcomed us and treated us with respect. A dozen kids could ramble up and down the narrow aisles, picking up objects and inspecting them without getting bawled out or thrown out of the store. They had seemed ancient when I was a child. They must now be in their eighties. I hadn't been here for a long time, and I now regretted not visiting them. I might not have a chance to see them behind the counter again.

Bobby Lee and I went back out into the sunlight. Hank looked at me and raised an inquiring brow. I shook my head, walking past him and Fray. I joined Jasmine, who was peering into the stolen car's interior. She was standing near the driver's door.

"Is this all we got?" she asked.

"This is it." We both stared at the red late-model sedan. "If it was stolen last night, I hope the creeps spent the night in here tossing and turning, rubbing their scent all over. If not, the dogs might scent trail back to the owner in Waycross," I remarked idly.

"Waycross is sixty miles away. I surely hope not," Jasmine replied.

"Let's collect scent samples and give it a whirl. Nothing ventured, nothing gained."

We went back to the vans to pick up our backpacks. We pulled out square pads of sterilized gauze individually wrapped, a pair of thin rubber gloves, and a pint-sized Ziploc.

I first rubbed the pad lightly over the steering wheel and the driver's seat, wearing the gloves. She held open a Ziploc while I stored it inside. Then I held one for her while she took a scent sample from the passenger's seat.

Hank and Fray walked over just as we finished.

"What kind of car did Miz May Belle drive?" I asked Hank.

"A blue Saturn. Couple of years old."

I couldn't distinguish a Saturn from a Ford until I got close enough to read their names, but I nodded my head sagely. If Bobby Lee started to approach a fairly new blue compact, I would know we had a strike.

Fray emitted a raspy chuckle. "That little piece of material is all you got? You won't find squat."

"Really?" I voiced politely. "When did you become an expert on bloodhounds?"

"Just common horse sense. I've watched the sheriff's dogs work in Waycross. You need an object that's permeated with the perp's scent, something that's been worn several times, like a cap or a jacket. Even with those, the dogs can easily lose the scent."

"This isn't Waycross, and these aren't just dogs. They're purebred bloodhounds and expertly trained with the correct credentials and with several finds that have been proven in court. They're heads above those flea-bitten half-breed mutts that Waycross tries to train."

I was being sweeter than pie. Butter wouldn't melt on my tongue. Fray's eyes narrowed. He recognized a challenge when he heard one. He reached for his wallet and pulled out a twenty.

"Care to put your money where your mouth is?"

"Oh, I wouldn't want to take your twenty," I said with a slow drawl.

"I didn't think so." He was actually smiling.

I reached into my inside chest pocket, flipped open my wallet, and pulled out five twenties.

"Let's don't talk trash. Make it a hundred," I countered crisply.

Fray glanced into his wallet and riffled the bills with his thumb. He counted out four more twenties.

"Hand them to Hank. We'll let him hold the stakes."

"Don't you trust me?" he asked, trying to sound like one of the boys.

"Not as far as I can throw you," I answered nicely as I strolled away.

Jasmine caught up to me when I stopped at the double doors of the store.

"That was a foolish bet," she said softly.

I held up a hand. "I know, I know. I shouldn't have done it, but it felt so damn good at the time. My guy and your gal will just have to come through for us."

"We hope," she qualified.

"Let's get started."

We returned to the car. Jasmine stood back and let me start Bobby Lee first. I knelt in front of him, pulled out my bag of deer jerky, and placed two pieces on my glove. I held my hand under his nose while I whispered.

"This is business, Bobby Lee, we're working."

The jerky that I fed him was the signal that he was to track. His tail became animated and his lower body moved with the rhythm. He was doing his jiggle dance of happiness. He loved the hunt.

I held the small square of gauze under his nose with the bag only cracked open. I didn't want to remove it and plant my scent there. He lowered his head and began the search, working in a tight figure eight pattern with his nose just above the ground. I played out the long lead and kept him from tripping on it when he would suddenly decide to turn. His sweeps began to get larger, from eight to ten feet apart. I felt a sinking feeling in my gut. He didn't seem to be having any success.

After a few passes and just before I could present the pad again to reinforce his scent memory, he paused momentarily—lifting his face to the breeze—put his nose down, and charged across the parking lot as if he were being chased by a hungry alligator. The hunt was on.

8

It's Not a Perfect World

January 4, Wednesday, 4:00 P.M.

Under clear hot sunshine and a lessening breeze, Bobby Lee and I had hoofed a good two miles. After a short halt for water and to catch my breath, we were back to picking them up and putting them down on the tarmac of Highway 301.

Our caravan was strung out over several hundred feet. In front of us Deputy Stringer was in the unit fifty yards ahead, straddling the yellow line and barely moving. He was matching our forward progress, driving slowly and forcing all oncoming traffic to slow and pull over; most drivers came to a complete halt to gawk.

His activated flashers were adequate, even in bright sunshine. I had listened to the *whoop-whoop* of the siren until the last break. I had Hank to tell him to knock it off; I was ready to yank my hair out from the monotonous repetitive refrain. The blessed silence was soothing to my brow. The aspirins I had swallowed earlier were helping.

Hank's unit was several yards behind us, with Fray lounging beside him. Deputy Tom Selph was driving my van. Tom was not what you expected to see in a deputy sheriff. He was short, slim, and wiry. His pale skin and thick glasses made him look like a shoe salesman, not a macho officer called to a robbery in progress. He raised half-breeds of

Rhodesian Ridgebacks and Bluetick hounds. He wanted Bobby Lee so bad he wouldn't take no for an answer. After viewing Bobby Lee's sightless tracking skills at four months old, Tom had set out on a quest of ownership. His last offer had been a thousand. I had laughed and said, "Not even if you threw in a new Porsche." This morning he had upped the ante to two thousand. I had only smiled.

Jasmine brought up the rear of the procession in her van. When the road curved, I could see a long line of impatient drivers behind her. Some were wising up and turning onto the crossroads to find a different route to their destination.

My right shoulder muscles were tightening up. When locked onto a viable scent, Bobby Lee went full out. I swear my right arm felt six inches longer than my left. I was applying a constant restraining hold on the lead, trying to maintain a reasonable pace for both of us, especially for me. Good bloodhounds will trail till they drop. Of course I wouldn't allow that to happen. Anyway, it would probably be me that dropped first.

I was already worried about the shock of the rough-surfaced pavement on the pads of Bobby Lee's feet. I had inspected them on our water break. At the first sign of a limp, or pad splitting, I would pull him off the scent. This was not a life-or-death scent trail. I would put our health on the line to save a human life, but not just to apprehend a couple of felons. It was less than a mile before the side roads stopped feeding off this main drag. Then, with more distance between turnoffs, I could use the tactic of "leapfrogging," which meant that Bobby Lee and I would get to ride between intersections.

Striding along behind this drooling miracle of fur, hide, and muscle, I felt awed at his great ability to pull one scent out of the ozone that had traveled several feet above his nose at speeds of fifty miles per hour or more hours ago, recognize it, and follow it mile after mile. I'm a take-charge person, as people so often tell me. Some even have the nerve to say I'm bossy and opinionated. But following behind Bobby Lee, trying to get him to slow down, I'm second string, and feel very humble when I see him doing what is impossible for all humans and most other beasts.

He surprised me when he turned right off the highway. It was unexpected, and I stumbled along for several feet hauling backward automatically before I realized we had lost our escort in front. A quick glance back to the left confirmed that Deputy Stringer was still slowly creeping along, unaware that he had no followers.

I had been studying Bobby Lee, not looking up at our surroundings. The small lane crossed a wide deep ditch, and turned into the large parking lot of Porky's. I had no idea that we had traveled so far so quickly. Porky's is a large barn-like structure that houses a bar and grill and a very spacious dance hall. Beer and wine only. It is *the* place to go on Friday and Saturday nights. Good barbecue and ribs. Three bouncers to break up the many fights on weekends. The stomping grounds for singles. Pickup heaven. Redneck territory, all others enter at your own risk.

Even on a Wednesday afternoon, I saw a double row of parked trucks and cars. We were an acre away from the building when I put on the brakes. I had spotted two vehicles that would qualify. Blue and compact. By the time I had Bobby Lee halted and sitting on his haunches, clearly showing impatience at being called off the hunt, Hank was by my side.

"You looked as if you were just going to stroll into the front door," he announced without taking his eyes off the scene before us.

"No, I was just wondering if you had put out an APB on the car."

"Of course I did!" He sounded a mite testy. "I have four deputies on patrol and two here with me. With twelve on the roster I don't have an inexhaustible supply! They can't be everywhere!" His voice had risen with each word.

"Where are the police when you need them," I murmured, doing a little tweaking.

"The city boys couldn't find their ass with a road map," he stated shortly.

He turned to get his men into position. I could hear Stringer backing up on the highway.

"You done?" He knew I was, this was a courtesy.

"Done, done, and done," I answered sweetly. "We will wait breathlessly on the sideline."

"Wouldn't like to block this exit with your vans, would you?" His voice held a smile.

"You have got to be kidding! My insurance agent would have a stroke. Thanks, but no thanks."

I directed Tom to back my van and park it a good distance from the only exit from the huge parking lot with the front end facing Porky's. Jasmine pulled her van beside mine. We both nodded at Deputy Selph as he took off to join Hank. I gave Bobby Lee water and loaded him in the van, fastening his harness to the ring bolted in the floor behind the seats. I pulled out a ripe pear and quartered it for him; I didn't want him to gobble it whole. I looked for carrot sticks but I must have left them in the crisper at home. Jasmine slid into the seat beside me.

"Think they're in there?"

"Bobby Lee turned in, I had to physically pull him off the scent. I see two cars that might be a blue Saturn compact. I can't tell from here. They could be here, been inside and gone, or simply circled the parking lot. I can't decide whether they're sharp or stupid. Three miles away from an assault in a known vehicle? Some get-away. However, they went undetected for more than three hours, and were found only because of a dog with a gifted nose, so who knows?"

"So we wait."

"We wait. I'm as close to the action as I care to be. How about you?"

"Absolutely," she agreed. We both were staring intently at Porky's entrance.

I reached for another pear and started quartering it. I hadn't had any lunch, and now that I was cooling down from my hike, I felt empty inside. It also gave my hands something to do while we waited. I sensed a movement, and a suppressed lip-smacking sound from behind me. I bit into a morsel of pear, and handed back the other three pieces to Bobby Lee, who gobbled them gently from my fingers.

I craved a cigarette. I still missed the nicotine, especially during times of inactivity and stress. I bit my lip and watched the bar. Two patrol units approached the drive from the direction of town and turned in quickly, being as silent as possible. One proceeded to where Hank had his men. The other took a position in the middle of the lane leading off the highway. The officer opened his doors on both sides and remained seated. That meant that Hank had Fray and three men to back him up. I wondered if Fray was competent in the field or just a loudmouth pencil pusher. There were a lot of booths and dark corners inside Porky's. It was always dark as a cocktail lounge at midnight, even in the middle of the day. An army could hide in there.

I could tell that Jasmine was getting antsy. She wasn't exactly fidgeting, but she wasn't sitting still, either. I felt soft movements and a spring squeaked in protest.

"You wanna help them?" I tried for casual. It had been a long ten minutes.

"Do you?" she countered.

"We'd probably be in the way."

I looked at my watch. Another minute had slowly ticked by.

"Shit," I uttered in resignation, and bailed out of the van, turned, and pushed my seat forward. Jasmine almost beat me to the pavement.

"Put Miz Melanie in the cage directly behind your seat, close the outer shutter, and take your keys."

I unhooked Bobby Lee and loaded him in a cage, giving him a boost on his fanny when he pulled his newly found nosing routine instead of sailing in quickly. I was impatient to get there, after wasting so much time convincing myself I wanted no part of the entry and search.

I pulled the .32 free, opened the cylinder, and checked the load. Yep, six rounds. I held the gun down by my side and glanced at Jasmine. Her .38 was in her hand in the same position as mine.

"Do we really want to do this?"

Jasmine managed a laugh. She was cooler than I was.

We were still a hundred feet out in the lot when Hank and his assault team of four entered. It seemed just a short time later when the jukebox was silenced with a screech. I winced. I bet that record was shot. It sounded as though the needle had scored the entire surface before its movement ceased.

We reached the door and stood with our backs braced against the wall on opposite sides. We now had our guns in a two-handed grip pointing upwards.

"On two," I whispered.

On my second nod, we both hit the double doors side by side and crouched low in the gloom, giving our eyes time to adjust to the darkness while trying to cover everybody and anything that moved.

The stools in front of the bar were occupied and most of the drinkers had spun around, and sat wide-eyed and silent as they watched the uniformed men yell instructions, deploy, and run through the room to the dark dance hall and the bathrooms beyond.

Tom had a problem. He was covering the entire counter area and someone had entered behind him. I yelled fast.

"Me and Jasmine are behind you. Help the others, we have these guys covered."

He moved without turning and took off in the gloom. Jasmine and I slowly straightened, keeping everyone in view.

"Hank will eat him alive, and us, too," Jasmine whispered softly where only I could hear.

"Maybe not," I whispered optimistically, but I knew she was right. The three of us had already broken several rules and had tossed aside procedure. I decided to enlighten the present population.

"Listen up, gentlemen. Stay seated, and all will be explained shortly. You're in no danger as long as you don't move."

Uh oh. An unsteady drunk laboriously climbed down from his stool and stood weaving and peering in our direction. It was Sam Johnson, or his brother, Bob. I had trouble telling them apart. Both were short, fat, bald, shiftless, and usually tanked. Jasmine and I were in a shadowy area.

"Don't let loose of the catch dog!" I yelled. I had pronounced each word distinctly so his alcohol-clouded brain could decipher the message. It was worth a shot.

"Dog? You have a doggie? Here doggie, here doggie."

Oh, God. A sentimental drunk dog petter. Just what we needed! Obviously, the only word he had heard was *dog*.

I inwardly groaned and slid towards Jasmine.

"Do the best you can, you've got it," I whispered as I passed behind her to go stop Johnson. He had taken a couple of lurching steps towards the sound of my voice. I holstered my gun and stepped in front of him, getting in his face while shaking my finger.

"Go sit down!" I thundered.

I was an inch taller, but he outweighed me by a hundred pounds. He reached out, clamping both arms around my shoulders. Unfortunately, I was the only stationary object in his sight. He swayed. I tried to brace myself, but his weight overpowered me and I went over backwards with him on top of me. I heard yelling and movement. The air whooshed out of my lungs and I couldn't breathe. Next came the sound of a shot, and then all hell broke loose.

9

Into Each Life Some Rain Must Fall

January 4, Wednesday, 5:00 P.M.

My head hurt. My stomach hurt. My right knee was killing me. I started inventorying the rest of me. I was sitting on the dirty floor in Porky's, my back pressed against a large beam that supported the ceiling. Hank was squatting in front of me, making churlish remarks.

"Quit yelling," I said with feeling. "I'm not deaf!"

"I'm not . . ." He stopped and started again, lowering his voice somewhat.

"Are you all right?"

"Feel like a million." Memory came flooding back.

"Who got shot?" I asked anxiously. "Jasmine? Is Jasmine okay?"

"She's fine, but no thanks to the three of you. What in the hell did you think you were doing? It's a God's wonder that y'all didn't get somebody hurt!"

"Where's Jasmine!"

"Relax. When she saw that you weren't hurt, she went to check the dogs. According to the bartender, and a few others who were sober enough to notice, no strangers have been inside since noon."

"Who fired the shot?"

"Jasmine. She shot at the ceiling. She was trying to stop the panic.

When you tried waltzing with Bob the drunk, they thought they were in danger of getting shot by a woman, and scattered like quail being flushed from cover."

I noticed his tone soften when he mentioned Jasmine. At least it was more pliable than when he was discussing me.

"You like her better than me," I accused him.

I heard a hint of humor in his voice, I wasn't looking his way. I had no desire to see his displeasure.

"You're feeling better."

"How long was I unconscious?"

I rubbed my head and felt where it had hit the floor. It was sore, but I didn't feel any bump or blood.

"You were never unconscious, just had the wind knocked out of you. Bob weighs a ton. You just weren't tracking too well for a time."

He stretched out a hand and pulled me to my feet. I started struggling to get out of my rescue suit. I wanted to check my knee, it was still throbbing. I got the top of the suit below my butt and Hank spoke.

"Sit."

I lowered myself in the nearest chair. He picked up a leg and pulled the suit free. He repeated the process on the other.

I felt sweaty and abused.

"Where is everybody?"

"In the parking lot playing musical cars. Miz May Belle's Saturn is outside. When a patron finds out he doesn't have a place to sit out there, we'll know what the perps stole for transportation."

Fray walked up talking. "You have an irate citizen outside who can't find his car. It's a dammed good thing, because he's too drunk to drive."

Hank left, and Fray stood grinning at me.

"Hand over the loot, Sidden, you've lost the bet."

"It ain't over till it's over," I remarked as I headed towards the john. I could hear echoes of his laughter bouncing off the empty walls till I hobbled into the restroom and locked the door.

I worked my jeans below my knees and sat on a commode while I tenderly prodded my right kneecap. I guess one of Bob's knees had connected with mine. It ached, but it wasn't cut or swollen. I came out the loser because my system wasn't fortified with booze. With that thought, I decided I needed a couple of beers, maybe ten or twelve of them.

The pain-easing brews would have to wait. I had two felons I needed to find. My knee would limber up with exercise. Maybe.

When I stepped outside, I was dismayed at the darkness, I was expecting sunshine. Glancing at my watch, I saw that it was 5:30. I looked around for Jasmine, and saw that she had pulled my van closer to the building, and she was in hers moving it next to mine. I walked over, trying not to limp.

She alighted and studied me.

"You look terrible."

"That's because I feel terrible. Hank chew you out?"

"Not like I expected. I shot a hole in the ceiling!"

"It's not the first bullet to ventilate Porky's ceiling and I doubt it will be the last. Don't fret over it. He wasn't mad at you for the bullet, he was furious with me and my feeble attempt to control a drunk."

She hugged her shoulders nervously. She had on a warm jacket. She had removed her rescue suit, but I didn't think the early first dark made the air feel that chilly.

"You don't have a clue, do you?" She searched my face. "When Hank came running in and saw you lying beneath that drunk he was like a crazy man, yelling and carrying on, trying to get him from on top of you, and holding you like he'd never let go!"

"Yeah?"

"Yeah."

"He probably thought you had shot me."

She threw up her hands and started giggling. I was glad to see her relaxing, she must have been scared out of her gourd to fire her gun.

She read my mind.

"It was the only thing I could think of," she said, defending herself.

"You did good. A lot better than me. Next time I'll know to keep my distance from a drunk, especially a fat drunk. He squashed me like a bug!"

Suddenly I felt better. I looked around and spotted Hank and Fray standing beside Hank's vehicle.

"Let's join the boys," I suggested. We strolled over and both of them watched us approach.

Deputy Tom Selph stepped from the rear of the parked cars to intercept us while we were still several yards away from Hank and Fray.

"Jo Beth . . . "

"Tom," I interrupted kindly, "I wish you would believe me when I say Bobby Lee is not for sale. I'm not trying to work you up to a higher bid. Honestly, you, or your bank, doesn't have enough money."

"I'm beginning to believe you," he said, frowning with concentration as if he was searching for the right words.

I waited him out. What now?

"I want to ask you something else."

"Ask away," I answered lightly.

"I've got a bitch, mostly lab and bluetick. She's the best tracker I've ever worked with, and she's due to come into season any day now. I was wondering what you'd charge for a stud fee. We'd have the best trackers in the county!"

He saw my expression, and hurried on. "I'd give you pick of the litter, and five hundred. How about it?"

I took a deep breath and held onto my temper. Tom didn't know that he had just uttered the most disgusting proposal that I had ever heard in my life. He was not deliberately trying to insult me. He was ignorant about the care and diligence that bloodhound breeders took to keep the bloodlines pure. I would no more put Bobby Lee at stud to a mongrel bitch than spread wings and fly over the moon.

"I'm sorry, but it's impossible. Responsible breeders don't sully the lineage."

"She's a truly gifted bitch!" he said, looking as though his animal had been insulted. "She's not sullied!"

Feelings are easily hurt when someone censures your dog. My heart went out to him.

"Tom, I'm sure she's a champion at heart. No disrespect meant."

He let out a pent-up breath. "Then I guess there's none taken." He mentally wrapped himself in his dignity, turned on his heel, and walked away.

"I'm proud of you, Jo Beth. When I understood what he was asking, I held my breath. I thought you were going to crawl down his throat!" Jasmine was pretending to wipe a sweaty brow.

"Lately I've been trying to think before I leap. Sometimes it works."

We had arrived. I focused on Hank, ignoring Fray.

"Tracking has been called on account of darkness. The Weather Channel predicted eighty percent chance of rain tonight, with some local thunderstorms, medium to heavy. I think they'll be on the money, I smell rain in the air. We could try again at daylight, but our chances are slim and none. Do you agree?"

"Yep, we'll call it a night. Stringer took Bob home. We have an APB out on the stolen vehicle. It's some other county's problem now, they could've traveled a hundred miles while we were searching. Thanks for your help."

"I'll bill you," I returned with a grin. "Oh, I almost forgot. Bobby Lee and I didn't finish tracking down the felons. Fray wins the bet. Pay him."

Jasmine and I turned to leave.

"I knew you'd be a sore loser!" Fray was braying like an ornery mule.

I paused, turned, and gave him an enigmatic appraisal, moving my eyes slowly from button to button down his chest to his zippered fly, then back up to his face.

"He who laughs last . . . "

We got out of there.

Jasmine didn't speak until we reached the vans.

"I've already mentioned that I was very proud of you, haven't I? That was classy."

"Being noble has its drawbacks. I feel soiled and thirsty. It also kept me from scratching his eyes out."

I took a longer route back home. I went out 301 till I reached Baker's Mill Road. I drove past the whitewalled fence and stopped in the driveway blocked by the closed wrought-iron gates.

I peered into the darkness, looking for some sign of the inhabitants, if any. It was too early for the moon, and the sky was partially blocked with fast-moving storm clouds. I couldn't see zip.

I cranked up and moved a hundred yards farther to a clearing where the view wasn't blocked with large trees.

I pulled over on the verge, turning off the headlights. I found the binoculars under the passenger seat. I climbed the small ladder at the rear of the van and moved to the middle of the roof.

I scanned the terrain, putting the glasses where I thought the mansion stood. I was keeping an ear cocked for engine sounds of approaching traffic. I'd look damn silly and a trifle suspicious if I were caught up here in the glare of headlight beams of a passing motorist.

I didn't spot any lights on in the house, only the outside nightlights. I moved the glasses a little to the left and saw a faint reflection of light on water. Swimming pool. It didn't look as though the family had moved in.

Back inside the van I saw several large drops of water hit the windshield. I turned to Bobby Lee and messaged his jowls.

"It's nutritious goop for you, a hot tub and cold beer for me. Let's get to it." He was snoring before we were halfway home.

10

Digging for Dirt

January 5, Thursday, 9:00 A.M.

It was still raining when I pulled up in front of Miz Alice Trulock's modest bungalow at 136 Ashbury Avenue. I tied a clear plastic rain cap over my frizzy curls, to try and keep them from getting frizzier. Fat chance.

I had left Bobby Lee at home. His hesitation at climbing in and out of the van was getting on my nerves. His too careful approach was depressing. It was as if he had just recently discovered he was blind and was determined to be prudent. It had me worried.

I had on a denim jacket, and decided to skip the plastic rain cape. I ran the short distance of twenty feet to the small open front porch, dodging small puddles here and there in the yard. I could see that an armadillo had spent last night diligently digging holes in the lawn.

A half-grown armadillo can root more than 200 holes with his long pointed snout in an eight-hour period of foraging for food. Lawn people who take pride in their pristine level landscapes have been known to break down and cry when they came out to get their morning paper and find their lawns pockmarked with small craters. The only way to repair them was with a wheelbarrow full of dirt, a shovel, and lots of patience.

I was searching for the doorbell among all the musical wind chimes, figurines, hardy plants, statues, and colorful wooden plaques that were overcrowding the small stoop. The door was swung open before I found it. A tall gaunt woman with reddish-orange hair, wearing too much makeup and attired in clinging red knit tights and a matching top, stood holding onto the screen, her small mouth held in a perfect oval of inquiry.

So much for my character read on what a retired office manager in her sixties would think of my appearance. Compared to her, I was stylish. I always made the mistake of judging older women by the dress standards of my long-dead mother. I still remember the shock and dismay on her face when she saw a stranger in church wearing a red pantsuit to a funeral when I was eight years old. From the murmuring and unforgiving whispers that rolled through the church when the ladies spotted the inappropriate outfit, I was sure they were going to burn the offender at the stake for being a sacrilegious heretic.

"Miz Trulock? I'm Jo Beth Sidden."

"Right on time. Come in, come in," she replied, pushing open the screen door.

"I see you had a visit from an armadillo last night."

"Oh noooo!" she wailed, brushing a large wind chime aside in her haste to view the damage.

All the dangling objects were hung too low. Only a midget could have maneuvered through the maze without stooping, or sweeping them out of the way.

"They should have a bounty on their armored heads!" she fretted. "Damn them anyway! I spent half a day last week filling up holes and stomping dirt!"

"I know," I soothed. "It really is aggravating."

She sighed. "Let's go have a cup of coffee. If it doesn't rain tomorrow, I know what I'll be doing."

The interior of the house was decorated much like the porch. Heavy dark wood. Earlier period pieces with too many small side tables, curio cabinets, and crocheted doilies on every surface, including the arms and backs of the stuffed couch and chairs. We threaded our way through the obstacles, the beaded curtain in the doorway between the living room and the hall, and finally into the cheerful kitchen.

It was painted bright yellow, with a deep purple trim around the ceiling. A garish combination that surprisingly worked. Potted ferns hung from the ceiling, and they were high enough that you wouldn't have to worry about getting a concussion if you walked underneath. She used a scrubbed wooden butcher's block for her table. It was pushed against one wall, with only three chairs with plaited rattan seats visible. She didn't do much entertaining in her kitchen. The table had coffee cups for two, and half of a homemade five-layer chocolate cake with chocolate icing. I mentally surrendered. One thin slice would have at least 650 calories. I have no defense against chocolate on chocolate.

"Would you care for a piece of cake?"

She had seen my greedy gaze.

"Yes, please," I said with no hesitation. She cut a thick slice, and I dug in after she poured a strong brew of beechnut coffee into my cup.

"Can't abide that weak swill they serve in restaurants nowadays."

My mouth was full of cake and I couldn't answer. I just bobbed my head in agreement.

"It really makes my blood boil to hear that the man who killed Velma Mae and the Sirmons baby is back here walking the streets."

"Did you know the nursemaid?" I asked between bites.

"Well, we spoke on the phone. I don't think I saw her in person more than two or three times. I remember running her to the doctor's office once. The baby had a cold, and Mr. Newton was in court."

"Was she competent?"

"I suppose so, I never heard anything different. 'Course, Mr. Newton never confided in me about his problems at home."

I thought I heard something in her voice. I decided to leave it to later on in the interview.

"Tell me about Calvin Newton. What was he like?"

She idly stirred her coffee, and seemed reluctant to speak.

"He's been dead almost thirty years," I reminded her softly. "It's not like you would be violating his confidence after all these years. Don't you think that he would want to correct any miscarriage of justice, if there has been any?" She looked startled.

"You don't think that man killed them?"

"I think that under heavy pressure, there was a rush to judgment in his case. No physical evidence, no eyewitnesses, and a lot of conjecture."

I had been cautious in my choice of words. I didn't want to plant the seed of doubt, I'd just let it lie there and see if it grew roots.

"I didn't hear any voice to the contrary back then. We all thought he was guilty. I think we were relieved that it was a transit and not a local, and the whole ordeal was settled. I know I was, and Cal . . . Calvin seemed to feel the same."

She looked at me, and gave a little shrug of her shoulders.

"I started thinking of him as Calvin after he died. An old maid's prerogative."

"You liked him, didn't you?" I smiled to encourage her.

"Very much. You could say I had a few fantasies that didn't pan out. We were the same age, and he was a widower and I had never married. Some women get silly when they are in their thirties and can't seem to land a husband. I was one of them."

I liked her honesty.

"But it was not to be?"

"Calvin had his heart condition, and his memories of Celeste. He had a child to raise that he felt lukewarm about. I'm sure he never saw me. To him, I was part of his office . . . one of the fixtures."

"He wasn't a doting daddy?"

"I think he resented her. She survived her birth, but Celeste didn't."

"He and Celeste were that much in love? A grand passion?"

"That was the biggest surprise of my life. I never thought so before her death. This was before I was having any dreams, or expectations about him. You know how you can think you know a person, how they will react? They seemed comfortable with each other. An average marriage. Devoted is not one of the adjectives I would have used in describing them. He was a very self-contained person, and didn't talk freely about anything personal. After her death, he appeared to draw into a shell, becoming even more taciturn and reluctant to talk about Celeste or his daughter. I decided that he really truly loved her, and resented Patricia Ann."

"You could have guessed wrong. What if he was relieved to be free of the marriage, and those thoughts made him feel guilty? Wouldn't he have acted the same way?"

Her eyes lost their focus, and I knew that she was back in the second half of 1964 and trying out this new thought. After several minutes, she was back. She gave me a searching appraisal.

"Do you really think so?"

"It fits the facts. People seldom change that dramatically, from comfortable to obsessed. What made you think he resented Patricia?"

"He never mentioned her. I would ask about her, and he would give me short answers, usually changing the subject. He didn't carry any pictures of her. You know how quickly children grow and change. I made all of his appointments, and kept reminding him to have her picture taken. He never asked me to get any made. He never asked me to help him find a nursemaid or baby-sitter, either."

"Unusual way for a man to act," I agreed.

Alice Trulock frowned and straightened in her seat, drawing a deep breath.

"What is it?" I asked.

"I just remembered one of the few times I ever saw the baby, and what happened in the office. I don't know where it came from. Out of the blue, I guess."

"What?" I was hoping for something useful.

"I'll have to explain something first," she said, sounding uncertain of her newfound knowledge.

"I worked for Calvin for eight years, right up until the day he died. I ran the office, hired and fired the help, and handled all the office finances, even before his marriage to Celeste. He never checked my figures, looked over my shoulder, or received any complaints from his tax consultant's firm or lawyer. I knew he trusted me. He was rich enough that he didn't have to work. He was also prudent. He was careful with money, he didn't spend a lot, or sell any land. His real estate is where his fortune doubled. After five years in his employ, he signed a power-of-attorney for me so I could handle his affairs if he was hospitalized with his heart condition, and this was after he married Celeste.

"I wanted you to understand he did value my services, and had complete confidence in me. I didn't want you to think I was greedy, or was soured about the will. He left me a hundred-thousand-dollar trust fund that started paying me a sufficient amount of money when I retired, so that with my Social Security, I have a comfortable life. In fact, I could have a steak every night and go on an exotic cruise every month without damaging my bank account. However, I enjoy reading and working in my garden, which I can do here, so here I stay."

She gave me a rueful grin and refilled our cups. I was full of chocolate and good coffee. I pushed the familiar and ever-present craving for nicotine to a back burner, and concentrated on what she was telling me.

"I knew that Calvin had no close relatives and wouldn't trust his fortune to a distant one he had never met. He didn't make friends easily. In fact, he didn't have a best friend, or someone he was close to. Towards the end, he seemed to depend on me more and more. I assumed that he would make me the executrix of his will, and I would be Patricia's guardian. I thought that the only reason he hadn't mentioned it to me, or asked me if I would assume the responsibility, was that he would have to acknowledge his impending death, and that he was simply putting it off as long as he was able."

I was hearing new facts that I was not aware of. I had assumed he and his gardener were joined at the hip. He had made Bryan Sirmons his executor, and the guardian of his only heir, Patricia Ann Newton. My ears prickled. Could I believe Alice's version of events? I couldn't judge until I had spoken with Bryan Sirmons, who was moving back to Balsa City any day now to take up residence in that large white house on Baker's Mill Road. Obviously, she was presenting the facts according to her perception. Was she right or wrong? I had no idea.

"Now I can tell you the incident that I just remembered. It was early afternoon about two months before the kidnapping. Mr. Sirmons came into the office with a baby on each arm. He had a camera around his neck. He announced that he wanted Calvin so they could take some pictures. He said, 'Calvin always gets home after dark, we need bright sunlight for these babies.' I wondered at the time why Calvin stayed so late at the office. I knew he wasn't working on any pressing case. I decided that he was avoiding going home and being in the same house with his baby. I knew Velma Mae lived in, and Calvin didn't have to take care of her personally. It was another fact to prove that he resented her.

"Calvin came out and made some excuse why he couldn't go outside to pose for pictures. Mr. Sirmons paid no attention. He walked over to Calvin and forced him to take Patricia, he wouldn't take no for an answer. It was in November, and it was cool. Her blanket was green, and Loretta's was yellow. They could have been twins."

Alice smiled at the memory.

"Calvin looked so uncomfortable, I could tell he wasn't used to cradling her. But why the memory returned to me came later, when they came back inside. I didn't hear all of the conversation, just something that Mr. Sirmons said. 'Calvin, you're all she has left. She deserves it.' I was looking at Calvin while Mr. Sirmons was speaking. Something happened to his face. He looked very solemn. Then his face cleared and he smiled at Sirmons. 'You're right, as always. That's what I'll do.' Then he handed Patricia back to Sirmons, and went in his office and closed the door."

I waited for her to continue, but she didn't elaborate.

"That's it?"

She nodded without speaking.

"What do you think he meant?"

I was in the dark here. I couldn't see any way that remembering those couple of sentences could have enlightened her.

"Don't you see? I think that had to be the moment that Calvin decided to leave the care of his estate and daughter to Mr. Sirmons. It wasn't a rejection of me, he saw that Mr. Sirmons cared for *his* daughter, as well as his own. It's bothered me for thirty years. I'm glad I remembered."

It might have answered her question, but I still had many.

11

This Makes the Cheese More Binding

January 5, Thursday, 1:00 P.M.

Jasmine and I were eating a small tuna salad. I had described the gastronomic delight I had had with my coffee earlier in great detail.

"You are making me salivate," she complained. "Just hush."

"It was worth every calorie," I rhapsodized.

"You'll gain a pound by Saturday."

"That was mean and petty."

"Maybe two."

She always had to have the last word.

Jasmine got to rinse the plates and place them in the dishwasher.

"What did what's-her-name, Newton's office manager, tell you?"

I stopped brushing up cracker crumbs from the tablecloth and recited.

"That Newton had his heart condition, a dead wife he was either nuts about or felt guilty about for not missing her, and a daughter he resented or wouldn't give two hoots in hell for. Take your pick."

"You didn't care for her conclusions?"

"Everyone has opinions, including me. I just don't know who has the right ones."

"Well, at least you're getting practice to become the great detective that you aspire to be."

I twisted the dish towel and popped her one on her fanny. She howled and splashed water towards me with her cupped hand.

I almost stepped on Rudy, who had been banished to the living room for begging. He had decided it was time to return, and we met in the doorway. I glanced back as he raised a paw and spat at me.

"My, aren't we friendly!" The phone rang.

I dropped into my desk chair and caught it on the second ring.

"It's Hank, Jo Beth. I need you."

"Have you noticed that it's raining?" I asked politely.

I relaxed and swung my feet on the desk.

"Tough titty. I use what's available, and you're it. Please get your tail over here pronto!"

"When it rains hard," I said patiently, "scent mantrailing is a no-no. The heavy water pounds the scent into the wet ground, or over into the next county. It all depends on how much wind is blowing."

"I have an abandoned car with a flat tire, with the driver's side door standing open in the rain. A woman's purse is in the front seat and the wallet is holding money."

I brought my feet to the floor, reaching for a scratch pad.

"Where are you?"

"I'm two miles east of Palmer Road and State Road Six's intersection. What's your ETA?"

Jasmine had entered the room and was hovering, and listening intently.

"Gimme . . . thirty minutes."

"Jo Beth? I haven't told you what's in the back of the car. A child's safety seat."

"What makes you think a child was occupying it?"

"A diaper bag up front, and a bottle of milk on the floor in back."

"Shit."

"Ditto."

"See ya."

I depressed the bar and started dialing the number for the weighing room. Wayne and Donnie Ray were planning to peel eggs after lunch. The trainers were already back in the field. The front gate sounded its strident alarm.

"Just great! Check to see who's arriving."

Jasmine had turned and was already racing to the kitchen window. On the fourth ring I slammed the receiver down and pressed the panic button wired to the right side of my desk. This activated both the outside lights to continuous blinking and a constant *whoop-whoop* wail of impending doom. It sounded as if we in dire distress. We just might be. I ran to the kitchen and joined Jasmine and we both peered into the driving rain.

Johnson's Feed and Seed's delivery truck was rounding the curve. I didn't recognize the driver, but I saw him well enough to know it wasn't Bubba. Jasmine and I relaxed our vigil.

My ex-husband, Bubba, was the reason for all the elaborate security precautions and nail-biting anticipation of danger. He had been quiet for too long. I have to stay constantly alert to survive. It sucks, but it's a fact of life that I have to live with.

The truck in our view was a flatbed, and I could see stacks of fifty-pound bags of dog food, which are damned expensive, as the tarp billowed and floated above them with each surge of wind.

"We're going two miles east of State Road Six after it crosses Palmer Road. Tell Wayne to load Ashley and Melanie. Full twenty-four-hour gear. Tell Donnie Ray he won't be going, it's too wet to film. I'm going to get dressed. Be sure and dress warm. It's suppose to turn cold tonight after the rain."

I knew that Wayne and Donnie Ray would arrive breathless any second now, and loaded for bear. I yelled back over my shoulder as I left so she could hear me above the din of the alarm.

"Tell Wayne that if those sacks of dog food are even damp, to refuse delivery!"

In the bedroom I quickly changed into pantyhose, jeans, and a long-sleeved fleece-lined sweatshirt, and pulled on two pair of thick white socks. I grabbed two extra pair to take with me. I can't mantrail a lengthy search in waterproof boots, I knew my feet would get wet.

The alarm was silenced in mid-whoop. I smiled when I thought about them scrambling for weapons. The false alarm was good practice. I wondered if Wayne had chosen the shotgun, or Donnie Ray. I decided that Donnie Ray would have grabbed the .38 that I had taught him how to shoot. He sometimes wore it when he accompanied me on a search that was videotaped.

I took two bandannas, raised my shirt, and tied one around my middle against my skin, and stuck the other in my pocket for wiping rain from my face. I removed my .32 snubnose revolver from the nightstand, loaded six rounds, putting another six in my pocket, and strapped on my holster.

I raced to the kitchen and laid out twelve slices of bread. I lathered on mayonnaise and mustard, added boiled ham and thin slices of baby Swiss cheese, slapped them together, and wrapped them in aluminum foil. I had survival food in the backpack I carry, but you need plenty of nourishment on a wet cold afternoon keeping up with a bloodhound. We might be out for two hours, or two days. I went prepared.

I met Wayne on the porch. He had pulled the van close, and had my rescue suit so I wouldn't get wet. I pulled it on, distributed my items in the right pockets, and knelt so I was nose to nose with an anxious Bobby Lee.

The alarm and hurried activity had alerted him. I had not raised a foolish bloodhound. He smelled my rescue suit and knew I was leaving. His anxiety was caused because I hadn't sent him to fetch his two leads hanging on their nails on a post behind me. He could stand on his hind legs and retrieve them.

"Sorry, sweetheart, not today. Would you please go inside and stay warm this once, as a favor to me?"

I gave him a hug, feeling a lump in my throat. I knew I was wasting my breath. I climbed into the van, signaling a well done to Wayne, without glancing towards Bobby Lee. I couldn't bear to see him sitting there so stoically while nursing a broken heart. I got out of there.

12

One Step at a Time

January 5, Thursday, 2:00 P.M.

Traffic was light to nonexistent. I made good time, arriving only ten minutes later than my estimate. Hank had the road blocked from travelers and the others that seem to gather at all scenes. Gawkers. Seth Andrews, a reporter for the *Dunston County Daily News,* and a branch special news reporter from Waycross TV.

I steered around a patrol unit and advanced to Hank's cruiser. He ran through the rain and flopped beside me. His rain slicker was Day-Glo yellow, the same color as my rescue suit. We were the only two spots of color on a dull gray afternoon.

I briefly eyed the small white car on the verge fifty feet in front of me as each swish of the wiper blade revealed its presence. I turned off the motor. One of the dogs shifted his weight, turning over in his sleep. They could zonk out in a hurricane. I felt a strange reluctance to break the silence. Hank lit a cigarette. I turned the key and lowered the window several inches.

"Will the smoke bother you?"

"Not any more than Chinese water torture."

I grabbed his arm as he reached to put it out.

"I'm kidding. Feel free to pollute my air. Who found the vehicle?"

"Would you believe Deputy Rigdon? He was returning from serving a warrant."

"That's a break, we aren't usually that lucky. At least the car and the immediate vicinity aren't contaminated, in case there is anything left to be contaminated, after all this rain."

"What makes you so sure that Rigdon followed procedure?"

"I personally saw Deputy Charles Rigdon royally screw up—not once, but twice. He wants my approval so much he can taste it. This time he went by the book, and you can bank on it."

"You're right on both counts." Hank chuckled. "He did everything correctly, and I've had to reassure him several times that he did good."

"Give me what you've found out so far."

"Naomi Zeckermann, twenty-seven, is presumed missing. The car has a flat on the right rear. The left front door was found open. Keys in the ignition. Purse still containing money on the seat. Diaper bag on the front seat, which I only observed through the window. Child protection seat in the rear, and a baby bottle half-full of milk abandoned on the floor. Jacksonville PD says her phone has voice mail. They have sent a man to check the neighbors, to see if there's a husband. She has one credit card that lists the name Jerome, and he's also listed as having the same phone number as hers. They haven't responded with any more information. So far, that's it."

"What do you think happened?"

"Well, abduction springs to mind," he said, removing his rain hat to scratch his dark hair. "We've checked the hospital, and the nearest house in either direction. We've alerted garages that have tow trucks. Rigdon said the engine still had some warmth, but not much. We should have heard from someone if a friendly gave her a lift."

"Sounds like she was a very unlucky lady," I said, feeling a smattering of goose bumps on my arms. "Along comes a spider, and sits beside her."

"We have our share of perverts in Dunston County, just like any other place. She could have been very unlucky that the first person passing took advantage of the situation, but there could be another explanation. Let me show you."

Hank squirmed around in the seat, pulling up his raincoat, and awkwardly reached in his back pocket. He handed me a ladies' wallet. I opened it and saw a picture of a light-haired woman with large eyes looking back at me from a Florida driver's license. She appeared much younger than twenty-seven. I read her measurements. Five-two, 115 pounds. Her hair color was blonde and she had hazel eyes. I added a few pounds to my estimate, remembering she had a baby on a bottle. Maybe a little plump, with glowing health.

"So, she's very attractive. Maybe she was spotted by a deviate in the big city, and he followed her till he could get her in a secluded area, and then picked her up? Is that your other guess? If so, he's the one that lucked out with the flat tire on this lonely stretch of road."

"There's another option that sounds even worse," he said. "Look at the car again, Jo Beth."

I obediently turned the key and activated the wipers.

"It screams abduction," Hank reasoned. "Open door to the elements. Without that touch, it could have sat there for hours without causing alarm. The tire's flat, and it's off the road far enough not to be dangerous for passing traffic. You could think, gone to get the spare fixed, didn't want to change it in the rain, went to a relative's house and will return to fix it later, et cetera."

"Are you saying *she* planned it?"

"Maybe she wanted to disappear."

I stared at the picture. I didn't want this petite woman and mother of a small child to be devious.

"No way," I murmured. "You didn't mention a spaceship and aliens who wanted to run tests. Isn't that a round burnt spot over on the verge?"

"I'm paid to think of the downside," he said.

"This is about as down as you can get," I agreed. "I just don't want her to be a hustler. She looks like a victim to me."

I flipped over the plastic sleeve, and a small copy of a family portrait came into view. Naomi, and I assumed Jerome, had a laughing baby between them that looked as if he was maybe six months old.

"Did you look at this one?" I asked.

"Just remember what happened in South Carolina not too long ago. Woman who drowned her two sons?" Hank replied softly.

"Oh, God," I said, shaking my head. "That's gross!"

"Shit happens."

A tapping on my window made me give a startled leap. I lowered the window and Deputy Rigdon leaned towards the opening.

"Howdy, Miz Jo Beth. Sheriff, you have a call from Jacksonville PD."

Hank took off, and I smiled at Rigdon.

"Think it'll rain, Charley?"

"It's missing a good chance!" he said laughing, with water dripping off his chin.

"Thanks for keeping it clean," I said, gesturing towards the abandoned car.

"Hope it helps!" He loped off to follow Hank.

"It won't," I muttered to myself.

I focused on the car and felt helpless. Too much water had fallen too fast. Not much wind, but Christ. Water was standing in every dip and depression, leveling the landscape. A solid sheet of water was covering the road. Most would drain off, if it ever stopped coming down, but it just kept on coming.

I unbuckled my seat belt and moved into the aisle and dug out my waders. I wrestled them on. I hated to wear them because they made me clumsy and kept me from going at a normal gait, but the rain had taken away any chance of fast trailing, and at least my feet would stay dry. I managed to bang a knee and an elbow with my gyrations. I rubbed and cursed.

Hank piled into the passenger seat, bringing back with him the smell of damp clothing and nicotine. He twisted in the seat to see what I was doing. I unfastened Melanie's cage and said, "Unload." She bounced carefully into the confined space, wiggling her rear with delight, while I attached her long lead. Ashley released an excited whine, bumping into his aluminum door.

"Sit," I told Melanie, so I could edge around her.

"Sorry, champ, not this trip," I whispered, to quiet Ashley. "Maybe next time." I stuck my fingers in between the squares, and got slobbered on.

Wiping my hand on my bandanna, I returned to the front and moved my seat back for more leg room.

"Jacksonville PD talked to the next door neighbor. She knew where the husband worked, and I just finished talking to him. Mrs. Zeckermann was on her way to Waycross to visit her mother with their eleven-month-old son, Andy. The neighbor said she pulled out at eleven. Taking into consideration the rain, and having to watch a baby in the back seat, I'd guess she hit this stretch somewhere around twelve-thirty."

I held my arm up to the window, to better view my watch. It was ten to three. The light was getting worse.

"When did Rigdon find the car?"

"One-thirty."

"An hour window, about two and a half hours ago. Not bad if it wasn't raining," I said, sounding like doom and gloom.

Lightning split the sky, flooding the atmosphere with instant daylight, followed almost immediately with a deafening roll of thunder.

I jumped a foot. "Damn," I yelled, suddenly angry.

"What's wrong?" Hank looked surprised at my outburst.

"Both dogs are terrified by thunder and lightning. In fact, if there's lots of thunder and lightning, *I get terrified!*"

Hank laughed. "Remember Miz Feagle's definition in her ninth grade science class? God's wink and him clearing his throat?"

"Yeah, yeah, well, it hits us in our gut. While you're sitting on your tush high and dry in a car that is insulated by rubber tires, we'll be standing in water surrounded by tall trees."

"Good point. Wait till it's over."

"Next you'll be telling me to take up knitting."

I shook my head to clear it. It wasn't getting any earlier out there, and what light was present would only last another couple of hours.

"Let's get things straight while we're dry," I suggested. "If we pick up a scent, send Selph with Jasmine and I'll take Rigdon. A separate car in front for each of us. Have you got enough men?"

"Half the force is here," he answered dryly.

"I'll try a radio check right away if we start trailing. If we get lucky, I don't want to pull them off the scent to give directions. Be prepared for us to move out, but it sure as hell won't be fast wearing these dang cumbersome waders. Tell Jasmine to put hers on, and pocket load the flashlights."

He opened the door and left. I dug out the five-cell and my battery head lamp, and crammed them into zippered pockets. I opened the rear door of the van, and Melanie jumped to the wet pavement, glanced up at the heavy rain, and shook her long ears.

"Keep your head down, babe, there's a lot more up there."

I had a plastic rain cap tied under my chin. Water was running down my face like someone had emptied a bucket over my head. I shortened up on Melanie's lead and clomped towards the car. I had several quart- and gallon-sized Ziploc bags folded against my chest, protected by my rescue suit. I tied Melanie's lead to the rear bumper of the small car with enough slack so she could huddle under the trunk ledge if we had another colorful and noisy display of electronics.

I walked to the driver's door and leaned my upper body inside out of the downpour. The driver's side was wet. I leaned farther and drew the diaper bag closer. I found a full bottle of milk, several diapers, a sleeper with attached feet, and a travel-size pack of wet wipes. I packed two diapers and all the rest into various pockets. I felt stuffed. My pockets were extended.

A white sweater was lying on the back of the passenger's seat. I held it to my nose, and smelled the faint aroma of baby powder and burp. She had worn it. I rolled it tightly, bagged it, and put it inside my suit. I pulled out the car keys and selected the trunk key before I straightened in the rain. Jasmine was approaching. I opened the rear door and saw a blue pacifier on the back seat. I brought it to my nose. I smelled milk, I thought. A fuzzy teddy bear was in the child's protection seat. The nap looked as if had been drooled on. I packed both in a gallon-sized bag, and passed it to Jasmine. I leaned near her face.

"I'm gonna check the trunk."

I walked to the rear and keyed the lock, raising the lid. There were two small valises on the carpeted surface. I moved them over and flipped back the carpet cover. I mentally had my fingers crossed. I was praying that the spare tire would be missing. That would mean that Naomi Zeckermann and her Good Samaritan were sitting in a kitchen near here, drinking coffee and waiting for the deluge to lessen before they drove in to have the tire filled with air.

The spare tire was there and after smacking it with my fist, I decided it had plenty of air. Another theory down the drain. I closed the trunk and motioned Jasmine to follow me. She untangled Gulliver's lead from Melanie's and we walked back to where three yellow-covered men waited about thirty feet back. I motioned them close and yelled over the sound of the rain.

"We both are going to try to pick up a trail. If it goes east or west on the road, stay about fifteen feet behind us. If it goes into the swamp, close it up fast, and stay right on our heels. You try first, Jasmine!"

She turned back to the car. Deputy Tom Selph started around me, and I put a hand on his shoulder.

"You watch out for her, you hear?"

He knew what I meant. His voice was soft, so he leaned closer so I could hear him.

"You can't tell till you step in it. You know that, Jo Beth."

"Just make sure you keep her and Gulliver safe!" I shouted.

He shrugged and it sounded like he said, "I'll try."

Rigdon and Hank looked mystified and stared at me.

"Miz Jo Beth? What did Tom mean, 'You don't know until you step in it?'"

"Quicksand," I answered grimly.

13

"Gimme a *Q*, a *U*, an'a *I*, *C*, *K*"

January 5, Thursday, 3:10 P.M.

"Quicksand?"

Rigdon's eyes widened in shock. I didn't glance at Hank.

"This strip of swamp from Jason's pasture over to Highway Three-oh-one is boggy and has quagmires. I just mentioned it to Selph *in case* the search left the road. Don't sweat it. We haven't picked up any kind of scent yet."

I glanced at Rigdon's feet. He was wearing polyethylene-coated boots with thick rubber-gummed soles.

"Do you have gloves?"

"No, ma'am."

"Wayne keeps an extra pair in the van. Look in the storage cabinet behind the driver's seat, top shelf. Bring my backpack."

Hank kept pace and stopped me with a hand on my shoulder.

"What made you mention the swamp?"

"Because we didn't explore the myth of the swamp monster rising from the slimy depths, and spiriting away Naomi and Andy," I answered lightly.

"Don't mention him to Charley, he's jumpy enough now," Hank replied through thinned lips. "Feeling fey?"

"This rain has me spooked," I admitted. "And this deserted highway and the encroaching darkness aren't helping any. Eight will get you five that it's a swamp search *if* the dogs find a scent."

"What tells you that?"

"Dammed if I know," I replied truthfully.

Hank stopped walking. We stood silently, waiting for Rigdon's return. When he ran up, he held my backpack as I shrugged my shoulders and fastened the belt around my middle.

Hank called, "Good luck!" I gave him a wave as I walked away.

Joining Jasmine and Gulliver, I gave her the bag with the baby's stuffed bear and pacifier, and moved close.

"The baby is your responsibility," I yelled. "His name is Andy, and he's eleven months old. I'll try to scent-trail the mother, Naomi. They were here approximately three hours ago. If we start trailing, radio check within ten minutes. I'm Joe and you're Slim. Okay?"

Her grin revealed her beautiful white teeth, and momentarily lifted my spirits. Every time Jasmine starts a mantrailing search, I worry about her. I had little hope of Naomi's scent lasting through this air-scouring downpour, and even less for Andy's. His feet didn't touch the ground and, being much smaller, would emit less of a trail of flaking skin, hair, and body odor. I prayed that she never tumbled to the fact that I was always trying to protect her. She would resent it if she knew.

I untied Melanie, and fed her two pieces of deer jerky. I pulled out Naomi's sweater and thrust it under Melanie's nose. I didn't worry about it getting wet; dampness would release more scent.

"Seek, Melanie, seek!"

I raised my voice, and put some excitement in my speech. Bloodhounds don't recognize our words, they take their cues from the tone that the trainer uses.

"Let's find her, girl, go get her. Seek!"

I bagged the sweater and fed Melanie two more pieces of jerky. She put her head down and got to work.

Repetition and infinite patience are required. My head and my back would be throbbing before long. This part was tedious and boring, but I couldn't let my voice reflect how I felt, for Melanie would quickly lose interest. You must always stay up and alert to keep their attention on the search. Bloodhounds can feel boredom and lack of enthusiasm, just like us humans.

"Come on, girl, find Naomi, seek, Melanie, seek!"

We had made a complete circuit of the automobile. I sensed Jasmine somewhere behind me. The minutes lengthened into a quarter of an hour. I bent, straightened, and repeated my request over and over, rubbing Melanie's ears, patting her briskly, and trying to keep her focused.

I glanced behind me and couldn't see Jasmine. I took a few clumsy steps and looked again. I expected to see her through the car windows as she popped up from giving a command. Nothing. I arched my back and stretched up to my full height, and still couldn't see her. I stared up the road and then down. No Jasmine or Gulliver. I frowned, and started quartering the landscape. She was thirty feet away, crossing a small drainage ditch and angling toward the trees!

OhGod, ohGod, Gulliver had picked up the baby's scent! My mind reeled in shock. I saw Selph hurrying to intercept her before she passed from sight into the thick growth. My first thought was to jerk Melanie from her slow prodding stroll and catch up to them. I wanted to scream with frustration. In trying to protect Jasmine, I just might have set her up for a bad traumatic scene.

My mind visualized what she might find. A dead baby tossed carelessly behind a shrub; a nuisance abandoned, and a battered mother raped and mutilated. I took a deep breath to steady my nerves. I no longer had to fake the urgency in my voice.

"Find her, Melanie, find her, seek, seek!"

Melanie took another lungful of the sweater's odors and lowered her head. She widened her circle pattern. She held her head near the pavement, then the grass on the verge. Just as I was ready to bolt, my beauty lifted her head, then lowered it, and started to pull for more freedom.

I freed a few feet of lead. She scampered for the ditch with me clomping behind her, trying to keep my balance. I didn't want to interfere or break her thin grasp on the scent she was literally drawing from the ground by manipulating her scoop-like ears.

I struggled to keep upright and restrained from pulling backward on Melanie's lead. She had no idea that she would soon intercept Gulliver's trail. She wasn't following him, she had found Naomi's trail.

My heart was beating furiously, and I knew I was risking a fall, or worse, a turned ankle, but I didn't draw her back. Melanie slowed when she discovered Gulliver and Jasmine's scent trail. It gave me time for a couple of deep breaths before she again lunged forward. I couldn't see if where we were entering was the same spot where Jasmine vanished from view. I didn't have the luxury of scanning the branches of the thick shrubbery for bent fronds or trampled grass. I gave a quick backward glance as we ran into the dark wet growth. Charley was six feet behind me. The noise from the rain had covered his approach.

Melanie stopped suddenly, and I almost ran up her backside. I raised my eyes and peered through the bushes, bending a titi branch that was blocking my vision. Jasmine was just ahead and not aware of our presence. She had her head lowered, and was resting her hands on her knees.

"Are you all right?" I called anxiously as Melanie and I crashed through the foliage.

"Just catching my breath," she yelled as she straightened. She gave me a rueful grin as the three of us approached. I now saw Selph standing to her left.

I gave Melanie the command to rest twice before she reluctantly complied and sat on her haunches.

"I'm having trouble keeping my balance in these waders!"

"Tell me about it," I replied. I nodded at Tom.

Charley moved close enough that I could hear and see his labored breathing. A fine mist was evident each time he exhaled. The rain hadn't diminished or slackened, the tall trees were absorbing almost half of the volume. It was old growth and thatched together high above our heads. Constant drips surrounded us, but it was much quieter than out in the open. The air was growing colder by the minute.

Three faces were white blobs in the gloom, with the wet shiny rescue suits and the men's bright yellow slickers looking as if we were giant blooms of a riotous flower gone mad.

I tried the radio, to see if Hank could hear us.

"Search One to base. Over."

"Base to Search One. I read you five by five. Over."

"Search One and Search Two traveling together. Over and out."

"Base out."

I glanced at the dark shapes that surrounded us.

"We might as well pull out our lights while we're stopped. We'll be needing them soon."

I glanced at Rigdon and Selph.

"Did you two bring flashlights?"

Charley looked stricken. "No," he uttered.

"Me neither," admitted Tom. He sounded sheepish.

Deputy Charles Ridgon was the All-American male, clean-cut, boyish, and impatient to prove his manhood. At twenty-eight, he sometimes seemed to have the intellect of a pubescent teen, but he had two redeeming qualities. A desire to be helpful, and a good heart.

Deputy Tom Selph, however, knew better. He had experience, traveled around the block many times, been there and done that. At fifty, he had more experience in living, and this primeval quagmire called the Okefenokee, than the three of us combined. Short, thin, wiry, and wearing glasses, he was not a typical-looking deputy sheriff in southeast Georgia, but he could out-macho them all. Two tours of 'Nam, twelve years on the force, and a lot of grit in his craw. He had no excuse for not being prepared for this search.

He spoke before I could tell him so.

"I didn't think the dogs would come up with anything, so I was just watching. I wasn't prepared when she hightailed it into the woods. Sorry."

He never addressed her by name (did I mention that he was born and raised right here in Georgia?). He had been with the department long enough to know Jasmine's history. Probably had arrested her himself more than once when she was walking the streets. I forced back a censure. I didn't need dissension among the troops, not out here in this godforsaken, snake-infested morass with darkness approaching.

I said a silent short mantra to control my bile. *I won't get upset, everything is peachy, and we'll make out. Amen.*

"Jasmine, give your five-cell to Deputy Selph, and hook up your head lamp."

I turned my back to Rigdon and undid my belt. He eased the pack off my shoulders and held it while I dug out the long powerful flashlight and my headlamp. I stuck the six-volt battery in my left pocket and ran the wire up to the clamped light on my forehead. I adjusted it to shine on the path in front of me, then turned it off. It was dusk in here, but not dark enough for the lamp to be effective. The dogs would now have less light on their path, and I resented the handicap. I took a long drink from my canteen and passed it to Rigdon, who declined. Jasmine neither drank nor offered any to Selph. Good girl. It's not politic to slight the person holding sustenance on a possibly long trek.

"Let's start. I'll go first, Rigdon next, then Jasmine and Selph."

My heart gave a lurch.

"Jasmine, when we were arranging the packs last month and you suggested leaving out the twenty-five-foot coil of nylon rope because of its bulk, did we?"

"No, you refused to take out anything," she said with a mild disapproving tone.

I drew in a relieved breath.

"Dig it out."

I turned my back on Rigdon.

"I don't think we have to take the pack off, it should be near the top. Can you reach it?" I squatted to make his chore easier.

"I have it," he remarked, and I readjusted my shoulder straps.

Noticing that Jasmine was balancing on one leg to rest her backpack on her bent knee, I told Rigdon to help her.

I stepped over to Selph and nudged him a couple of steps back.

I got in his face, using susurration.

"Lose her or the dog, and you die." Seeing his startled expression, I added, "It's a promise."

I turned back and handed my rope to Charley, raising my voice so all could hear.

"Unwrap it, and fold it so you can tie it around your waist. If, God forbid, Melanie or I get stuck in a bog, I want it where you can get to it fast."

I opened the bag of treats, gave a handful to Melanie, and put her back on the scent.

I walked behind Melanie, keeping her lead short, where I was almost on her heels. It was slow going. I deliberately kept Melanie down to a fast walk. She was close enough to the ground that she wasn't experiencing clinging branches, but we were having to walk with one arm up, to push aside foliage so constricting it seemed as if we were trying to negotiate through a thick hedge.

Rigdon activated his flashlight, and I glanced back at him. He had the beam on his hand. I saw a smear of blood.

"Put on the gloves," I said sharply, and kept walking. First aid could wait till later, when we stopped to rest. A large gallberry bush loomed ahead, and Melanie moved to my right. I had to stoop to clear the bottom limbs. A thick blackthorn vine at my waistline stopped me on a dime. Rigdon plowed into me, and I almost went down.

"A machete is in a sheath on the left side of my pack," I told Rigdon.

He turned on his light to remove it. I grabbed it, holding the beam on the vine as he hacked at it.

"Careful," I cautioned. "Wayne keeps those babies razor-sharp."

When the vine parted, I checked the time. It was five minutes till four. We were making lousy time. I tried to visualize the people in front of us whom we were trailing. At least one man, and a terrified mother holding her child. It didn't make sense, unless the man was a local and knew the swamp. No sane stranger to the swamp would head into this mess.

Back to trailing, I stumbled through rough terrain and tried to find an explanation for us being out here. When we didn't find bodies a few feet into the brush, I knew that this passage didn't compute. I wondered if there was more than one abductor. One or more, where was their transportation? There hadn't been any abandoned vehicle on the stretch anywhere near Naomi's car. Hank had checked. Was he, or them, walking along the road, hitchhikers dropped by a confederate who then drove away, or had they appeared in a puff of smoke? I shook my head and tried to find a logical explanation.

I heard a startled cry of "Jo Beth!" And a call of "Yo!" Almost simultaneously. I tugged Melanie to a halt, turned her around, and we reversed our steps and hurried back several feet. Jasmine and Selph weren't in view. I stopped and listened.

"Over here!" Selph shouted.

I located the sound and turned to my left. I saw where they had bent back a branch and trampled grass. I put my headlamp on their path, and we walked several more feet before I saw them in the beam of my headlamp.

Melanie and Gulliver greeted each other like long-lost relatives. Selph's hands were on his hips, and Jasmine had a bewildered expression.

She lifted a hand and dropped it.

"I thought Gulliver was just skirting the vines when he turned right from the path you took, but he just kept on going to the right! I let him go several feet before I pulled him off the scent! We got glimpses of your light and saw that you were going to the left!"

"Are you sure he just didn't lose the scent, and he's scouting to pick it up again?"

"Absolutely. Gulliver didn't hesitate, he turned right and was acting normal. You know how agitated he gets when he first loses a scent he has been following. He would have whined and ran around in circles."

She was right. He wouldn't have remained silent if he had lost the child's scent trail. I pulled out my bandanna to gain some time to think. I wiped my cold face dry of rain, and tried to reason. Melanie was following Naomi's scent, and Gulliver was following the baby's scent. The dogs were telling us that mother and child had split up a few yards back, and gone in different directions.

It couldn't have happened. I firmly believe in a mother's love. It would have been over Naomi's dead body to be separated from her baby. We weren't even close to either one, or the dogs would have alerted us by their loud baying.

I juggled the facts, and arrived at only one logical conclusion.

My gut received a shot of hot acid, and it rumbled in protest.

I couldn't meet their eyes.

14

Damned If You Do, Damned If You Don't

January 5, Thursday, 5:00 P.M.

"My guess," I said slowly, feeling my way, "would be that Naomi's trail will end somewhere to the left, where she was assaulted and killed, or badly injured. The abductor then returned this way by a different route, and only joined his former tracks a few feet back, and returned in this direction carrying the child."

I was madly trying to formulate a game plan. If we continued like we were, it would mean sending Jasmine, Gulliver, and Selph after the abductor. That was unacceptable. If I took over Jasmine's search and handled Gulliver (I couldn't switch the dogs to different scents, it would confuse them), it would imply I didn't trust Jasmine's abilities. I wanted to protect her, but how?

The dogs were unconcerned and resting. Three humans were waiting in silence that was steeped with impatience. I had to give it a try. I turned and faced Jasmine.

"I think you and Tom should wait here while Ridgon and I check to see if Naomi is dead or dying. Then we all can concentrate our efforts on the baby."

We were all shining our lights at waist level, more or less, to be able to see facial expressions without blinding anyone. I tried to look competent and omnipotent.

"I believe we'd be wasting valuable time when we could be tracking the abductor and finding the child." Jasmine's voice was cool. "Or maybe you think I'm not capable?"

"It would be wasting time," Tom agreed.

Rigdon was smart and kept silent.

Shit. Now I'd have to try and repair the damage my ridiculous suggestion had caused.

"I was running hunting dogs in this swamp while you were still in diapers," Selph added indignantly.

Christ, he was letting me know that *his* expertise had also been impugned.

"Listen up!" I said quickly. "My suggestion wasn't meant to imply that either one of you were incapable. I had several reasons for making it (in a pig's eye), but will bow to age and beauty. We'll continue as before, with fifteen-minute radio checks. Okay?"

Jasmine nodded with a hesitant smile, and Tom appeared mollified. I silently pulled down my waders' shoulder straps and unzipped my suit far enough to untie the bandanna around my waist, placed it in a bag, and held it out to Jasmine. She did the same, and I put hers in my pocket and resettled my straps.

"Take care," I said.

"You too."

Rigdon and I stood and watched as Jasmine put Gulliver back to mantrailing, and they moved out of sight.

"What's with the bandannas?" Rigdon asked.

"In case we need to find each other. Let's go, Charley," I said, with resignation.

Back on the trail breaking new ground, past where we had already trod, the rain seemed to lessen. About time. The ground, however, was getting soggier. Melanie gave a whine and nosed at something directly in her path. I tightened up on the lead, and adjusted my headlamp.

"What is it, girl?"

It was a lady's brown shoe, a slip-on with elastic at the heel, and half-full of mud.

Rigdon peered over my shoulder. "Do you think it belonged to Mrs. Zeckermann?"

"Yes. Melanie wouldn't have paid any attention if it wasn't the scent she was seeking."

I knocked out most of the mud, bagged it, and slipped it in a pocket, and we continued. The rain seemed to finally be over, but we were still sprinkled with water falling from the trees. The wind was picking up.

On the first check, Jasmine sounded chipper.

"Slim to Joe. Over."

"Joe here. How's it going? Over."

"Slow but steady. Gulliver's still trailing. You? Over."

"Fine. Watch where you step. Over and out."

"Will do. Out."

My gut didn't relent and ease its nagging, even on hearing they were doing fine so far.

The swamp is never quiet. A bullfrog can make a sound almost like a grunt from a bull gator. With hundreds, possibly thousands raising their croaks into the wind, it can get downright noisy out here. The lonely harsh cry of a screech owl rose above the clatter. The bushes rustled and cracked. Crows called their warning of our approach. Birds disturbed on their roost gave panicky flutters and rose higher to escape our trespass. Other unidentifiable cries could make me jerk the light on my forehead off Melanie's path, and turn to the scan the darkness. Rigdon's light was played around us more than on the ground in front of him. We were both skittish and jumpy. The swamp belonged to its critters and natural inhabitants after dark. We were the unwanted intruders.

"What was that?" Rigdon shouted after a particularly throaty roar.

"If I didn't know they were extinct in these parts, I would guess a hungry panther," I answered half in jest.

"Jesus," he said, sounding shaken.

I smiled. His first nighttime excursion into Okefenokee was an experience he wouldn't easily forget.

Melanie was three feet in front of me, and I was two steps into the muck, before I felt the deadly pull on my feet. Melanie let out a terrified yelp and I felt her lead tighten, as she was frantically trying to pull free of the suction pulling her downward.

I threw myself backward, trying to gain inches of her lead, hand over hand, and my muscles strained to their limit. First rule: present the widest part of your anatomy to the surface and don't waste your strength trying to struggle. I had read that somewhere, and had imprinted its image on my brain in case I ever needed it. I remembered, and wished I could explain the theory to Melanie, who was pumping away at trying to dog paddle her way out of peril. I screamed at Ridgon.

"Get the line on her! Around her stomach, not her neck!"

My lamp was directed upward and I couldn't see shit. My feet cleared the surface. I dug in my elbows, scooted a few inches back, and gained another precious hand span of her lead. I kept a death grip on Melanie's lifeline and managed to twist my head to the left.

The beam of light reflected off Rigdon's bulk as he passed above me, momentarily groping my stomach. He had dropped the light to untie the rope. He couldn't see, and was running his hand down her lead to guide him. He took another step towards Melanie and passed from my sight.

My immediate fear was that her lead would part from the harness connection. I imagined the light metal clasp bending from the pressure and the leash pulling free. I knew that most of these sinkholes were shallow, usually no more than two or three feet. Melanie measured twenty-six inches to her shoulder, not counting her head. Three feet would be deadly. A lot of deer were discovered out here, with their heads still above the surface, bloated in death. Their hearts gave out from struggling to get out, or they starved to death. No one was sure.

"Get the rope around her middle, behind her legs," I screamed into the darkness. I strained my neck muscles, trying to lift my head, but the weight of my backpack kept me down. I was trying to put my light on them. I dug in my elbows and twisted up on my left side.

"I'm working on it," he yelled back. His voice was high and full of panic. I tried to remove all anxiety from mine.

"Good dog, Melanie. Stand still, girl. Steady. Good dog. You'll be all right."

She wouldn't understand the words. I was trying to calm her terrible struggles.

My light rested on Rigdon's back. I could only see Melanie's tail, held high, and whipping back and forth like an out-of-control metronome. Her continuous high whine of terror pierced my heart. I managed to hold the light steady and ignored my screaming neck muscles.

Melanie's lead suddenly went slack, and my heart stopped. In the next second, Rigdon's bulk landed a foot from my left ear, and his scream seem to pierce my eardrums.

"Pull!"

I placed my fists hand over hand, laboriously reclaiming inches, my shoulders on fire.

"Now, pull," he shrieked.

At the height of our combined endeavors, I heard the suction break with a noisy pop and Melanie began moving toward us. I lunged for her head and missed, as my gloves slid through the slime to her belly. I wrapped my arms about her middle. She was all over me; her slobber was mixing with my tears as she drooled, whined with relief, and licked my face.

I sat up, shrugging my backpack off my shoulders, and unbuckled the waist strap. I wiped my face and blew my nose. Melanie chose that moment to shake the mud and slime from her coat. I had to clean my face and neck again.

"God, Charley!" I said with fervor, "You saved Melanie's life! You're my hero! Thank you, thank you!"

He rolled over, collected the heavy flashlight, and sat up. He didn't utter a word.

"Charley? Are you all right?"

"I'm resting, give me a minute."

His voice trembled, and he sounded close to tears. I babbled on about his bravery, giving him some time to recover, until I saw in his flashlight beam a smear of blood on his hand. I scooted over and grabbed his right arm and adjusted my light on his palm.

"Oh, Charley," I groaned as tears sprang to my eyes, "why weren't you wearing the gloves?"

Both palms were scored with deep burns from the nylon-braided rope. Thick mud covered the wounds, which were leaking clear fluid and blood.

His voice was husky. "I was sneaking a smoke. I knew you didn't allow cigarettes on a search."

"I quit three months ago. You should have said something, I would've stopped."

"I was so scared," he whispered. He ran the back of his hand under his eyes, smearing the leaked moisture and mud.

"Ah, Charley," I said, enveloping him within my arms, "all men are scared. The brave ones are those that can still function despite their fears."

I cleaned and dressed his hands with gauze. Melanie had curled into a wet ball.

"How about a sandwich?" I asked.

"You brought food?"

"Always prepared."

At the smell of food, Melanie moved closer. I fed her bits of my sandwich.

"Do you have any dry cigarettes left?"

He fumbled in his slicker pocket and produced a crumpled pack and a lighter. I took them from him, lit one, and took a deep drag. Nothing had ever tasted so good. I placed it in his mouth and handed them back.

"Don't you want one?"

"Boy, do I, but I just took the hit to calm my nerves. With three months under my belt, I can't waste them."

"Won't the dog smell the smoke?"

"We're in the open with enough wind. She'll be fine."

I checked the time. I was ten minutes late on calling Jasmine. Our quicksand adventure had made me forget to call. I dug out the radio, and tried twice to reach her, without success. Now I understood why she hadn't called me. Moisture, malfunction, or whatever; we now couldn't connect. I put it away with disgust. Half the time, it didn't work out here. I'd try again later.

Rigdon finished his cigarette, and I helped him pull the gloves over his bandages. He did some flinching, but didn't mention being in pain.

"Can you take aspirin and codeine?"

"For colds and in cough syrup, yeah."

I dug out a Number Three Empirin Compound, and made him take it.

I was tempted to take one myself. My arm and shoulder muscles were screaming foul with every movement, but I decided against it. The temperature must have dipped five degrees in the last two hours. I guessed it was around 37 to 40 degrees now, and it was early. If it kept dropping, I would need all my wits to function.

"Now we have to find out how our abductor, and Naomi carrying her child, got around this sinkhole."

"Maybe they didn't."

He was staring at the dark pit we had avoided.

"Well, we know the abductor and the baby made it, or Jasmine wouldn't have had a scent trail to follow."

"I should have said, maybe the woman didn't make it."

"These quagmires are not very deep. Normally, they are only two to three feet in depth. 'Course, there are exceptions, but we'll know for sure if we find her scent on the other side of this puddle."

I adjusted my light at my feet and put Melanie back on Naomi's scent. She backtracked several feet and wandered forward again, working her nose back and forth, and stopped several times, to test the ground. Back within two feet of the mud, she moved right, and I whispered encouragement in her ears.

We went around a clump of growth, and then went back to the left. I wondered if the abductor had led us to the brink of the quicksand, to possibly throw off the dogs; but not knowing if the person knew dogs would be used, it was useless conjecture. He might have felt the pull of the mud, backed up, and detoured.

After ten minutes of torturous passage with little gain, Melanie froze, sniffed again, and raised her head to announce she was near her target.

I yelled with delight at her wonderful baying. We surged forward. I prayed that Naomi was still alive. I knew that she could be dead, but I longed for a miracle. I tottered forward, careless in my haste.

Melanie ran up to a prone mud-splattered figure lying face down to the left of the path. With her excited baying and drooling tongue, she was trying to rouse her target. She wanted her pats and hugs for a successful quest.

In the bright circle of my light, Naomi didn't move.

15

Trouble Comes in Threes

January 5, Thursday, 6:15 P.M.

I pulled Melanie back, heaping praises and gave her a quick hug before I tied her lead to a thick limb of a nearby gallberry bush. She was so excited, she continued baying. I knelt beside Naomi's body.

Rigdon was kneeling by her other side, trying to remove his gloves.

"Don't take them off," I said sharply. "I'll check her out. It's too cold not to wear them and you might not be able to get them back on."

"She's dead, isn't she?" His voice held sadness.

"It looks that way."

He held his flashlight on her back. I took a deep breath and rolled her over.

I thought I heard something, but Melanie was still baying, and I wasn't sure. I jerked off my right glove, and placed my fingers underneath her jaw, feeling for a pulse. She opened her eyes and groaned.

"She's alive!" I exclaimed to Rigdon.

"I heard her! I heard her!" he yelled.

Naomi's mouth was moving, but I couldn't hear her.

"Charley, go hug Melanie, and tell her to hush! Naomi's trying to speak!"

I leaned closer to Naomi's face. Her eyes widened, and she gave me a terrified stare.

"You're safe, Naomi, I've come to help you. Tell me where you hurt."

"Who are you?" She was whispering, but I heard her this time, because Rigdon had finally got Melanie quiet.

"I'm Jo Beth Sidden, and my bloodhound tracked you. You're safe now. Are you hurt?"

She spoke louder. "She has Andy! She took my baby! You have to find her and get him back! Is he here? Tell me!"

"She's not here, and you're safe. We are looking for Andy now. You have to tell me where you are injured."

"Forget me, you have to find her, she's crazy! She has a knife! Please find my baby!"

Tears were leaking from her eyes and puddling in her ears.

"Where are you hurt?" I yelled to get her attention.

She moved her right hand to her left shoulder, just below the collarbone. I shrugged off my pack and quickly undid the belt, dragging it close.

I gently removed her hand and unbuttoned her blouse. She was so muddy that I would have missed the wound if she hadn't pointed it out. The rain had removed the blood, and washed the area clean of dried blood. There was a two-inch gash about three inches from her clavicle. Her teeth started chattering. She could be going into shock, or simply bone-chilling cold. I knew I had to get her warm, and patch the shoulder so she wouldn't lose any more blood. Her blouse was short-sleeved, and she had been wet for over five hours.

"Did it bleed a lot?"

"I think so. She stabbed me in the car before she pulled me out. I was trying to get away from her. With the rain it was hard to tell, it just kept washing it away. She took Andy and I followed her."

"Are you dizzy? Weak? Nauseous?"

"All of them when I was walking, but now I'm cold." It was difficult to understand her speech. She was shivering and having trouble pronouncing the words clearly.

I pulled out the rescue sled and started to spread it out beside her. Rigdon was hovering.

"How can I help?"

"I'll tell you in a minute."

I unzipped the long tubular bag and removed the small inflatable bags. I was tucking one side of the sled under her as far as it would go down the length of her body.

"Get on my right side, Charley. When I say to, roll her up on her left shoulder. Use the back of your hands and forearms; don't try to use your palms. Now!"

My right hand braced her shoulder, while my left frantically stuffed half the material down the length of her body.

"Now lower her, easy, easy. Now move back."

I crawled over her, pulled the crumpled half from beneath her body, and straightened her. Her gash had started bleeding. I ripped open two sterile gauze four-by-four pads and placed them on the wound.

"Hold the compress firmly with the back of your fingers, use steady pressure to stop the bleeding. That's it, good."

"Shouldn't you zip her up so she can get warm?" Rigdon inquired, sounding anxious.

"As soon as I finish."

I grabbed my small pair of scissors and cut open her lightweight wool slacks at her left hip. I put my face near hers.

"Naomi! Have you ever been injected with morphine?"

"Yes."

"Did you have any reaction?"

"I don't think so." It sounded as if she was fading and I wasn't sure if she knew what I had asked, but she was getting the shot. It was going to be a tough rough trip back for her.

"Hold the light for me," I told Rigdon.

In its gleam, I tore open the disposable syringe and filled the barrel. I cleaned her hip and popped in the needle. It was the second time I had ever given a shot. The first one went into Jasmine, when she broke her leg during a search. I hoped this rescue turned out as well as hers had. I opened more sterile pads and bandaged her shoulder. I fished out a handful of Hershey's Kisses and starting removing the wrappers. I leaned close.

"Can you chew and swallow some chocolate?"

"I think so."

I pressed one against her lips. She opened her mouth and started chewing. I set the candy aside, and started inflating the small pillows and tucking them around her, starting at her feet.

The sled is made of the same material as my rescue suit, a thin variation of Kevlar. It is impenetrable except by bullets. The bottom is heavy smooth galvanized rubber. Melanie can pull it in an emergency, but it's easier to put the braces on and do it myself.

When I had her packed in tight with pillows, I zipped it up to her neck. It has a hood, but I wanted to question her before she went to sleep.

"Naomi, can you hear me?"

I was talking loudly and with authority. I wanted her total attention.

She swallowed. "Yes."

"Was the woman alone?"

"Yes."

"Was she dropped there by a car, or was she walking?"

"She walked up and startled me, I didn't hear her because of the rain. I want my baby!"

"Listen to me, Naomi. A team is searching for your child as we speak. I promise you we will find him. In a very few minutes, you're going to get sleepy. Don't fight it. The trip out is going to hurt. You'll be jostled, a lot. Do you understand?"

"Find my baby." Her tears returned.

"You have my word! Now quit crying and listen! This is important! What did she look like?"

"She was a monster, huge."

"How tall?"

"Over six feet."

"How much did she weigh?"

"A lot. Gross."

My stomach spasmed. It couldn't be.

"What color was her hair?"

"Light brown, I think. It was wet."

Naomi closed her eyes. Her head tilted to the left. I was losing her. I put my hand on her chin, straightened her head, and adjusted her pillow. She was falling asleep.

"Naomi! Stay with me for one more question! Did she giggle a lot?"

I had to lean close to hear her whisper.

"The knife was bloody before she stabbed me." Her face relaxed, and her jaw sagged. She was out like a light.

I sat back and stared at nothing.

"Give me a cigarette," I told Rigdon. He started fumbling, and I leaned over and pulled them out. I got his going and passed it over. I lit mine, and took a long drag.

"Ernestine Whitley," I whispered. "It doesn't seem possible."

"You know the woman who stabbed Mrs. Zeckermann?"

"I went to school with her. She wasn't in my class; she was two grades above me. She got a late start, so she must be thirty-five, thirty-six, now. She is mentally retarded. This was back before they put them in special classes and gave them more individual help. They let them join in classwork, passed them every year, so they could be among friends. 'Course, Ernestine had few friends. The girls made fun of her, and the boys ignored her."

"Are you sure it's her?"

"The last time I saw her a few months back, she weighed in the neighborhood of three hundred pounds. She has long stringy light-brown hair, and I think she lives somewhere around here. It's her."

I took another drag. I wasn't aware I was crying until my eyes blurred.

"A couple of sixth graders jumped on me one afternoon after school when I was in the second grade. She picked them both up and shook them. They went screaming to the teacher. Ernestine got into a lot of trouble over it. They took her out of class for a while, but they finally let her come back."

"You liked her, didn't you?"

"She was simple, but very sweet. I felt sorry for her."

"Well, she had one friend." Rigdon smiled at me.

"No, she didn't," I said harshly. "She began following me around during recess, and the kids started teasing me about it. I told her to stop, but she wouldn't. So I called her Doughface, like the other girls, and she eventually quit."

"Hey," he said, noticing my tears, "you were just a kid. You didn't know better."

"Yes I did. I just couldn't take the peer pressure. I caved in because I wanted to be liked by all the other little beasts in my class."

I stood up, pulled out some jerky, and fed Melanie a handful.

I sat smoking the cigarette, feeling guilty. But enjoying every puff. I thought it strange that I was working on two cases of kidnapped babies, which had happened thirty years apart. One died and I was only seeking the truth of who committed the crime. The other baby could be dead, too, and if Ernestine Whitley was the killer, there wouldn't be any justice meted out here, either. She would never stand trial. I shook off the morbid thoughts.

"I think the shot has Naomi zonked. I'm gonna try the radio again before we start."

I was shocked when Hank answered almost immediately.

"Base to Rescue One, you're five by five. Over."

"Has the husband arrived yet?"

"About thirty minutes ago. Over."

"Can he hear me?"

"No, he's near the fire. Over."

"Get an ambulance rolling, she's been stabbed and lost some blood. She may go into shock, but I don't think her injury is life-threatening. I'm bringing her out in the sled. The scent trail split. We went after the mother, and Jasmine and Tom went after the perp and baby. Have you heard from Jasmine?"

"Nothing but you trying to reach her a while back. I wondered what had happened. Over."

"Hank, I have some bad news. J. C.'s not with you, is he?"

Lieutenant J. C. Sirmons was Hank's second-in-command in the Sheriff's Department.

"He's back at the station. Why? Over."

"Isn't he related to Miz Pansy Whitley?"

"She's his aunt on his mother's side. Why? Over."

"You better keep this off the airwaves. I think you need to send a unit to check on her."

"Why? Over."

"It was a woman walking down the road who stabbed Naomi, abducted her, and now has the baby. Naomi said the knife was bloody before she was stabbed. The description fits Ernestine."

"Jesus! I'll send a man to her house. Over."

"Keep trying to raise Jasmine. Explain about Ernestine. It should take us about an hour. See you."

"We'll be waiting. Take care. Out."

I turned to Rigdon. "You'll have to carry the backpack. I'll have my hands full with Melanie and the sled."

"I can pull the sled," he stated.

"Not with those hands, you can't."

I held the backpack, adjusted the straps, and buckled the belt. I attached the sled harness and untied Melanie. My hands felt raw and irritated from Melanie's rescue. The suede was soaked, and mud had oozed through the stitches. I didn't have an extra pair, and no way to clean these out here. They would have to hold up to Melanie's pull and guiding the sled until we got back to the road.

"Take us home, Melanie. Load up, girl. Take us home."

We started the trek back to civilization.

16

The Price of Terror

January 5, Thursday, 7:30 P.M.

The temperature had taken a nosedive or the wind chill had increased. Whether it was 32 degrees or not, it *felt* as if it was freezing. My rescue suit was keeping my body warm, but my face was so cold I couldn't feel my nose, and my hands were numb inside my wet gloves. I knew Rigdon was suffering. His serge uniform pants above his boots had become wet with slime during Melanie's rescue and had probably dripped into his boots, wetting his feet. His hands had to be throbbing from the rope cut, plus aching from the cold. His gloves were as wet as mine were.

His shoulders were strained from the tug-of-war with the quicksand, and he had a thirty-two-pound pack on his back. I remembered that he had tired quickly last summer as he had lugged my pack for some minutes, in the heat of a July day. The cold didn't make it any easier. He hadn't complained, but when I had last sneaked a quick look back at him, his face looked chalky and drawn in the reflection from his flashlight. Just clutching the heavy five-cell must hurt his damaged hands. I noticed that he switched it back and forth often.

I figured we had another quarter-mile of rough going until we reached the road. I called a halt by stopping and facing his light. I wasn't feeling too chipper myself. Holding Melanie back in her fast break for home and guiding the sled over the roots, straw, and mud, plus dodging around obstructive bushes, I, too, could use a break.

I was now facing into the wind. As we ceased crashing through the foliage, I heard noises resembling our passage almost directly behind us. I took two fast steps back to Rigdon, clicked off my headlamp, plucked the flashlight from his hand, and turned it off. I pointed it back down the trail we were traveling. There was no moon. The sky above us was just a tad less dark than at ground level. I pulled off my right glove with my teeth, unzipped my suit, and slipped my hand near my shoulder holster.

"What is it?" Rigdon whispered.

I sank my elbow into his stomach to warm him to be silent. I waited until the noisy thrashing was almost upon us. My eyes were adjusting in the darkness, and I felt I would have the advantage when I switched on my light.

Just as I was preparing to click it on, the round beam of a headlight cleared a bush about twelve feet away. I hit the switch to reveal Gulliver and Jasmine, who were blinded by its glare.

"Jasmine?"

"Oh, thank God, I found you." Jasmine was sobbing as she blundered towards us.

Gulliver dodged around me to rub noses with Melanie. Jasmine stumbled forward, and I quickly dropped the light from her eyes. I grasped her shoulders.

"What's wrong? Where's Tom?"

"He's dead, and it's my fault!" she blubbered.

Her eyes were wild, and she was shaking from head to toe. My mind absorbed the shock. I reacted instinctively and grabbed Gulliver's lead. Jasmine swayed.

"Help me," I grunted to Rigdon while I tried to hold her upright. The flashlight was knocked from my hand by one of the leads. Rigdon jumped behind her, supporting her body as she crumpled.

"Have you got her?" I asked anxiously. The dogs were entangled around my legs.

"Yes, I've got her."

"Put her head between her knees!"

I couldn't back up; I would step or fall on Naomi in the sled behind me. I was being pulled in all directions. Fighting for balance, I couldn't adjust my headlamp to see how the leads ensnared me. Both dogs were fighting to get free. I guess they sensed her terror, and were confused. I sidestepped, releasing and dropping the sled harness. I remained upright, and managed to clear my legs. I backed up until I hit an obstruction. I looped both leads around the bole, tying a hasty slipknot in case we had to leave in a hurry.

It was hard to get a deep breath. My heart was hammering in my chest, and my head was pounding. I retrieved the fallen flashlight and trained it on the rescue sled. I unzipped the hood. Naomi was snoring in her drugged sleep. I pulled down the zipper and checked her bandage. The dogs' paws had missed her, or they hadn't broken open the stab wound. There was no leakage on her dressing. I covered her.

I switched the light to Jasmine and Rigdon. She was sitting, and was slumped against Rigdon. I undid the waist strap and worked her backpack from her shoulders. Then I removed my pack from Rigdon's back.

Her head was lowered. She had lost her rain cap, or had removed it. Her soft curls were plastered to her scalp with mud. She was covered with more mud than both Rigdon and me. I remembered a smear of blood on her cheek, and crawled behind Rigdon and dug into my pack for the first aid kit.

Immediate and compelling action had kept my mind clear. Now I had to find out the fate of the baby, Tom, and Ernestine. On my knees in front of Jasmine, I opened the kit. She was sobbing weakly, like a lost soul.

"Hey," I said softly, lifting her head, "don't try to talk. I'm gonna clean your face."

She sat like a wounded child, face upturned, and endured my ministrations stoically, trying to hold back her tears, save for an occasional hiccup. With the mud removed, I discovered two scratches. A shallow line on her forehead, and a deeper one on her cheek.

"This is going to burn," I warned as I dabbed both with antiseptic. I covered them with Band-Aids. I dug out her bandanna, tying it under her chin. It would keep her ears covered and somewhat warmer. I held my canteen and made her take several sips, until she shook her head.

I took off her gloves and mine, and rubbed her cold hands, trying to generate warmth. Her eyes looked haunted.

"Feel better?" I asked.

"The . . . thing . . . just kept raising the knife and stabbing him, over . . . and . . . over," she whispered.

Her eyes closed and she shook her head, as if she was trying to block some terrible vision.

"Jasmine, listen to me," I said in my best lecturing voice, "start at the beginning. Tell it in a logical sequence. We need to know everything. It will make you feel better, I promise."

Jesus. What I knew about psychology could be written on a thumbnail. I said it to soothe and appease. I could only hope I wasn't doing her any damage.

"We were tired and cold. We had just halted to eat the sandwiches when Gulliver strained forward and started baying." She swallowed and continued. "I was trying to hold Gulliver back and quiet him at the same time. We had disagreed earlier on whether I should enforce the silent command. Selph said we should let Gulliver sound off, it alarmed most people, and it might shake up the kidnapper we were following."

Jasmine looked me in the eye. "You were right in not trusting my ability. I should have had Gulliver on a silent approach. Selph was older and had more experience. I listened to him, instead of relying on my gut feeling. My decision got him killed."

"Nonsense. If I had been there, I would've done the same as you," I vowed, lying through my teeth.

"Would you?" She looked uncertain. "Are you sure?"

"Positive." I put every ounce of certainty I could muster into that one word.

Her tense expression relaxed as she searched my face.

"I was so sure I screwed up," she whispered.

"You didn't. What happened then?"

"I couldn't silence or control Gulliver, he just went bananas. He was jumping and twisting and howling, all at the same time." Her voice lowered and she frowned as she returned to her narrative.

"He has never acted that way before. It scared me. I fell in the mud and he was all over me. I finally got him by the neck and held on tight. His bays turned into high-pitched whines of fear. He kept trying to twist from my grasp."

I didn't rush her.

"All I had was the headlamp. I couldn't understand why Selph hadn't put the flashlight on us, to see what was going on. I was on my knees and confused. I turned my head behind me to locate Selph . . . He was face down in the mud, about twenty feet away. This . . . thing was above him, and the knife flashed as it moved up and down, up and down."

Jasmine's eyes were on me, but I was not what she was seeing.

"I only had a brief glance. A bush blocked part of my line of vision. The thing was gigantic! Suddenly it stopped, as if it just noticed the light. It rose to a terrible height. I got my gun out, snapped off my light, and tried to silently turn Gulliver around. *He started dragging me!* I lost the gun, trying to get control. His terror was contagious. Without the gun, I couldn't make myself return, even if Gulliver had allowed me. He made a wide circle around the danger and started back this way, and we ran into you. I botched the search. I'm sorry."

Rigdon patted her shoulders awkwardly with his damaged hands, and I wiped her face and let her cry. I spoke earnestly, telling her that she had no control over what had happened, and to quit blaming herself. When she calmed down, and I was sure that she was registering what I was saying, I told her about Ernestine.

"It . . . she was so *big!*"

I recalled my earlier mention of a swamp monster to Hank, and felt shame. Jasmine and Gulliver must have felt as if they had seen one. Gulliver had smelled her madness. If a dog can tell when an epileptic is going to have a grand mal seizure—minutes before it occurs—it's possible that Gulliver could sense her madness.

I lit a cigarette for Rigdon, and pulled out two granola bars and persuaded Jasmine to eat one. I munched on mine and tried to map out what to do next. I could not walk out of this swamp without trying to rescue the baby. It was not that I was this brave, bigger-than-life hero. The very thought of Ernestine skulking behind a bush turned my knees to jelly. To leave, I would have a different opinion of myself. A smaller and weaker portrait of who I perceived myself to be.

Also, there was Tom Selph, lying somewhere ahead in the trail. He hadn't volunteered for this duty; I had requested his services from Hank. He was, in all probability, dead. But since I had put him in the place where he was killed, I was going to make damn sure that he was dead before I slept. I couldn't live with being told later that he survived for several hours, alone, before expiring.

So I would continue. I wanted to do it alone. If I went back with Jasmine and Rigdon, Hank would not allow me to return without him and half his department behind me. With the knowledge of Selph's fate, at the hands of a knife-wielding psychopath, I would be leading a trigger-happy horde that would make more noise than our high school marching band.

I owed Ernestine an act of kindness, because I had been too gutless to offer it in grade school. The Bible mentions, your sins will find you out. Mine had just come home to roost.

Jasmine had finished her granola bar, and we both drank water. I excused us, and Jasmine and I walked several feet into the brush and went through the disrobing process we had to perform every time we peed.

"Jasmine," I said, as I pulled up my clothes, "I need to ask you a question, and you must promise me to tell me the truth. It's vital. Are you able to lead Rigdon out of here? He won't be much help. Melanie walked into quicksand, and he waded in and pulled her out. He wasn't wearing his gloves and his palms are deeply scored with rope burns. He's not able to put any pressure on them."

"Yes," she answered.

"And pull the sled with Naomi?" I sounded doubtful.

"I was scared, Jo Beth, not faint from exertion. I'm rested, and over my fright. I'll be fine."

I believed her, because she said what I wanted to hear. I checked the time as we walked back. It was ten after eight. Hank would be sweating our return. He knew that I kept the radio off and he couldn't instigate calls; but he would give me hell when I returned because I didn't keep him informed. I was forty minutes late on my estimated time of arrival. That wasn't all he would have to yell at, but I'd be like Scarlett in *Gone With the* Wind—I'd worry about it tomorrow.

I told Rigdon that he would be going back with Jasmine and Melanie. I opened Jasmine's backpack and cut two eight-foot lengths of new rope. I had wrapped up my muddy one and buried it near the sinkhole. It was too soiled to store inside my pack.

"Jasmine, help Charlie out of his slicker and tunic. Leave his shirt sleeves buttoned."

I tied a rope on each rear corner of the sled, then fastened a loop on each end. I pulled out two three-inch Ace bandages that were two feet in length. I wrapped both his elbows, just like they were sprained ankles. Round and round, till I had them well padded.

"Put his coat and slicker back on, Jasmine, while I demonstrate how this works."

I nestled the loops in my elbows and held my forearms aloft. I pulled on my left, then my right, to turn the sled.

"I think it'll work."

"Why didn't you do this sooner, so I could help you?" Rigdon was indignant.

"To tell you the truth, I just thought of it," I announced wryly, "or I would've.

"Hear me out before you raise any objections," I said to Jasmine and Rigdon. "I'm going after the baby. I have an advantage that neither Jasmine nor any one else around here has. I know Ernestine. I went to school with her. I may be able to talk her into giving me the baby. If I went back, Hank would insist on sending in the troops, and then I'd have no edge at all."

"After what you told me about her, you think you have an *edge*?" Rigdon looked at me askance.

"Listen, blabbermouth, do you want to discuss what we shared in confidence a short time ago?" I spoke half in jest. "If so, I'll start."

Jasmine was dividing a questioning glance between us.

"Did I miss something?"

"Not a thing," Rigdon returned bleakly. "Just a joke between Jo Beth and me."

I gave them both a confident expression.

"Jasmine, Hank will try and talk you into leading in a posse. Don't listen to him, and don't let him call Wayne with the excuse that I need backup. Promise?"

"Do I have a choice?"

"Absolutely not."

"I promise."

"Atta girl. Tell me about the woods. What is it like there? How long did you think you spent coming out?"

"I can't judge distance traveled as well as you. I would say that it took half the time coming back as the total journey coming in. Does that help?"

"Good enough. Same type of terrain, or was it lower?"

"About the same, except just before we . . . encountered the wom . . . Ernestine. There was a small pond with a beach around it. White firm sand. It seemed like we had crossed over into a new country."

"Was there a clearing large enough for a helicopter to land?"

"I would think so, there were no trees close to the water. It looked as if someone had dug a fish pond."

"How close to Selph's body?"

Jasmine faltered. "Ah . . . perhaps . . . a hundred feet."

"Let's rearrange the packs. I'll take yours. We'll leave mine, no sense lugging it back tonight. Wayne and Donnie Ray can pick it up tomorrow."

I pulled out a large trash bag to put over my pack. I took Naomi's shoe, her sweater, and Jasmine's nonworking radio and crammed them in my pack. I put the baby's scent articles, the stuffed bear and pacifier, in my suit pocket. The sleeper, diapers, baby wipes, and milk bottle went into the backpack I was taking.

Jasmine slid my backpack into the trash bag while I held it open. I secured it with a twist and placed it behind a tree.

"I guess we're ready to roll."

I watched Jasmine and Rigdon awkwardly manhandle the sled, turning in the small space available. She fed Melanie some deer jerky, and gave her the command to head home. Jasmine turned and waved before they disappeared from view, and I waved back.

I eyed Gulliver.

"Well, it's just you and me, buddy. Shall we go slay the dragon?"

17

Bleak Just Got Bleaker

January 5, Thursday, 8:30 P.M.

Leaning near Gulliver's ears, I began the time-consuming, tedious refrain to start a silent search.

"Shh, hush, no, no, shh, hush, Gulliver. Hush."

I was weary, my back and shoulders were aching. I fantasized about a gallon of hot coffee and a foot-long cigarette. I trudged along, leaning over often, and whispered again, and again. I had to backtrack until we intersected the original trail where Gulliver following the child's scent had veered right and our trail to Naomi had turned to the left.

I had to trust that I would find it quick. The trail we were on was fairly easy to follow. The sled had bent the grass, and left an occasional rut in soft mud. The way the wind was now blowing, the bent grass wouldn't stay down long, and when it returned upright, the ruts would be hidden and the visual track would disappear.

When I thought we were close, I gave Gulliver some jerky and let him sniff the stuffed toy. I was trying to put him back on the baby's scent trail. If he missed it, or couldn't pull that one particular smell out of the air and isolate it, I would be out of options.

I was also worried that he would freak out again when we neared

Selph's body and Ernestine. I just didn't know what he would do. Bloodhounds are not machines. They are as diverse as people. Each search turns up new problems. You learn from experience, and fail as often as you win. Mantrailing is not a precise science.

Up and down went my weary back. My canteen felt lighter, and I knew my water wouldn't last much longer. Whispering, and the extra exertion with the cumbersome boots, were drying my mouth. I had another pint bottle inside the pack, but it might be a very long night. I started taking smaller sips and holding them longer on my tongue. I didn't have to share with Gulliver. He stopped when he was thirsty and lapped out of puddles. It didn't bother him that it was dark in color and tasted of leaf matter and roots.

I decided to give my back a rest. I leaned down and whispered for a brief halt. I didn't want to pull him off the scent if he had found it, I just needed a temporary respite. He ignored me, and continued slinging his ears and walking forward. My pulse quickened. He must be back on the baby's scent trail! I hadn't realized that we had reached the split in the trail, and were now following Jasmine and Gulliver's original path.

I began to take in some slack on the lead. He had been working about two to three feet in front of me. I shortened his lead until we were almost side by side. I mentally groaned at what I knew came next. I knew I couldn't blunder into Ernestine or Selph's body without some prior warning. I didn't fancy the thought of Ernestine jumping from behind a bush *after* we had passed, and coming up behind me. I switched the lead from my right to my left. I bent over until I could curl my gloved fingers over the base of his tail.

When working a scent trail, a bloodhound holds his tail in a high arch over his body. When he nears his target on a regular search, he bays his excitement. On a silent search, he could only signal his joy by rapidly twitching his tail and whipping it back and forth. This would be my advance warning.

Try listing to the right, wearing neoprene crepe-soled wading boots, as you monitor a loosely held tail of a dog in constant motion, keeping in step, and all the while toting a heavy pack on your back. It ain't easy. Just as my back signaled it wasn't going to take it anymore, I felt Gulliver's tail moving erratically sideways, instead of a smooth up-and-down motion.

I switched off my headlamp, pulled back on the lead, and went to my knees beside him. Holding his neck, I reinforced my "silent" command in a low whisper. I strained to hear movement above the wind. It was impossible. The wind would cover a careful approach. Well, if I couldn't hear *her*, it meant that she couldn't hear *me*, and the wind was still in my face. That meant that the bone-chilling breeze was blowing their scent here. Ernestine, the baby, and Selph's body were still in front of me. At least, I sincerely hoped to hell they were.

I was basing this tenet on Jasmine's description of a pond with a sandy beach. It had yet to appear. I could probably get closer with Gulliver before I left him, but I didn't want to take a chance. No way did I want to walk into Ernestine with her knife while Gulliver danced his berserk version of the Watusi.

In the darkness, my night vision returned. The cold front moving in had cleared out most of the cloud cover. It was going to be a cold clear night. I could now make out the dark shape of trees against the lighter skyline. The trail was still shaded and mysterious. I felt my way to the closest tree and found thick grass at the base. I tied Gulliver's lead around its trunk.

I fed him some jerky and hugged his neck. I crawled a few feet and heard a soft whine escape his large jaws. I froze. After listening awhile, I ventured a few more feet, but I didn't hear another. I stood and walked, staying in the shadows, with one hand outstretched so I wouldn't blunder into a tree or thick brush. I couldn't use my compass in the dark, so I was counting my steps. I was up to thirty-three when I could make out light-colored sand and the ebony-colored pond on my right. Jasmine had estimated one hundred feet to Selph's body. I had stridden a total of eighty steps when I spotted a small glow at ground level about twenty-five feet ahead.

It was the flashlight Selph had dropped when Ernestine attacked him. It was still burning. I took a few more steps and then started crawling. I didn't want to trip over him, or worse, step on him. The bright yellow slicker was easy to spot as I drew near. I kept swiveling my head from side to side as I approached, fearing that Ernestine would rush out of the darkness with her knife upraised.

He was on his stomach. When I crawled next to him, I could see the ripped slashes in the raincoat and dark black splotches on his back. Removing my right glove, I took a trembling breath and placed the tips of my fingers at the side of his neck. His skin was icy and didn't feel like flesh, more like marble in winter. My hand was shaking from tension and the cold. His head was turned to the right. I crawled around him so I could see his face.

The flashlight had fallen so that it was pointing in his general direction. There was enough light that I knew I was looking at death. His eyes were open and from the first glance I knew that he was gone, but I leaned close and forced myself to be sure. I worked my hand inside his slicker, then his tunic, and there was no warmth, pulse, or heartbeat. It seemed like I listened for a long time, hoping for some sign of life. It probably wasn't as long as I imagined. Time felt distorted. I decided to leave the flashlight burning. I hated to leave him in the dark, and it might tip Ernestine to my presence if it suddenly went out.

I crawled a few feet before I stood. I didn't want to be outlined in its glow if she was watching. I moved cautiously forward, leaving the light and Selph behind me. I would stop every few feet and listen. I was up to 107 steps when I saw the yellow flickering glow of a bonfire.

Advancing, I used each large tree and growth for cover. Peering around a thick clump of palmetto, I could see a small clearing in the trees and movement just on the other side of the fire. From where I stood, it seemed that she had something wrapped around her, and was sitting beneath some sort of lean-to. The fire was between us and I couldn't see well enough to discern what she was doing. I went back behind the razor-sharp fronds and removed my backpack. I took out my binoculars and stepped forward until I got a clear view.

Ernestine was sitting on a ruined mattress with a tattered patched quilt around her shoulders. She was cradling the boy to her enormous bosom. The glasses brought her so close, I could tell that her lips were moving. Her face still looked unformed, and unlined, as it had in grade school. Age hadn't marked her. She looked as if someone had carelessly stuck on eyes, nose, and a mouth, and forgot to smooth out the excess fat and arrange them properly. Her chalk-white flesh bulged around each orifice to the point that it looked painful.

A desolate chill formed in my gut. I could only see the back of the child's head. It was uncovered. They were six feet from the fire, which was radiating warmth, but not enough to dispel the wind chill and freezing temperature! I had tied a bandanna around my ears a couple of hours ago, and had the rain hat over them. They felt like icicles that would break at a touch, and I had been exercising. Jesus.

I quickly scanned the opening. Nothing grew within a twenty-foot circle of the mattress. Two sheets of rusted tin formed the roof. The poles to the right were listing at an angle, and looked ready to collapse with the next gust of wind. I couldn't tell if the bedding and quilt were wet or dry, but with no sides to shield it from the earlier rain, and no waterproof material within sight, it had to be wet.

No way to sneak up on her. She was constantly turning her head, as if to see or hear an intruder. She started moving jerkily back and forth in a rocking motion, and was staring down at the child, her mouth activated into overdrive. She suddenly thrust the baby out from her body with both arms, shaking it back and forth. Oh God, time to move!

Peeling off the awkward waders, I shucked myself out of the suckers with the speed of Mercury. I pawed through the pack, pulled out the last sandwich, and thrust the scent items, binoculars, and radio inside. I tucked the sandwich in a pocket and zipped my suit down to holster level, for quick access.

I strolled out of the trees, and when I knew she had spotted me, I pretended that I had no idea she was sitting in front of me. I had a huge grin plastered on my face, and a churning gut that was begging for some fizzy stuff.

Ernestine dropped the child on the mattress and rose to her knees, the quilt sliding behind her. She was in a short-sleeved T-shirt soiled with God knows what—mud, blood, or food stains—and stretch pants bursting at the seams. Her mouth was agape and her feral eyes tracked my every step.

As I drew even with the fire, I heard a reedy wail coming from the baby. Ernestine was so huge that lying beside her on the filthy wet mattress, Andy looked like a discarded doll, no longer remembered or cherished.

I began clapping my wet gloves together, slowly at first, then building up speed. I wanted her to focus on me, and it was also waking up my numb fingers.

Dancing on the balls of my feet, I began bobbing and weaving like a punch-drunk prizefighter, pretending I was having a grand ol' time. I didn't want to give her slow-witted brain enough time to wonder about my unexpected appearance.

I bounced forward to within six feet of her. I didn't know how fast she could move, but if she grabbed her knife and came at me, I was gonna run like greased lightning. If I could draw her away, lose her in the swamp, double back, and grab Andy and Gulliver, we had a chance. This was my game plan.

I looked straight into her eyes and pantomimed an exaggerated comic look of happy surprise that would have put Emmett Kelly to shame.

"Well, hi, Ernestine! Fancy meeting you here! How's tricks?"

18

Slaying the Dragon

January 5, Thursday, 10:00 P.M.

Ernestine glared at me, seemingly unable to move from the shock of my antics and hearing me speak her name. She stayed frozen on her knees, looking both ludicrous and deadly. A mind-numbed tank that could grind me into the mud with little or no provocation. I couldn't see the knife, and didn't want to remove my eyes from hers to scan the immediate area. I also didn't want to look at Andy, lest I drew her attention back to him.

"Aren't you glad to see me? Don't you want to play?"

I suddenly had a brilliant thought (at least, it was brilliant at first blush), but I would need my pack. I had to keep her off-balance. That was a laugh, she was about as off-balance as you can get.

"Who . . . Whacha doing here? This is my place! Go away!"

Her voice rumbled with indignation. We were communicating. Somewhat.

"I came to play!" I repeated slow and loud, trying to sound excited. "Come stand by the fire, it's cold!"

"Who'er you?"

I guess my face and voice didn't ring any bells. 'Course, I was in a bright rescue suit covered with mud, with a bandanna and rain hood hiding my hair. She also hadn't heard my voice in almost twenty-five years. I didn't know whether proving my identity would be a help or a hindrance. I could only try.

"I'm your friend from school, years and years ago. I'm Jo Beth Stonley. We used to play together? Don't you remember?"

"Jo Beth?"

She must be wandering down her version of memory lane, trying to place me.

"That's right, Jo Beth! We were friends and we played together. Wanna play a game?"

She scowled.

"I don't like you. You called me names!"

Ah, she remembered. Not a good move, Sidden, you should have remained anonymous.

"You didn't know how to play the game." I laughed. "All good friends call each other names. You can call me Frizzy. Remember how they called me Frizzy? Remember my hair?"

I whipped off cap and bandanna, pointing at my head. I forced a hardy laugh, and danced a fast little jig. With the dampness and high humidity, it should look like a brand-new permanent from hell.

Her lips formed the strange word before she tried it.

"Frizzy."

"That's right, Frizzy! Come to the fire. I have a goodie for you. Are you hungry?"

"I'm hungry!"

I had finally said the magic word. She straightened, and started lumbering towards me. I had to fight the urge to run. One swipe of her oak trunk-like arm, and I'd be picking hot coals out of my teeth. When she came close to me, and the warmer air by the fire, I could smell her. I cut my eyes upward and made eye contact. I wished I hadn't.

Her face revealed by the flickering flame was grotesque. My mind remembered a degrading comment I had once heard a good ol' sexist pig use to describe a blind date. "She looked like she had been hit in the face with a sack of rabbit guts." It was an uncharitable thought, but Ernestine's came close.

She looked at my empty hands and her mouth curved downward with disappointment.

"I'm hungry!"

"You have to play the game. Turn around and count to three. Promise you won't peek, and I'll make a big ham sandwich appear. Turn around and count to three!"

Nervous sweat popped out on my brow. My brilliant idea depended on her following my orders.

"I don't wanna. Gimme!"

She took a step closer.

I went back to my tippytoe routine and danced backward two steps.

"Turn around, count to three, turn around, count to three! I'll make it a ham and cheese sandwich! Play the game!"

She thought about it. I guess that's what she was doing. For all I know, she could have been trying to remember where she had put her knife.

She shuffled around and presented her enormous backside to me.

"Count, count to three," I sang gaily. "Don't peek, don't peek!"

"One . . . two . . . three . . . Gimme sandwich! I'm gonna peek!"

"Don't peek, don't peek. Put your hands behind your back, and the sandwich will appear!"

My voice sounded more hysterical than gay, but maybe she couldn't tell the difference.

She slowly moved her big arms behind her. I grabbed her right ham-like fist and shoved the sandwich in her palm. She snatched it, turned around, and began ripping the aluminum foil.

"I didn't peek!"

She grunted and then took an enormous bite of the sandwich, tearing at the bread and meat with her teeth, and cramming it into her mouth with her free hand.

"Ernestine? I've got a surprise for you, over by that tree," I yelled, pointing across the fire. Her head turned as if to see the tree, but she kept chomping away. Christ, she'd devour the sandwich before I could get back.

"I'm going to get your surprise. Don't move. Promise you won't move. Big surprise!"

She tore off another chunk of the sandwich. She didn't close her mouth as she chewed. It wasn't a pretty sight. She nodded her head with apparent eagerness.

"Don't move!" I called as I scratched off on a frantic twenty-five-yard dash. I grabbed my pack, slung it over one shoulder, and almost slid down in my turnaround. I hauled ass back to her.

The sandwich was gone, but she was still chewing, so I had made it back before she could think up some mischief. I dropped the pack at my feet and wanted to brace my hands on my knees to drag in oxygen, but settled for several deep breaths. I was trying to remember exactly where the AWRs were inside my pack. Several months ago, Jonathan Webber, an ex-lover, had given them to me. They are made of Velcro, and are called Alternate Wrist Restraints, or AWR. They are lightweight, and easier to carry and use than handcuffs. Wrap them around the perp's wrist behind his back, tighten, press the Velcro in place, and presto! Mission accomplished, with no keys. My pack held four. Jasmine's pack, however, held one. I had used mine only once before on some rowdy men on a bank of the Suwannee River. Jasmine hadn't ever used hers. Knowing Jasmine, it was at the very bottom of the pack. Christ, I'd have to unload everything to reach them, and do it quietly, since I would have to search while Ernestine counted to three. I took one last deep breath. It was nitty-gritty time.

"Ernestine, are you ready for your big surprise?"

I knelt in front of the pack and lifted the flap, and forced an insincere grin.

She nodded and went down on her knees in front of me.

I laughed and drew the pack towards me.

"Remember the game! Turn around, and don't peek! Turn around, and don't peek! Count to three! Count to three!"

She obediently started squirming around on her knees. The second she started her turn, I was hauling out items as fast as I could, first aid kit, baby bottle, radio, diapers, ground sheet, emergency water, signal flares, tool kit, rope, rescue sled, plastic bags, emergency rations, body bags, and other plastic wrapped items. No AWR.

"Don't peek! Don't peek!" I screeched in panic.

My hand reached the bottom of the pack, felt along the creases, and finally closed on the Velcro strip.

"Put both arms behind your back, put them back . . . atta girl!"

The second her wrists were close enough, I slipped the Velcro around one, jerked it tight over the other, and pressed the fabric together. I shoved her over on her right side before it could occur to her to try and stand.

Scooting away from her, I almost made it clear. She had released a startled yelp at feeling her hands immobilized, then began a keening cry that made my blood run cold. She drew her legs up, lashing out with a full thrust. She caught my thigh with a glancing blow with her left foot, which looked as big as a packing crate. If it had hit head on, she would have destroyed my femur. I saw stars. The pain telegraphed to my gut, making me feel nauseous.

She was squirming around in the muddy grass and making faster progress than I anticipated. I rose on weak knees and a throbbing thigh, and hobbled out of the range of her feet. Staying just beyond her kicking length, I led her away from the pack and my supplies strewn everywhere. When she was at least eight feet away, I limped back quickly and gathered the rope and tool kit.

I unrolled the cloth with fitted sections and opened my knife. I cut two lengths of rope and approached Ernestine warily. She rolled around until she could see me.

"Noooooooo," she yelled when she saw the rope, then went back to her deadly screams. She tried to keep her feet moving, but I made a loop and, timing her kicks, succeeded in snagging an ankle. I whipped the loose end around my wrist and managed to get it under her next thrust. I pulled them together and wrapped and tightened until I was panting from exertion. It would have been easier to hogtie a half-grown steer.

I picked up the baby bottle and moved near the fire. Scratching in the hot sand a foot from the flames, I placed the bottle upright and packed hot sand around it. I was thankful it was glass instead of plastic. I didn't put it close enough to warp the plastic cover from the heat the flames were generating. The wind was at my back. It should be safe.

I limped over to the dirty mattress and picked up Andy. He was lying with his eyes closed, whimpering restlessly, with a fist crammed in his mouth. He was wet, filthy, and smelled ripe.

"Hi there, Andy. How do a dry bottom and a warm bottle sound?"

I knelt, holding him on one knee, and spread out the thin plastic ground sheet I use under my sleeping bag. I placed Andy on it and stripped off his clothes and dirty diaper. I gave him the fastest wipe-down on record, applying the baby wipes on his bottom half more thoroughly than the top. His lips looked dark in the circle of my headlamp. They were blue from the cold. He needed to be dry and under cover quickly.

Freshly diapered and in his sleeper, he still fussed, appearing logy and confused.

"Soon now, Andy. Just hang on a little bit longer."

I unrolled my sleeping bag and placed Andy inside it, but left it unzipped. Stripping to the waist, I removed my gun and holster, tucking them under the sleeping bag. I peeled off my cotton fleece-lined pullover and slipped it over his head. The cold air gave me goose bumps and I zipped up my suit, shirtless. I pushed up the sleeves of my shirt until Andy's hands appeared. I took Jasmine's extra pair of socks, slipped them over his hands, and stretched them over the bulky sleeves. I zipped up the sleeping bag, leaving a six-inch slit for air.

I had lots more housekeeping to do, but Ernestine and the cleanup could wait. I went to check Andy's bottle. My hands were like ice, no good trying to ascertain the warmth of the milk there. I wiped off the bottle, attached the nipple, and squirted a small amount on my skin just above my bra. It felt cold. It went back into the hot sand.

I had been trying to ignore the hideous sounds that Ernestine was bellowing. I had heard once that madness gave a person the strength of ten. I now believed it. She didn't even seem to pause for breath.

I got the sled and spread it near the fire. I walked over to Ernestine and considered the next task. I had to move her near the fire and get her tucked in. She weighed almost one-sixth of a ton. Christ. I didn't have the strength or inclination to drag her.

While I was standing there, she rolled towards me and lashed out with her feet. She was strong as well as humongously obese. Who was the joker who said the bigger they are, the harder they fall? He was way off base here. She lunged again, and I stepped back further. I'd let her body do the walking. I was pooped.

I went back for the sled. I tried to time her rolls, keeping away from her feet. I missed several times and finally got lucky. Either she was tiring, or she needed a respite. I got half the sled under her, and with the next attempt to roll got the other half over her shoulders. It took me several more attempts before I was able to bring the zipper up and over her body. It was a tight fit. I sure didn't need the inflatable pillows! Inside the bag, she couldn't get her knees high enough to get any leverage.

I used my foot to push and roll her the rest of the way to the fire. Her eyes were glowing red in the firelight. I shuddered at the look she was giving me. The Ernestine I once knew didn't live there anymore. My pity was tempered with aggravation. She had cost me a lot of hard work; I was so tired I felt ready to drop. I wiped off all the muddy items from my pack that had been scattered, replaced them, and threw Andy's dirty diaper and sleeper in the fire. I staggered around, checking to see if I had forgotten anything.

I inspected Andy and Ernestine and both were secure. I started limping my two-hundred-feet-or-so journey to bring Gulliver to the camp. He was ecstatic to see me, but voiced his disapproval of moving nearer the strange noise that was making his hackles rise. He moaned his reluctance in a cross between a growl and whine. I led him near the sleeping bag and tied his lead to a heavy length of log I couldn't budge on a bet. If Gulliver was spooked, he could, but he wouldn't make it far—thick brush would halt his progress.

I wearily checked the bottle again. A gourmet might have argued that it wasn't the correct temperature, but I doubted if Andy would be finicky at this point. I wiped it free of ash, and hobbled over to the sleeping bag. Andy was still awake and trying to gnaw a sock-covered fist.

"This will taste better, big guy."

I picked up the head of the sleeping bag with Andy nestled in it, and held him while he guzzled down half the bottle. I raised him to my shoulder, and after a few pats he burped for me.

I put the cap on the bottle, saving the rest for early morning. One more chore. I was nodding off in mid-thought. I pulled the radio out of the pack.

"Rescue One to Base, Over."

I glanced at my watch while I was waiting, for the first time since I had walked out of the swamp and confronted Ernestine. It was ten minutes past midnight.

"Rescue One to Base. Over," I repeated.

"Base to Rescue One. Over," Hank replied.

It was wonderful to be reunited with the outside world, however tenuous the connection.

"Hi, Hank," I said slowly, dreading to impart the news.

"He's dead?" We were both ignoring transmitting protocols.

"Yes. I'm sorry, Hank. He must have died within a few minutes. It was quick."

"I knew it . . . just kept hoping . . . The baby? Ernestine?"

"Andy just finished half his bottle, and is warming up. He's been wet and very cold for several hours, and could get sick later, but now he's dry, and catching some z's."

"That's great news! What's that noise?"

"Ernestine is producing the noise. She doesn't care for the fact that she's bound hand and foot, and confined in the rescue sled. She'd rather be munching on my arm for a midnight snack."

"I'm impressed. How did you manage that?"

"With guile and artful deception. I just wish she'd shut up."

"I'd gag her," he said grimly. "She stabbed her mother at least a dozen times. It was bad, Jo Beth. Are you sure she's secure? Don't pity her and loosen her bonds or anything. I saw what she did to her mother, who loved Ernestine and devoted most of her life caring for her. It made me sick."

"She's secure, and I'll check often. I was tempted to gag her, but I'm afraid that she might choke or swallow her tongue. Her vocalizing will keep me awake and alert. Send in a chopper at first light. I estimate we're a mile or a mile and a half north-northeast of you. There's a pond with a clearing and a white sandy beach. I'm about a hundred feet north of the pond. At least three men are needed, and make sure one is a three-hundred-pound weightlifter. He's gonna have to drag Ernestine. They'll need a stretcher for Tom. How's Naomi, Jasmine, and Charlie?"

"Charlie's hands are a mess. He didn't screw up, did he?"

"He's a genuine hero, and don't you forget it. He waded in without hesitation and pulled Melanie out of quicksand."

"Good. Jasmine is fine. She wouldn't go home until we heard from you. She's asleep in the back of my unit. I'll send someone to drive her home. Naomi is doing well. They've given her blood and the doc says she'll be as good as new in a few days. Her husband is with her. I'll call and tell them Andy is safe as soon as we're finished talking. I'll notify Wayne and Donnie Ray, they'll arrange for the vans to be returned. Get some rest. I'll see you in the morning. You did good, Jo Beth."

"Thanks. Over and out."

"Out."

The night seemed darker after Hank's voice was gone. I dragged myself out of the bag to Ernestine's woodpile and added three big oak logs to the fire. I curled up beside Andy in the sleeping bag and pulled up the hood. I knew I wouldn't be able to sleep with danger so near. I was wrong.

The *whomp-whomp* of the chopper's blades roused me from a deep sleep when they flew low over our position at daybreak.

19

Another Day, Another Suspect

January 6, Friday, 3:00 P.M.

The phone was ringing when I came up the steps to the porch. I trotted into the office to reach it before the recorded message.

"Hello."

"How's the leg?" Hank inquired.

"Bruised and sore as hell, but I've lost the limp, since I've almost completed a full day's work. How's your day?"

"Not so great, we've been working on funeral arrangements. I called to tell you that Tom's service is being held at All Soul's, on Sunday at two P.M."

"Thanks. Who's taking care of his dogs? If you need a place for them, we have room in the clinic."

"His sister drove over from Tifton. She's his nearest relative. She's gonna stay at his place until she can sell it."

"What happens to Flora Mae? Weren't they living together?"

"Tom's sister tossed her out this morning."

"Doesn't she have any rights?"

"Not a one. I called Wade. He says Tom named his sister to inherit. Of course, the will was written early last year, before he met Flora Mae. Another good reason to marry, instead of just moving in."

"You're a fine one to talk!"

We had lived together, briefly, some months back.

"I was willing to marry. In fact, I still am."

"In my book, the good doesn't outweigh the bad."

"I'm amenable to change."

"In a pig's eye!" I took a breath and hastily continued. I had stated my denial too vehemently. "Anyway, who's asking you to change?"

"I thought maybe we might be discussing terms."

I laughed.

"No way. I guess Naomi and her hubby were glad to see Andy."

"You should have stuck around and delivered him yourself. They wanted to thank you."

"And give Sizemore an exclusive for the evening news? I hate that little bastard! I'd end up kicking him in his nuts, just like Jasmine did the last time he got obnoxious."

"You are missing some good publicity."

"I'll live."

"I was hoping that you would invite me to dinner tonight. Miz Jansee is cooking, isn't she?"

"Nope, she doesn't start until Sunday afternoon this month. You can come to dinner, plus bring it. It'll be Jasmine, Susan, and me."

"I love you girls separately, but not together. I'll pass. You gang up on me."

"Coward."

"I freely admit it. By the way, I got Hanson Aldridge's current address for you. He's staying with Miz Cora Pendleton. You want her number?"

"Yep."

I wrote it down, and we ended our conversation.

I pulled the phone towards me, but it rang before I could dial.

"Hello."

"Is this the lady that raises bloodhounds?"

The voice was refined and pleasant. No Georgia twang. A mature female.

"Yes, I am. How can I help you?"

"I heard all about that thrilling rescue last night of that little boy. Someone told me that bloodhound puppies are adorable. I wish to purchase one."

"May I ask why?"

"Why?" Her voice faltered. "Because I want one. Do I have to have a reason?"

"Yes," I said simply. "And it must be a valid one."

"I beg your pardon? You own a kennel and breed them for sale, don't you?"

"Yes, ma'am, I surely do, but only to people that fit certain criteria."

"What criteria?" Her voiced was full of surprise and impatience.

"May I ask your age?"

"Well, this is ridiculous! What does my age have to do with anything? I'm buying a dog, not adopting a child!" She laughed at her joke, and sounded uneasy.

"If you can't answer my questions, then I'm sorry, but I won't sell you a puppy."

"Fifty-six," she replied coolly.

"Who would exercise your dog?"

"I would, of course. My dog died recently after twelve years of good care. I walked him every day."

"Are you aware that a bloodhound needs to run at least two miles, twice a day?"

"I can afford to pay someone to exercise him. Any other questions?" Her voice had turned tart.

"Did you plan on letting him live inside?"

"Of course!"

"Ma'am, a bloodhound puppy can destroy your home with the same ease as a raging tornado, only he's a tad slower. His slobber will peel varnish off antiques, ruin valuable rugs, and destroy your drapes and furniture. He chews up and swallows everything he can pull to the floor, up to and including a travel alarm clock. I had one that ate mine once."

"I paper-train my puppies, and teach them to behave."

"How tall are you, and what do you weigh?"

"I'm five feet two inches tall and weigh a hundred and ten. Next question?"

"You won't be able to train him. An exuberant puppy could knock you off your feet at five months. You could no more handle a grown bloodhound than you could a half-grown tiger. Take my advice and get a smaller breed, something cuddly and manageable."

"Missy, I'm appalled at your attitude! If you won't sell me a bloodhound, I'll find someone else who will!"

I took off the kid gloves.

"I know all about you without asking another question," I said harshly. "You, and several hundred like you, hear about a rescue and suddenly crave a bloodhound. It's a current craze and has dire consequences. This adorable creature ruins a valuable possession, eats like a horse, and grows to an unmanageable size, weighing one hundred twenty-five pounds or more. He ends up in a pound, or sold to an unscrupulous puppy mill owner who breeds them like rabbits. The dog has to be rescued by responsible owners or admirers of the breed. If you live near here, the rescuer will be me. No, lady, I will not sell you a bloodhound!"

She hung up without another word.

I hoped I had put her off the breed. She wanted the dog for all the wrong reasons. If she were persistent, she would find someone who would sell without questions, just like I did when I first opened the kennel. But I wised up fast, and now make sure that I check out who buys the dog, how it will be treated, and its environment.

I went to the kitchen and grabbed a Diet Coke. I dialed Miz Cora's number. She was home and willing to speak with me. I called Donnie, and told him when I'd be back.

Miz Cora lived just two miles down the highway from me. When I arrived at her small house, I found that it was tucked directly behind an old building that years ago started out as a motel. It had been converted into rooms for single gentlemen. The grounds were neat and trimmed, and the paint on the rental and house was adequate, but it looked as if it belonged to a bygone era. Independent owners couldn't make a small motel work on Highway 301. The large chains had run them out years ago. It didn't look very profitable, even as rented rooms.

I rolled down the window for Bobby Lee. It was forty-seven degrees, and as warm as it was going to get today. Tonight's low was supposed to drop to eighteen degrees.

"Enjoy, but it goes back up on the way home."

He moved over as far as his seat belt allowed and stuck his large head out the window.

"Don't bark at strange dogs," I warned.

Miz Cora came to the door a long thirty seconds after I rang the doorbell.

"Come in, Jo Beth. I had to set a pot off the stove. Come back to the kitchen. I'm cooking. Seems that's all I do nowadays is cook. I've got a full house!"

Miz Cora was big and a careless dresser. She had to be sixty-five if she was a day. Nothing matched or looked new, but she was clean and so were her clothes. She was blowsy, with hennaed hair showing gray near the roots, and had a cheap wave that needed trimming and shaping. No, I was wrong, it needed a miracle.

I was expecting relatives to be sitting in the kitchen, but when we entered, we were alone. She moved to set the pot back on the burner.

"I feed them twice a day, nine A.M. and five P.M. Some of them don't eat much, but some do. Keeps me hopping."

Now I understood her comment about a full house.

"You cook two meals a day, for six men? Do you have any help?"

"Not with the cooking and bed making, cleaning and laundry. My gentlemen guests believe that's woman's work, but they do keep the yard up, make some basic repairs, and paint, when I can afford the paint," she said wryly.

"I hope you make enough profit, to expend that much energy?"

"Profit?" She leaned her head back and gave a loud guffaw. "What kind of an animal would that be? I haven't seen a profit around here in years! I'm doing good when it doesn't take all my Social Security check just to feed these yo-yo's."

"Why would you spend your own money, and all this effort, if they don't pay you enough?"

Somebody had to wise this woman up.

"You'll have to raise your rates so you make a decent profit. You sound like it's taking most of *your* income. They're taking advantage of your good nature."

"Honey, let me tell you, half of these ol' coots can't hit the bowl when they piss, and can barely dress themselves. If anyone is taking advantage, it's me!"

She saw my startled expression and her heavy frame jiggled with bawdy laughter. She looked just like Bobby Lee when his whole body writhed with ecstasy at the beginning of a search.

"Look at you, you're blushing!" She slapped the table with her pudgy hands. Most of her fingers were adorned with cheap flashy rings. Her nails were polished a glossy red, but they were in need of another coat, and two nails were broken and needed some repairs with an emery board.

"You go back and tell them tightass bitches that call themselves Christians to mind their own damn business and quit trying to pry into mine! You bought those rumors they've been spreading, huh? Want some coffee? It's fresh."

"Rumors?"

It was the best response I could muster. I felt like Alice when she fell down the rabbit hole. What the hell was going on here? She hadn't asked me what I wanted to talk about when I called, and I was waiting to broach the subject when I arrived. Obviously, Miz Cora thought I was on a different mission.

"Didn't the do-gooders from the Holiness Baptist Church send you to find out how I was robbing these dodos of their Social Security and pension checks? How I'm their guardian, cash their checks, and keep all their money?"

Now Miz Cora was the one with a confused look.

"I came to ask you to introduce me to Hanson Aldridge so I can question him about a murder that took place thirty years ago," I blurted.

"Lord God, me and my big mouth! Sorry, chile, for jumping down your throat for no reason. I try not to pay attention to their silly rumors and nasty whispers, but lately they've gotten under my skin."

She patted my shoulder, stirred her pot, and explained over coffee.

"Me and Mac, that was my husband, we kicked up our heels in this town for thirty-six years before cancer took him. It'll be five years ago in March. There wasn't a blessed day that he didn't come home from the mill, slap me on my fanny, and ask me what's cooking? When he died, I missed him like crazy.

"I'm too old to go looking for someone new, so I sat home and stewed. We didn't have kids, didn't feel we wanted any. I don't sew and can't abide a bunch of women sitting around talking about their latest operation. What I missed most of all was our talks at the table. Breakfast and supper. A man's talk, there's nothing like it.

"We bought this place right after we married. We always planned to fix up the rooms and rent them out, we just never got around to it. I finally lit on the bright idea that I could fix up the rooms and rent them to old geezers, and I'd have plenty of table talk.

"Hah! I should have paid more attention to them, sitting around on benches around town, and I wouldn't have been so hasty! Talk? These geeks are waiting for the bottle, or cigarettes, or their prostate to finish them off. I'm working my tail off and getting little in return, I tell you. Don't know why I bother!"

"It's been five years," I ventured. "Why don't you ask them all to move?"

"Where would they go? The Salvation Army will give them one hot and a cot. None of them make enough to eat out, much less rent a room! Every time one of them croaks, there's another waiting with his hat in his hand, unable to fend for himself. I've got my health, and enough money to manage, but if groceries keep going up, I'll have to start serving them soup, which sure isn't a meal that starts my kind of conversation!"

"You're a good woman, Miz Cora."

"Nah! God and me aren't on speaking terms, but he's got it figured out real good. He keeps making these dumb bunnies that can't take care of themselves, and then makes dumb suckers like me to take care of them!"

20

A Surprise from a Boozehound

January 6, Friday, 4:15 P.M.

As Miz Cora walked me to her rented rooms, she filled me in on Hanson Aldridge.

"He's a drunk. I bank his check the third. I buy his toilet articles, six cartons of cigarettes, and depending on the days in the month, thirty or thirty-one pint bottles of Southern Comfort. He gets his daily bottle after breakfast. He's learned that no excuse will pry another from my locked hall closet.

"Dr. Sellers and I weaned him down from a quart a day last year. He has to eat a little, morning and night, or he doesn't get the booze. He's gained ten pounds this past year. Doc says that he's as healthy as you can expect for a man who's been on the bottle for over twenty-five years.

"The pint a day is his maintenance dosage. Sometimes one of the others will get a windfall from a relative and share the wealth. It doesn't seem to affect him, to increase his intake on those rare occasions. He talks freer, is all.

"You can buy him a pint at Ray's liquors, right down the road. His memory is fair to middling. He'll remember some things, but I doubt if you can get any details from him. Mac and I talked about the kidnapping way into the night a lot of times back then. They questioned Hanson, but he wasn't involved. He had a nice car dealership here in town, and a beautiful wife. She divorced him about a year before the crime. They say she cleaned him out, with Calvin Newton's help. He was her lawyer. There were two reasons they questioned him, the fact that he was seen near All Souls the afternoon of the kidnapping, and he had threatened Newton several times in front of witnesses."

"I appreciate your help," I murmured.

When we came around the corner of the building, there were two men sitting in the weak sunshine in wrought-iron chairs.

"Hanson!" called Miz Cora.

A tall man rose and walked to meet us. I was expecting a stumbling, disoriented drunk. He walked slow and straight, and didn't look confused. His face was flushed. He had on an outdated suit and white shirt. As he drew nearer, I could see the shine on the suit, and a frayed shirt collar, but his eyes looked normal. He whipped off his hat, and his gray hair appeared clean. He gave us a tentative smile.

"Yes, ma'am?"

"This here is Ms. Sidden. She wants to ask you some questions. I want you to give her truthful answers. She's gonna buy you a pint, but she knows that's your limit, so don't shine her on, you hear?"

Miz Cora turned to me.

"I serve supper at five. If you aren't finished by then, I'll keep his food hot 'til he gets back."

"Thanks."

I walked over to the van, unhooked Bobby Lee, and turned down the seat. I slapped the bent back.

"Back, Bobby Lee."

Nose down, he took his own sweet time, looking awkward as one leg slipped on the leather.

I motioned Aldridge to climb in. I walked around, got under the wheel, and attached Bobby Lee's harness to the ring bolted on the floor. The minute I closed the door and raised the windows, I could smell the whiskey. So could Bobby Lee. I saw him lean forward and take a deep sniff of Aldridge's sleeve. I felt like warning him not to inhale too often, he might get high on the fumes. I tried to breathe through my mouth.

"He's a big dog. I never saw a bloodhound up close."

"Yes," I replied shortly.

We drove to Ray's Liquor Store in silence. I reached under my seat for my wallet.

Aldridge cleared his throat. I looked his way.

"I could remember a lot better with a quart."

"What would you remember?" I asked wryly. Miz Cora hadn't told him what I was going to question him about.

"Well, it all depends if you're working for the man in the blue truck, or the woman in the red car. I saw the accident real good. It happened right in front of me."

"Accident?"

"Yes, ma'am, I gave the officer my name and address. I was expecting someone to drop by."

"What can you tell me?"

"Whatever you want to hear," he said, giving me a cunning smile and a broad wink. "If you work for the man in the blue truck, the woman in the red car plowed right into him. If you work for the woman in the red car, she was going down the road, not even speeding, and this blue truck ran the stop sign and hit her. With a quart, I can remember lots of details."

I gave him a smile. "I'm not here because of a traffic accident. I wanted to pick your brains about a thirty-year-old murder and kidnapping. Now you've disappointed me. I won't be able to believe a thing you tell me, since I find that you can lie easily for an extra pint of Southern Comfort."

He was silent for a minute. I watched him shrug his shoulders in defeat.

"I can tell the complete truth on any question you ask just as well as I can lie. A quart would buy me about three more hours' sleep tonight. Pint or quart, you'll get the truth, if that's what you want. But buy the pint . . . please. I've been tasting it in my mind ever since Miz Cora said you'd buy me one." He was pleading, his voice filled with tension.

I got out, slamming the van door. The clerk behind the counter watched me though the plate glass as I walked in, and searched the shelves for pints with the Southern Comfort label. I picked up two, placing them on the counter with a twenty.

"Miz Cora won't be pleased," the man informed me as he rang up the sale and counted out my change.

"You mean, because I bought *two* pints?"

"You got it," he answered, smirking.

He picked up a pint and started to bag it. I reached for the other one and slipped it in the back pocket of my jeans.

"You're mistaken," I corrected nicely. "See my other passenger in the back?" I turned around and pointed. Bobby Lee had stood when I exited the van, and you could see his big mug clearly through the glass. He was listening for my return.

"It's for him. I don't allow him to share a bottle with anyone."

"The dog?"

"You got it!" I said crisply, and gave him a pleasant nod as I departed.

I drove to the park. The sun had lost its warmth. The temperature must be 40 degrees by now. It was gonna drop like a stone. My denim jacket felt good.

"Let's sit over there," I said, pointing to a picnic spot consisting of a cement table, cement benches, and an overhead cover. I tied Bobby Lee's leash to a metal post. The park was deserted because of the soggy turf from yesterday's downpour and the current cold. The honky-tonks and bars would do well tonight. Payday in a small town.

I sat on the table, resting my feet on the bench. Aldridge left as much distance as possible, lowering himself at the far end. He lit a cigarette, and offered his pack.

"No, thanks. Tell me about your participation in the murder-kidnapping crime in 1965."

I found it interesting that he didn't object to the way I had worded my inquiry. No hasty denial of innocence. Of course, even if he was guilty, he should feel safe after all this time, and I had to keep in mind that his brain had been soaked in alcohol for thirty years. Subtle nuances might just float right over his head.

"I still owned the dealership then. I knew it was doomed, had known it for a year. My wife divorced me the year before, and she got everything she wanted, and more. Newton told her additional ways to gouge me, than even she could dream up. I blamed him more than her. She was just dumb and greedy. He was cold and calculating. I let everyone know what I thought of him. He ruined me. He knew I couldn't survive. I often thought that they . . . "

He shook his head and gave me an embarrassed smile.

"Sorry, you wanted the true story, not all the random thoughts I had in those days.

"I had a customer that had a beef about the factory finish on his new Chevy. The afternoon of the kidnapping, I drove out to his place to see if he was right. He had been bad-mouthing me at the country club. His house was two streets over from All Souls. He wasn't home, so I didn't have any way to prove why I was in the neighborhood.

"When they asked for reports of anyone seen in that area, someone turned in my name. I came back from lunch, and two deputies hauled me down to the Sheriff's Department. Sheriff Callis questioned me. The interview should have been routine, but I had had three martinis with lunch and the liquor made me run off at the mouth. I told the sheriff that I was glad that Newton's kid had been kidnapped, and it was a shame that she wasn't the one still missing.

"They gave me a rough time for several hours. I finally started sobering up, and they listened to my answers, checked out my story as best they could, and released me. The aggravation just made me hate Newton more. End of story."

"Did they ever come back with more questions?"

"No, ma'am."

"Well, you had participated, however briefly, and must have followed the case closely, especially after you were interrogated. Did you attend the trial?"

"I had a business to run, I couldn't go, but I read every word in the newspapers, and listened to what was being said."

"When Samuel Debbs was arrested, tried, and convicted, did you believe he was guilty?"

"Most everyone did. Once in a while, someone would voice doubts, but all in all, people were satisfied. We just went back to our lives, and didn't think too much about it."

I straightened. My sensory antennae were quivering in the breeze. They smelled evasion.

"You didn't answer my question."

"Sorry, I thought I did. What did I miss?"

"I'll shorten the question," I said grimly. "Did *you* think that Samuel Debbs was guilty?"

He shrugged. "I remember having this weird thought, that maybe Calvin Newton and Bryan Sirmons had worked as a team. But later I realized I was using my anger against Newton, and was trying to wish him guilty."

He pulled out his pint from his pocket, still in the paper bag, and took a swig. I thought over what he had said. He knew something, and I was gonna dig it out of him if it took me all night.

"That would account for Calvin Newton. Why would you think that Bryan Sirmons was involved?"

"I remember that I compared him to me. We were close to the same age. I was twenty-seven and he was twenty-nine. We both needed money. He didn't have any, and mine was being siphoned out of my business by my ex-wife and her lawyer."

"Not good enough," I said harshly. "I think you're bullshitting me. Get with the program. I'm paying you for truthful answers."

He stared out at the creek, which was almost flooding its narrow banks from the rain. The rush of water sounded restless as it made its winding journey out of the Okefenokee.

"I need to ask a question first."

"Ask away."

"What if another person saw someone, just like the person saw me and turned in my name, but didn't report it to the authorities? Would that person be guilty of a crime?"

I chose my words carefully, because I wanted what he was holding back—and if we paused to get a legal opinion I just might lose the chance forever. Truthfully, I didn't have a clue, but I'm one hell of an improviser.

"Picture this. A woman is standing by a riverbank and sees a small boy fall in. The mother turns and tells the woman she can't swim, to save her child. The woman refuses to help. The woman observer could see the child was in danger, the mother requested assistance, and even if the woman was an excellent swimmer, she is *not legally required to act.*

"Someone could have knowledge of someone else in the area, be aware the sheriff wanted that information, but that person is not *legally culpable* for not reporting it. Does that answer your question?"

"Yes. It really shook me up when I read about the crime. I saw him turn into the same street that All Souls is on. The paper said he was somewhere else."

"Who?"

"Bryan Sirmons."

21

Girls' Night In

January 6, Friday, 5:00 P.M.

"Are you sure?" I was skeptical. The Sheriff's Department had documented where Sirmons was the entire afternoon of the kidnapping. He'd been cutting a tall field of grass several miles away from the house that would have taken him all day. He couldn't have been in two places at the same time. However, without an eyewitness it could be possible, I guess. The men who did the checking weren't around to tell me how thorough their checking had been.

"Pretty sure."

"What does that mean?"

"I didn't know him personally. About six months before the kidnapping he came in wanting to trade in his wreck of a truck. He got there late and the salesmen had already left. I looked at his jalopy and gave him the bad news. It wasn't even listed in the Blue Book any longer, meaning that it had no value as a trade-in. He said he couldn't manage the down payment, so that was that."

"How positive are you that you recognized him that afternoon?"

"It wasn't him that I was looking at. I recognized his beat-up truck. I knew that it was the same truck he had been wanting to trade in earlier. I was in the business, Ms. Sidden. I looked more closely at the cars people owned than I did at faces. The salesmen had to check with me before they could firm a trade-in value. At that time I could tell you value of any vehicle on wheels."

"But you couldn't swear that you were positive that he was the one you saw driving it."

He shrugged. "It was his truck. Unless he loaned it to someone, it was him behind the wheel."

As little as I knew about the law, I knew that his identification of Sirmons by his transportation alone wouldn't have been damning, but it might have caused some doubts and a more thorough scrutiny of his explanation of where he had been all afternoon. At this late date, I didn't have anything to raise anyone's eyebrows.

I drove Aldridge back to Miz Cora's. I handed him the pint from my hip pocket.

"Don't make me regret this. I want to stay on Miz Cora's good side."

"So do I," he said with a grateful smile. "I won't get in no trouble. Appreciate it. Thanks."

I've always been an easy touch when I heard what I thought was an honest plea. Sucker is my middle name.

I drove over to Baker's Mill Road and slowed at the front gate. It was half past five and the big white house was ablaze with lights. Both stories were lit up in warm-looking yellow oblongs. Bryan Sirmons and Patricia Ann Newton were back in residence after thirty years. I watched from the gate until car lights swept into view, turning into the driveway from the rear of the building.

I drove a sedate thirty-five, and watched as a van passed me with a swish of tires on the way to Balsa City. It was the delivery van for Alice's Flower Pot. Alice, a schoolmate and friend, had picked up some new business. The same van would be coming tomorrow to the kennel to deliver my new silk arrangements that Alice replaced every three months. I sighed. Another bill to pay, and the two tardy checks hadn't been in today's mail. If they weren't in tomorrow's I would be forced to call them Monday. Purchase of the bloodhound included the seminar training for a week, but they knew it was due in advance. Trainees would arrive Sunday afternoon.

Back home, I fed the animals, had a leisurely soak in the tub, and was almost finished blow-drying my hair when I heard Susan Comstalk's yelled greeting from the office.

"Coming!" I hollered, and hurried around the corner in time to see her back disappearing out the office door. She had on a loden green wool coat that I hadn't seen, and a sweatsuit the shade of cranberries. My sweats were navy blue and well worn. Jasmines would be a shade of pink, her favorite color. Either electric, salmon, or pale. They both dressed better than I did, even though there would be no males and just the three of us to enjoy their splendor.

Susan was striking. My age, with flaming red hair subdued with dye to a rich auburn glow, and she wore bright green contacts. I had gotten so used to them over the years, I had to concentrate to remember their original color. At 5'9" she was two inches taller, with smaller, fuller boobs than mine. I envied her boobs, flamboyant colors, and ability to coordinate her wardrobe.

She owned and managed Browse and Bargain Books. She didn't have to buy her clothes with her profits from the store. Her parents gave her a hefty allowance, which she promptly invested in the latest fashions. She called her many purchases "bait," so she could net a brilliant catch.

Susan's parents owned a horse ranch a few miles out of town. She rode each weekend and worked out in a gym, faithfully, two or three times a week. She had been actively searching for a male to share her life ever since Harold, her ex, had ran away with a high school senior seventeen months after he and Susan were married. My marriage had lasted three miserable years only because I worked hard at trying to save it.

I didn't go looking for a man, I was sitting back and waiting for Mr. Right to come riding up on his white horse in full armor and sweep me off my feet. Our different approaches had netted us the same results. Zip, nada, none. Jasmine also spurns all offers. So the three of us regularly spent every Friday, the big dating night, clad in sweatsuits, eating pizza, drinking our choice of alcohol, and discussing our week—with only ourselves for company.

Jasmine arrived and helped Susan bring in an overnight case, a folded dress carrier, a cosmetic case, and a jewelry case, all in matching leather. Susan's first trip had been to bring in the jumbo deep-dish pizza from Pete's Deli.

"Moving in?" I asked with amusement.

"You've neglected me all week. Your failure to call has produced an abundance of news. Two glasses of wine will not cut it. I'm going to drink beer, beer, and more beer. Your usually empty guestroom is not occupied, I trust?"

"Be my guest."

"'Bout time," she grumbled.

Jasmine winked as she passed. It should be an interesting evening; Susan only drank beer when she was pissed at someone. I slid the pizza into the heated oven and checked the fire in the living room. It was drawing nicely. I can build a great fire, which is my only domestic success. I opened a cabinet under the bookshelves and tossed out half a dozen pillows onto the carpet in front of the fire. I lit the candles on the credenza and coffee table. I went back to the kitchen and placed Jasmine's bottle of wine, wineglass, and two beers in styrofoam holders on a tray and returned.

Susan and Jasmine were already lounging on the pillows. I poured wine, handed out drinks, and flopped down beside them.

"I've starved all week, just dreaming of a hot slice of pizza," Susan announced.

"We sometimes have it on Wednesday," I said smugly.

"And Monday, Tuesday, and sometimes Thursday," Jasmine added tartly.

"God, Sidden, you're gonna weigh two hundred, eating junk food all the time!"

"Enough about me. Tell us the news!" I hastily replied. It wouldn't do to get her started on my faults. She was my worst critic.

She did. All through eating pizza, and past the first two beers. It seemed her parents had been matchmaking again. They had introduced her to another bachelor rancher at dinner on Monday night.

"He's fifty-six if he's a day," she uttered with exasperation. "Tall and skinny, and had the unmitigated gall to ask me my measurements, sitting right there at the table while we were eating, with my parents smirking and nodding with approval!"

"You're kidding!" I replied with delight.

"That's not all," Susan added. "He pulled his reminder out of his pocket, and wrote the damn things down, every measurement, very carefully. I thought his next move would be to come around the table and ask to examine my teeth!"

I couldn't help it. I threw my head back and roared. I noticed Jasmine didn't join me. She just smiled and went back to looking pensive. She was still reliving Tom's death. I would have to convince her she was wrong in blaming herself.

"You haven't heard the best part," Susan continued. "He nailed me right then and there, to have dinner with him the next night."

"Couldn't you come up with some excuse?"

I wanted her to feel better and this was the best therapy, vocalizing her unhappiness at her parents well-meaning but intrusive meddling into her love life. They weren't getting any younger and longed for grandchildren.

"'Hell, no!' was what I wanted to yell, but I decided to be the dutiful daughter. I asked myself, just how boring could a two- or three-hour dinner be?"

"How boring was it?" I fed her the words she needed to complete her story.

Susan kept going. She was on a roll and enjoying herself.

"We were at Chesters. I had lobster, and it was delicious. He had talked constantly since cocktails, about his ranch, his horses, and his desire for an heir. He stated he wouldn't have considered marriage, but realized the best way to produce an heir was by, and this is a direct quote, 'picking the correct vessel to carry my seed,' unquote."

"He didn't!" I said in awe.

"He did," Susan uttered grimly. "My mouth was open with shock. I had no idea that he could top this asinine performance, but he outdid himself. He handed me a printed document and asked me to read it.

"Friends, we're not talking about a crisp, fresh-from-the-computer copy with pristine edges. These ten pages or so had curled edges and showed their age by their well-thumbed appearance. 'Rules of Marriage,' was the centered title."

"Be still my heart," I croaked breathlessly. "What did it say? You did read it, didn't you? Tell me you read it!"

"I'm ashamed to admit to reading it, but I was dying to see what the bozo had dreamed up. It was simple, really. He just required total submission, no excuses in the bedroom, accepting all his godlike decisions with panache and gratitude, and producing a male heir in the first attempt. In other words, no tickey, no laundry. It was a prenuptial agreement, for God's sake!"

Jasmine spoke for the first time since she had greeted Susan on her arrival. "Susan, please don't take this wrong, but why did you actually go out with him? You obviously disliked him."

"Let me answer this one, Susan," I offered. "Jasmine, Susan's parents want to find her a mate very badly. Susan goes along with most of their attempts at matchmaking because she doesn't want to have to shop locally and stay on a strict budget. Wouldn't pay to get them pissed off. They furnish unlimited charge accounts and twice-a-year shopping excursions in New York City. God forbid if she had to settle for JCPenney and Kmart fashions!"

The pillow landed on my face just a fraction of a second before Susan threw herself on top of me. I had a devil of a time trying to get her off me. She's as strong as an ox.

"Enough, I give, I give!" I yelled weakly when I could manage to breathe.

"Don't mess with me, Sidden, I'll eat you for breakfast!"

We drank more beers, and half-watched *Dark Victory* starring Bette Davis, which we had seen more than a dozen times. At eleven, Susan rose and bade us good night.

"I know I shouldn't ask, Susan, but I won't be able to sleep without knowing. What did you tell him?"

Susan gave an airy wave. She had consumed six beers. I had been fetching them from the fridge and keeping track. She wasn't feeling any pain.

"I embarrassed my parents. They tell me they can't hold their heads up and face their friends. I'm surprised you haven't already heard about it, Sidden. They also canceled all my credit cards, and any future trips to the Big Apple."

"I'm sorry, Susan, I've been real busy lately. They'll forgive you," I assured her, "they always do."

"Not this time," she responded, sounding tiddly.

I saw Susan's satisfied feline look appear.

"I tipped his bowl of bouillabaisse in his lap, laughed at his enraged roar, and made a dignified exit. I ruined my grand exit, however, by having to sneak back inside and hide in the powder room. I had forgotten it was Wednesday night, and our only taxi was out of service. At thirty-two years old, it was humiliating to be picked up by my father, fussed at all the way to the parking lot, and then all the way home."

"As soon as I lock up, I'll be back," I told her. "Walk with me to lock the gate?" I said softly to Jasmine.

"Nighty-night," Susan called as she walked carefully down the hall to the guestroom.

I threw on a coat and stuck my feet into a pair of boots. Outside, the cold air cleared my head. Jasmine kept her head lowered and kept pace with me in silence.

"I've given it a lot of thought, and I think I let a good man die because I froze in fear and couldn't function," she answered calmly. "I don't think I can do this any longer. You don't have another job open, so I guess I'll have to move, maybe relocate in a northern city."

"All right," I agreed, "let's discuss your actions. You said you froze. If you hadn't, what do you think you should have done?"

Her face looked troubled in the yellowish glow of the overhead nightlight. "I should have pulled her off of Tom from behind. Between the two of us we could have subdued her."

"He was behind you. You said Ernestine rushed out and started stabbing him, over and over. Is that correct?"

"Yes . . . "

"After the first surprise blow, Tom was out of it," I said brutally. "He couldn't have done anything to help himself or you. It was a large butcher knife, Jasmine; the blade was fourteen inches long, and almost three inches at the widest part. She had the strength of the insane. Any one of the blows would have been fatal."

"I should have done *something*!" she declared, stopping and staring off into the night.

"You *wished* you could have done something, I know, but believe me, she was too fast. If you had run up behind her, all you would have accomplished was getting you and Gulliver killed. Can't you see that?

"Listen, I'll make you a bargain. Stay on rescue for thirty days. If you still feel this way after a month, I'll switch you to dog training. I don't want to lose you, Jasmine. You're too valuable to me as an employee and a friend."

Her sobs filled the night. I held her and let her cry.

22

Balsa City's Angel

January 7, Saturday, 2:00 P.M.

This morning's low had been 18 degrees. With the warmth of the sun it had climbed to the present high of 35. Jasmine and I had spent a cold morning shopping for the groceries for seminar week. We had divided Miz Jansee's list and, with our gloves still on, had spent two hours in Winn-Dixie, filling baskets.

It had taken another hour to put the groceries away in the correct places so Miz Jansee wouldn't have a reason for not producing her great meals. Then, after lunch, I drove to the 600 block of George Washington Carver Boulevard.

Jasmine had declined to come with me. She said she had to study. She didn't come right out and say it, but acted as if I were on a wild-goose chase. I was now parked in front of Number 608 on the north side of the street. I was driving my black Ford Escort. The van with its large yellow Sheriff Department seal would have produced reluctance and suspicion.

I had left Bobby Lee at home for the same reason I had driven my car. When I conduct locker checks in the schools the black kids seem to resent the intrusion of the bloodhounds and me more than the white kids. They must view it as harassment. The whites whisper insults just loud enough for me to overhear, while the blacks look scared.

For more than two years, I had been fighting with the school board to introduce a series of visits in which Jasmine and I would give lectures on drug searches and explain how gentle the bloodhounds are. The school board wanted the kids scared and wary. They thought it helped. So the kids saw Nazi storm troopers with unlimited power over them, and we saw their hatred and resentment.

At 608 George Washington Carver Boulevard, I got out of the car and walked to the front door. This street had community pride. No trash in the yards, and most were raked clean of pine straw. Houses needed paint, but hardly any junk cars were up on blocks and the porches were bare of old stuffed furniture and broken chairs.

I knocked. The door was opened by a black woman in her thirties. She had a pleasant smile.

"Yes?"

"I'm looking for anyone who can remember Velma Mae Nichols. She was eighteen when she died thirty years ago. She lived here."

"I've been staying here for nine years. My mama passed six years back. I never heard her mention no Velma Mae Nichols. Are you sure she stayed here?"

"Yes, ma'am."

"I be sure that I never know her. Can't help you none."

"I'm sorry that I bothered you on this cold morning. Thank you for taking the time to answer my questions."

I gave her a grateful smile and turned to leave. I had taken several steps when she called.

"Wait." She wrapped her thick sweater around her thin frame, walked out on the porch, and pointed down the block.

"You see that dark green house? It be three doors down?"

"Yes, ma'am, I do."

"Granny Rose, she stay there her whole life long. Maybe she know this dead woman. You axe her."

"I surely thank you."

"You welcome."

She dipped her head and ducked back inside.

I drove to the green house. It looked better than any of the others on the block. The paint was dark green with white trim. The porch deck was painted a brick red, and four black rockers were spaced across the narrow porch. The front yard was free of leaves. I had glimpsed a bonfire burning in the backyard as I was arriving. Several children played there and looked like a flock of some exotic species, in their bright multicolored cold weather gear.

An old brass knocker was mounted on the front door. I clapped it, and the door was open immediately by a small boy who looked to be about eight.

"Is Granny Rose here?"

"Granny Rose!" he yelled, and scurried out of sight.

The woman who appeared in the doorway holding an infant wrapped in a pink blanket was the spitting image of Miss Della Reese. My mouth gaped. I was staring at an icon. She was wearing dark thick slacks, a long knitted tunic in orange, and a flowered bib apron over it, tied in back with a large bow.

"You needin' to see me?" she asked when I just stood there gawking.

"Granny Rose?" I stammered.

I apologized when I came to my senses. "The lady down the block told me Granny Rose. I assumed it meant your last name was Rose."

"I be Granny Rose Richardson, but it don't make no never mind, everybody calls me Granny Rose. Lots of white yunguns, too. Come inside, chile! We're letting out all the heat!"

I stepped inside, and as she closed the door I glanced around the living room. A beautiful fire was burning in the fireplace, but I didn't smell wood smoke. The walls were covered with framed photographs. Men, women, and children, both young and old, stared back at me. Every surface was covered with standing frames, some ornate and shiny enough to be silver, some cardboard covers, but most were products of the Dollar Store. My eyes returned to the fireplace. It was a gas log.

"I see you have a gas log," I said, turning to her.

"Sure 'nuff. My boy children 'cided it would save me a lot of work but I 'spect they were tired of choppin' wood and loadin' the wood box!" She gave a deep, belly-shaking laugh and patted the infant's back.

"What you think of my family?" She raised her free hand towards the displayed pictures.

"You must have a large family!" I exclaimed inanely. I was still off-balance from her likeness to Miss Reese.

"Well, I'd ten head and they'd twenty-seven head and there's where I lost count. I leave it up to my daughters-in-law to keep track!"

Before I could reply, the door was thrown open and two teenage girls entered. They were laughing and chattering until they spotted me. Both stopped talking and silently glared at me.

"Wacha be doin'? Mind your manners! Quit lookin' like an old persimmon!" Granny Rose was shaking her finger.

"She's the bloodhound woman!" one blurted, while the other shook her head vigorously in agreement.

"You be polite to my guest," Granny Rose said quietly. "You smile and say hello this very minute."

"They both struggled to furnish a ten-watt smile and mumbled a low greeting.

"Wacha need?" Granny Rose inquired coolly.

"Mama wants your grocery list. She says she has the money for it."

"Fine. I'll be right back." She turned to me. "'Scuse me a minute."

"Certainly." I smiled.

I looked at the girls, who were looking everywhere but at me.

"You got it wrong about me, kiddos. If you'd like to be fair, you could come to the kennel and I'll answer any question you want to ask. Deal?"

Neither one answered or even looked my way. Granny Rose returned with the list.

"Both o' you shamed me in my own home. Don't ever be doin' it no more."

They nodded and escaped out the front door.

"Come back to the kitchen, chile, and we'll have some coffee and sit awhile."

I followed her.

"Were they your granddaughters?"

"Great-grandchildren. Can't 'member their names nowadays. Just call 'em darlin', or sweetie, or chile."

I upped my estimate of her age another ten years.

I sat in a comfortable dinette chair at the end of a large formica table. A baby was sleeping in a small wooden cradle to the left of the large gas range. Granny Rose poured rich-smelling coffee from a huge blue-and-white-flecked coffeepot sitting on a low-turned burner into large mugs. She placed a spoon and a paper napkin to my right. A large sugar bowl and a can of Carnation evaporated milk were placed before me.

"Help yourself."

I hate canned milk. When I was very young, we were so poor that my mother drank her coffee black, so she could mix up a glass of canned milk diluted with water and a touch of honey for me. I drank it then because I knew she was sacrificing her coffee milk for me. I would drink it now because when in Rome . . . I added a pinch of sugar, trying to make it more palatable. It didn't help.

"Tastes and smells delicious!" I enthused. This was only half of a polite lie—it did *smell* good.

"Miz Richardson, my name—"

"No-siree-bob! I be Granny Rose, and you be chile. I be plumb forgot by tomorrow. Anyhow, I be seeing your likeness in the paper from time to time. It came to me when the children called you the bloodhound woman."

"That's nice of you," I murmured.

"Lets me axe you somethin'. You be the one that Jasmine Jones went to stay with after she sell her diner?"

"Yes, ma'am. Do you know Jasmine?"

"Since the day she be birth'd. How she gettin' on?"

"Just great!" I was beaming with pride. "She's more beautiful than ever and is so good with the dogs I don't know how I ever got along without her! I'll tell her you were asking about her."

"You tells her ol' Granny Rose sure be glad to lay eyes on her one more time. She ate many a bowl of soup in dis kitchen."

"I'll be sure to tell her. Did you know her mother before she died? Jasmine hasn't ever mentioned her. My mother taught me to never speak ill of the dead, but I thought it was terrible when she gave up on Jasmine and tossed her out on the streets when Jasmine was only twelve years old."

"She ain't passed! She be stayin' three streets over, and has been for more'n fifty year!"

"Her mother is still alive? But Jasmine's never mentioned . . ." I bit my lip.

"You be blamin' her?" Granny Rose had cocked her head and sat waiting for my answer.

"Of course not!" I spoke quickly. "I have never pried into Jasmine's past. I just assumed . . . It's none of my business."

"That's a good chile! Jasmine will tell you all 'bout it when she be ready. Mark my words."

I thought back over the past two years and remembered that all the girlish reminiscing and confidences had been mine. I would have thought the same as Granny Rose, but now I doubted it. After two years of close proximity without saying a word, she probably never would. It saddened me.

"Granny Rose, I need your help. I'm trying to find someone that knew a woman who lived on this street thirty years ago and can tell me about her. Maybe you'll remember her?"

"I'll try. Who she be?"

"Velma Mae Nichols. She was killed—"

"Hush, chile, no need to explain 'bout that chile. Thirty years back my memory be sharp as a tack. It's yesterd'y and last week I be hard to call back."

Granny Rose gazed into the past as she remembered.

"She was just a little slip of a girl, but proud of her job and worried, too. She be afraid she'd do somethin' wrong. I be all the time 'surring her that she helped her mama since she was five to raise six head. She be coming to me often and axing me for advice.

"She be here just a couple of days 'fore she passed. She be so proud of the babies she watched over, she brung me a picture for me to see. She only had the both of 'em for a few days. Yellow was her favorite color. She dress her boss man's baby in yellow. Everythin' she bought for the chile was yellow. She tole me that the boss man didn't pay no 'tention to his chile, and hopin' the yellow color would cheer her up. She be a good chile and now she be in heaven singin' with the angels!"

"Did she ever mention anyone hanging around or paying attention to the babies?"

"Lordy, chile, she be a little mama hen! She see somethin' like that, she be screechin' and yellin' all over the place!"

"Did she have a boyfriend?"

"That chile? She never had a minute for herself in her whole life. She be shy. She never got to lookin' at boys."

I couldn't think of anything else to ask. All I had learned was that the opinion of Alice Trulock and Velma Mae were the same, that Calvin Newton never noticed his child. Also that I could drop the theory that Velma Mae's boyfriend had done it, as she hadn't had one.

"I want to thank you for answering my questions. I'll tell Jasmine about meeting you and you'd appreciate a visit."

"You welcome."

As we walked to the door I complimented her.

"You have a lovely home."

"The yunguns pay me what they can for babysittin' and what'd they like, they put in fixin' up the place. It takes every cent for groceries. Sometimes there be twenty head eating my soup at noon, and half of 'em I don't know. No chile be hungry 'round here!"

She stood tall and proud.

"You're an angel, Granny Rose."

"Now you 'paring me with Miz Della I see on the television!" She laughed.

"You're both angels!"

I could hear her laughter until I closed the car door.

23

Time Out for the Trainees

January 8, Sunday, 5:00 P.M.

When I entered the common room that evening, Jasmine came to meet me. She looked splendid in a wine-colored two-piece wool suit and a silver lamé blouse. Her heels were three-inch spikes the same color as her top. I would buckle at the knees if I wore spikes for more than three hours.

"How was the funeral?" Jasmine asked in a low voice.

"Tom would have hated it. Much too long because all the politicians orated mightily. It had its moments, however. At graveside, Flora Mae half-read, half-cried a seemingly endless poem of many pages. Tom's hatchet-faced sister was so livid she started towards her, but Hank caught up to her and saved the day. I think she was planning on throwing Flora Mae into the grave with Tom. It ended in a shouting match between the two of them in the parking lot."

"Poor Hank." Jasmine looked sad.

"Yeah, he and Tom had worked together for almost eleven years. He said he'd be along when he could break away. He asked me why you didn't come."

"What did you tell him?" she asked, avoiding my eyes.

"The truth. I said someone had to be here to greet the trainees who were arriving this afternoon. I didn't tell him that you didn't want to go."

"That's not true! I just didn't want them whispering about me during Tom's funeral."

"No one blames you, Jasmine, so why should they whisper? You have to stop this now. It's unhealthy for you to cultivate guilt where none is due. Promise me you'll give what I'm telling you some serious thought, will you do that? If not, then I'll have to sic Hank on you, and you know what he would say."

"I promise." Her smile was slow in coming, but almost back to normal.

I glanced across the room to count heads. Three men were standing near the bar. The two tardy checks had arrived in yesterday's mail. One more male (as yet, we have not been blessed with a female trainee) was due to drive in at any time, and Wayne and Donnie Ray were picking up two at Jacksonville's airport.

"Did Wayne and Donnie Ray leave in time?"

"I helped them feed up. They left early. Are you ready to meet the trio already in residence?"

"Lead on," I said. I sucked in my gut and threw out my boobs and followed her.

On the way over I saw Miz Jansee working behind the steam table. Jansee Tatum was forty-five years old and always appeared worn out, used up, and ready to be thrown away. She had wispy thin brown hair and bony arms, and exhibited a cowed acceptance of her lot in life.

She had six children, ranging from eleven to twenty-nine years in age, and a no-good shiftless drunk for a husband who didn't supply any of his family's needs. She worked here part-time as my cook during the seminars and cleaned houses for the balance of her time, struggling to raise her brood. I urged her to take home the leftover food. It hurt her fierce Southern pride, but she did it for the kids' sake. I sometimes dream of taking a horsewhip to her worthless mate.

She had set the tables with salmon-colored linen cloths and tented wine-colored napkins in the plates. The crystal-like water goblets sparkled just like the real stuff.

The room was forty feet square. Three leather sofas, six black bar stools at the six-foot wet bar, and five easy chairs lined the walls. The jukebox was a 1955 Wurlitzer, and its multicolored lights cast a rosy glow. It had cost a fortune, but I knew I'd be paying for all this for thirty years, so I had purchased some things that I liked. Six much larger than life oil portraits of famous bloodhounds adorned the walls. A door on the south side led to Wayne's office, a door to the right rear was to the restrooms, and a door on the north side opened into the weighing room. The wooden floor gleamed with honey-colored varnish. The four dinning tables were three planks of twelve-inch white pine, six feet long, with twenty coats of clear polyethylene gloss, so the knotholes could be seen.

The twenty-four chairs were a vision of soft leather and chrome. The suckers had cost 100 bucks apiece. Four potted trees eight feet tall decorated the corner spaces. They were artificial. I have such a black thumb, I have been known to kill a cactus plant, which was guaranteed to be indestructible.

The kennels were behind the buildings. Wayne and Donnie Ray lived in an upstairs apartment twenty feet from the south wall and Jasmine's garage apartment was directly across the front drive from my house. The six individual units patterned after motel rooms were facing the asphalt courtyard and fifty feet to the left of my house. They were sleeping quarters for the six trainees, who were law enforcement personnel. They spent a week here learning to handle their animals before they took the department-owned dogs home with them.

Fifteen acres were fenced with eight-foot chain link, which was hot-wired, and five acres surrounding the buildings had a six-foot inner fence. The first gate near the road and second gate at the entrance to the compound had pressure plates. Any weight over thirty pounds triggered the alarms.

Five acres fronted Highway 301, and was where the small animal clinic sat with a small cottage set back fifty feet. I was beginning the seventh year of a thirty-year mortgage. The seminars were making money, even with my heavy payroll and expenses. I was comfortably writing in black ink and planned on retiring in twenty-three more years at the age of fifty-five, God willing.

The three men turned and faced us as we approached.

Jasmine began the introductions.

"Gentlemen, I'd like you to meet Jo Beth Sidden, your host and owner of Bloodhounds, Incorporated. May I present Deputy Sergeant Henry Scanlon, Clinch County Sheriff's Department, Homerville, Georgia."

"I'm glad to meet you, I've heard of some of your exploits," he answered, shaking my hand.

"We're practically neighbors. What is it, about eighty miles coming through Waycross?"

"Yes, ma'am, you're close."

Scanlon was married with two children, a ten-year veteran of the force. I get a detailed report from each law enforcement agency on their man well in advance of his arrival. Jasmine and I had memorized every detail. We had quizzed each other for the past two weeks. I think we had it knocked.

Jasmine indicated the man in the middle.

"I'd like you to meet Patrolman Carvel Manning, Athens Police Department, Athens, Georgia."

He was good-looking, three years in the department, and single. I bet the ladies adored him.

"I read about your commendation for the capture of an escaped felon from Illinois. That was good work," I said.

"I got lucky," he answered with a killer smile.

"Solid police work is my guess."

Jasmine started to introduce the only African-American attending this seminar. This one was divorced, two children, had partial custody, and had been a deputy for five years.

"Let me guess," I said with a 100-watt smile. "Officer Marvin Smith, Atlanta Metro Police Department, Atlanta, Georgia. Welcome."

He gave me a slow smile. "What gave me away?"

"At six foot two inches, you're the tallest trainee attending this session." My voice was a tad cooler.

"Good answer," he said in a lazy drawl.

"It's the way I am," I shot back.

Jasmine reached for his glass. "Let me freshen your drink." She led him away.

I blinked.

"I need a drink," I told Scanlon and Manning. "Care to join me?" I went behind the bar, popped a beer, and took a healthy swig. I made both of them fresh drinks. Bourbon and branch, and whiskey and Coke for the ladykiller.

"Ah, a star is born." I spoke in awe. Both men turned on their stools to look behind them.

Susan had arrived. She was carrying a black lamb's wool jacket so it wouldn't spoil the dramatic lines of her dress. She was a bright flame from head to toe. Ruby earrings, plunging crimson velvet bodice, and rippling red folds of chiffon over lustrous taffeta. Her shoes were narrow strapped sandals the same shade as the gown, with fuck-me heels. She turned a full circle in hanging her coat on the hat rack and glided over to the jukebox, where Jasmine and Smith stood gawking.

Susan turned with a swirl of her skirt and headed our way.

"Brace yourselves," I whispered softly.

"Hi, guys!" she said with a grin, perching on the end stool. "I'm Susan. Would you inform the bartender I'd like a glass of white wine?"

They both scampered off their barstools trying to be the first to introduce themselves.

I tsk-tsked. "Susan, behave. One is married."

"That gives me a fifty-fifty chance," she purred in a sultry contralto.

I heard the first gate alarm, now muted by the noisy jukebox. By process of elimination, this fourth man would be Agent Philip Wells, GBI, Georgia Bureau of Investigation, Tactical Drug Unit, currently working out of the Savannah Task Force. They were going to try a bloodhound. They used several other breeds around the state. This was an experiment, so I had decided to give them Edna, one of my favorite drug sniffers. She'd do us proud if the guy had any moxie at all.

Discounting the law of averages, the way my luck had been running lately it could possibly be Bubba coming up the drive. My .32 was in my nightstand. Having six armed guests arriving had seemed sufficient to repel boarders.

"Deputy Sergeant Scanlon? Yoo-hoo!" He finally tore his attention away from the red menace.

"Care to come with me to greet a fellow trainee?"

He and I strolled towards the front door. Just in case, I decided to issue a preliminary warning.

"Are you packing, sir?"

After a disconcerted glance, he admitted he was.

"A more complete explanation is part of my welcoming speech in the morning, but there is a slim chance that the approaching vehicle might be carrying my ex-husband, whose mission in life is to snuff out mine. Don't be afraid to shoot if necessary. He'll be armed with a lead-drilled-and-filled baseball bat and is extremely dangerous not only to me but anyone standing within range."

I saw him brush back his coat and adjust his chest holster, straighten up, and square his shoulders. Maybe I'd get lucky tonight and have Bubba blown away by a visiting lawman.

Nope, not tonight. The man emerging from the car was Wells.

"Rest easy, Deputy Sergeant, it's a fellow traveler."

I introduced myself and then Scanlon. The three of us went back inside.

While making the rounds to make sure that everyone was aware of the latest addition, Jasmine eased me aside.

"If you were trying to alienate the only suitable dancing partner for me around here, you did a good job," she whispered.

"The dude jumped to the improper conclusion that I was identifying him by his black skin. He thinks this honky is a racist," I hissed back.

"I corrected the situation, but you really can't blame him, it was a logical surmise. You could have done the same on the first two but you waited until the brother before you tested your skills because you knew you had a lock!"

"*Et tu, Brute?*" I gave her a questioning stare.

"What are you two whispering about?" Susan was drawn to intrigue like a cobra to the flute.

"Whether we Americans should pay our delinquent dues to the United Nations!" I turned on my heel and took a hike.

Two years together in April, and Jasmine and I just had our first quarrel. I felt sick. Me and my fast mouth and faster tongue! Outside I drew in several deep breaths of the clean cold air. I peered at the temperature gauge on the freestanding post located at the corner of the building. It was 38 degrees at a quarter 'til seven. I had about two more minutes of exposure before the chill bumps started to mottle my pale complexion and make me look jaundiced in spite of my careful cosmetic application. I looked at the early full moon now floating high above the horizon and wished for many things.

24

Stand and Deliver

January 8, Sunday, 7:00 P.M.

The first gate alarm sounded before I could enter the common room door. It could be Hank, Wayne, and Donnie Ray with their plane passengers, a lost traveler, or Bubba. I kinda wished it was Bubba. In the mood I was in I felt willing and able to take him on barehanded. Nah, that would be stupid. Maybe I should get a little closer to the door just to be on the safe side.

I recognized Hank's car and walked out to greet him.

"What are you doing out here without a coat?"

"Trying to catch pneumonia." I looked at him while I rubbed my arms for warmth. "Rough day, huh?"

"It was a dilly. Let's go get a beer." He wrapped his arm around my shoulders and we went inside.

I warmed up as I led Hank around, introducing him to the four men present. I eased out of the group when they started to play the game of who-do-you-know and went to check on dinner. Susan walked up while I was admiring the food on the steam table and handed me a beer.

"You looked like you could use one right about now."

"Thanks. You look gorgeous tonight, by the way."

"What's with you and Jasmine?"

"We had our first quarrel. I feel like a shit."

"Good, it was about a year and eight months overdue. Now, when the smoke clears you can quit tiptoeing around each other and relax."

"Don't quit your day job, Susan. I don't think you're cut out to be a diplomat."

"Thanks for sharing that thought. Well, well, more grist for my mill."

My eyes followed hers and saw that Wayne and Donnie Ray had arrived with their two passengers in tow.

"Put your tongue back behind your teeth. They're both married," I admonished.

"It's a cold night and I need a back rub. Tonight, my friend, I'm not necessarily searching for a matrimonial prospect. Perhaps I'll resume the search next Saturday."

"Susan!"

She didn't hear me. She was locked onto her target like a heat-seeking missile. I followed her across the room, thanked Wayne and Donnie Ray, and watched them disappear into Wayne's office. They weren't much for mingling with the guests. They'd rather read drag racing magazines and play endless hands of cribbage. I greeted the man whom Susan was ignoring.

"I'm glad to meet you, Officer McPherson, I'm Jo Beth Sidden, your host. How was your flight?"

"It seemed we no sooner got up there when we could feel us coming back down. Small planes make me nervous."

He and his flying companion were new officers entering the K-9 unit in Augusta's Police Department. Both were fresh out of the police academy. They were going to handle drug dogs.

The man Susan was monopolizing was Officer James Dinsmore, obviously a weightlifter from the thick tree-trunk neck and large shoulders under his sportcoat.

"Susan?" I tapped her bare shoulder and interrupted her come-hither approach.

"Let me greet Officer Dinsmore," I said, smiling. "I'm glad you could join us. I'm Jo Beth Sidden, your host. I see that Susan Comstock has already introduced herself. Let's go meet the others."

I took Dinsmore and McPherson away, leaving Susan with unfinished plans. She wasn't invited to dinner each night to pique their libidos or put a strain on their marriage vows. She was supposed to furnish conversation and brighten up the evening. Her definition of brightening the evening and mine were poles apart.

By the time I had the two officers with drinks and tucked into a conversation with another lawman, I saw it was time to eat. I checked with Miz Jansee.

"Are you ready for us to start loading our plates?"

"Yes'em, I just poured up the gravy."

"Good," I said beaming. "It sure smells good!"

Miz Jansee went to tell Wayne and Donnie Ray. I beat it over to Officer Dinsmore and hooked my arm into his.

"I want you to sit on my right tonight. I want to hear about your new K-9 unit in Augusta."

We were twelve. I always asked Miz Jansee to sit and eat with us, but she invariably declined. "Don't feel right," she informed me when she first started cooking the meals.

Supper was delicious. Fried chicken and pork chops, mashed potatoes and gravy, field peas from our garden last fall, also corn and collard greens, hot biscuits and cornpones. Dessert was peach cobbler and apple pie.

Tonight was just for conversation and getting to know the trainees. Tomorrow they would be paired with their animals and begin their training. Tomorrow night, we would show them the video Donnie Ray had made of the search for a missing woman. It made a good training film, and fortunately it had a happy ending. This was to give the trainees confidence that they, too, could be heroes and find people who were lost or abducted.

After supper was over, several went back to drinking. I was busy for a while mixing drinks, then I told them to help themselves and went to corner Hank.

I was avoiding Jasmine because I wanted to give her time to cool down before I approached her to apologize. She was right. It did look suspicious that I "guessed" on the only black person at the seminar. I thought that I had done it only because of his height, but had I really? His color was so obvious. Neither one of them, Marvin Smith or Jasmine, had thought so. Maybe it was there and I used it along with his height. I wasn't sure now.

When I got Hank isolated, I sat with him at an empty table and had coffee. He had a bottle of beer and gauging his demeanor, I decided he had drunk several. He sat loose-jointed and his eyes had a vague look.

"Are you sure you're all right?"

"Right as rain. What can I do you for?" He used the local terminology.

"I was wondering if you had tried to locate Sara Louise, Bryan Sirmons's wife?"

"The one that ran off with her bowling partner over thirty years ago? Christ, Sidden, she could have moved and married and changed her name a dozen times by now. How do you suggest I start, by asking one of my men to track her down? The case isn't open and we're always shorthanded. That's exactly the reason why I asked you to look into it, I can't spare any time, or men."

"I know," I acknowledged. "I thought maybe you could see if they knew where to notify her—if they did—when her child was murdered."

"Seems I remember something about the sheriff getting her address and calling. I can't be sure. I read it somewhere in the files."

"It wasn't in the files you gave me."

"Jo Beth, the follow-up slips on the case are filed on the day they are written. I went through the whole bunch and didn't learn anything important."

"Could I look through them?"

"Hell, no. Take my word, there's nothing there. I can't take them out of the storeroom—and you can't sit on the floor and leaf through them like I did, which was after midnight, by the way. Don't ask me to copy them, either. I'd be standing at the machine for a week! Why are you interested in her anyway? You think she came back, murdered the nanny who wouldn't have known her from Adam, kidnapped her daughter, and killed her?"

"Not at all," I stated with thinned lips. "The thought occurred to me, if Bryan Sirmons was involved in the kidnapping, he would need someone to help hide the babies while he was trying to collect the ransom. Who better than the mother that had deserted her several months before? The reason she left was money. Sirmons could have promised her a lot."

"Then why was the Sirmons baby killed? That doesn't make sense!"

"Maybe the child was killed by accident, then the facts would fit, wouldn't they?"

"So why kill the child's nanny?" he asked, staring at me with his head tilted to one side and trying to look patient.

"Maybe that was also an accident."

Hank grunted and drank some beer. "Lot of maybes."

"What if I told you I had an eyewitness who places Bryan Sirmons a couple of blocks from All Souls Church at the precise time the crime was being committed?"

He rapidly blinked and seemed to focus more clearly on my face. "Where was this witness thirty years ago?"

"Didn't want to get involved."

"How positive is this witness and do I know him?"

"He's pretty sure and I don't want to name him right now."

"Why?"

"Just because," I answered, being stubborn.

"It hasn't been a week since you heard about this case, and you now have two fresh suspects and a 'pretty sure' eyewitness. I'm impressed," he said lazily, and took another swallow of his beer.

"Just tossing out some theories, trying to get them to fit," I said casually. "Nothing definite yet."

"This eyewitness wouldn't be Hanson Aldridge, would it? Our resident drunk?" He gave me a wink.

"Nah," I lied. "He couldn't tell me anything new." I decided not to tell him about my interview with Alice Trulock, and meeting Granny Rose. He acted as if he thought I was spinning my wheels, which was too close to the truth for comfort. I would keep any new scenario to myself until I could figure out who done it. If I could.

"Can I join you?" Susan asked as she slid into a chair beside Hank. I noticed Jasmine was standing behind her.

"Yes to both of you," I said, sounding glad of being interrupted. "Sit by me, Jasmine."

Susan sat, and started bending Hank's ear about the funeral and the histrionics of the women in Tom's life.

I turned to Jasmine, who reluctantly took a seat on my side of the table.

"I apologize for the way I treated Smith, and you. I'm sorry. I've decided you both may have been right, I just might be guilty. I don't think I am but I could be without recognizing the fact."

"I'm sad that we both said hasty things. I'll forgive you, if you'll forgive me," Jasmine uttered under her breath. She was trying to keep this moment between the two of us. It was not to be, not with Susan within earshot.

"Are you two making up? Don't whisper. Hank and I want to hear." Her low throaty Georgia twang could be heard great distances with little effort.

"We'd talk louder if we wanted an audience!"

"Great balls of fire, she's now being mean to me," Susan joshed.

Hank glanced towards the six trainees, who were carrying on an animated conversation in a loose circle near the bar.

"You're excused, Hank," I said with a chuckle. "Go talk with your peers."

I didn't have to say it twice. With little ado, he hied over where the conversation didn't involve feminist infighting.

I saw Susan eyeing Officer Dinsmore.

"For shame, Susan, I'm disappointed in you. Quit trying to pick up Officer Dinsmore, he's too young for you."

"Six years difference in age means nothing after the parties get past puberty," Susan drawled.

"Just don't tempt him to break his marriage vows," I amended. "Let's talk about something pleasant."

Susan seemed excited.

"You'll never guess who I saw today! Try to guess."

"Jimmy Hoffa?" I ventured.

"Elvis Presley?" Jasmine added.

"Jasmine, you're too young to remember. This happened right around your birth. I met one of the wailing baby ghosts that grownups used to tell Jo Beth and I about to scare us into behaving. She walked right into the store Friday afternoon and introduced herself. We had a nice long talk. Bet you don't know who I mean!" She was smiling in anticipation of stumping me.

Like the thoughtless jackass I can be at times, I walked right into her surprise and stomped it flat.

"You mean Patricia Ann Newton, who lived in the big white mansion and survived her kidnapping thirty years ago? I've known she was moving back since last Tuesday. Didn't you?"

The minute I uttered the taunt, I knew I was in deep shit. Susan hates to be kept out of my quote, investigations, unquote. I hurriedly started composing an abject apology for the third time this night. One of these days I would learn to think before I blabbed quick answers.

25

Meeting the Golden Girl

January 9, Monday, 11:00 A.M.

After breakfast in the common room with the regular crew plus six trainers and six trainees, I spent two hours watching them working with their four-legged partners on a leash and learning how to give them simple commands.

At ten o'clock I called the new telephone listing that the local operator had supplied me, after she informed me there would be a seventy-five cent charge added to my monthly bill for using her services. Since it was a new number, just installed, and not yet listed in the directory, it didn't seem fair. It seems nowadays that everyone has their hands out for fees, assessments, and service charges. This is progress?

I told the woman who answered that I would like an appointment to see the lady of the house, to officially greet her and discuss community activities. I didn't say I was the Welcome Wagon hostess, I just let her assume I was. She left the phone and came back shortly and informed me that Ms. Patricia Ann Newton would see me at eleven this morning, if it was convenient. I said it was.

I pulled into the driveway and stopped at the front steps. This was my first invited visit. Two other youngsters plus Susan and I had dared each other until we were forced to climb the fence on one hot Saturday afternoon. We had crept down the drive, whispering nervously, and giggling to hide our fright. Heat lightning had been in the advancing clouds and when an unusual clap of thunder rolled in the heavens, we took off like scared rabbits. We must have been eight or nine.

The maid or housekeeper took me into a large formal living room and said Ms. Newton would be down shortly. She was around my age and a stranger to me. I wondered if she was a local I didn't recognize or if she had been imported from New York.

I sat on one of the pale pink brocade-covered armchairs, in jeans, sweatshirt, and denim jacket, and inspected my well-worn dirty sneakers. I could hide only one of them behind my denim-clad leg. I decided that one dirty shoe looked just as bad as a pair, so I put them side by side on the lovely antique rug.

The room was huge, much larger than my common room. There was a white piano by the south ceiling-to-floor windows. A fire was burning merrily in a fireplace large enough to roast an ox. Its brass-edged glass doors were closed. I would guess to preserve the pristine carpet, but it could be for another reason. I had never been in a house this grand. Even my lawyer's "Tara" didn't hold a candle to this house.

I had dubbed her the golden girl. This didn't mean she had blond hair. In the South, if a girl is very beautiful or very rich and everything seemed to go her way, she is called "the golden girl."

The woman who entered the room was not beautiful. She had plain features and looked apprehensive or nervous, maybe both. She was wearing carefully applied makeup. Her hair was shoulder-length and black, with fullness but no curl. Her eyes were dark brown. Her chin was a tad pronounced. Not a beauty, but she had clear skin and appeared to glow with good health.

She was wearing a pale blue sweater set with a fancy trim of tiny violets and a navy wool skirt. Her shoes were navy sling pumps with sensible heels. She seemed wrapped in muted colors, socially acceptable, and had an aura of haunted Victorian secrets. I was getting too fanciful about this modern poor little rich girl. She could be an empty-headed, self-centered bitch for all I know. Maybe I was viewing her this way because I knew her history. I could be projecting my estimate of vulnerability and sadness to her features and seeing it reflected back at me. All I knew at this moment was that I liked her and wanted to help some way.

"Ms. Sidden?" She came towards me and offered her hand. "I'm glad that you came to welcome me home. Even though I've lived in New York for thirty years, I always felt like this was home. I'm very glad to be back."

"Please call me Jo Beth. May I call you Patricia Ann?"

"Just Patricia, please. Won't you sit down, Jo Beth? Marion will bring coffee soon, or would you like something else? Tea, or perhaps a soda?"

"Coffee will be fine."

I sat back down on the wingback chair and she perched opposite me on its twin. There was an enormous coffee table in pecan wood, with a glass top and a huge flower arrangement of fresh blooms and buds of assorted colors on its surface. I knew they were real because I saw a drop of water near the gold-colored base. If Patricia kept the house stocked with fresh-cut flowers, my friend who owned Alice's Flower Pot would be able to take her winter vacation in Hawaii this year.

Patricia moved the flowers over to her right, just as I saw Marion enter the room carrying a silver tray with a coffee service.

"Thank you, Marion," Patricia said as she placed the tray between us.

Marion lifted a silver cover and revealed a plate with warm fruit-filled scones. I took a deep breath of the delightful aroma.

"They smell wonderful!" I proclaimed as I glanced up at Marion. Her back was to Patricia and she gave me a knowing grin and bawdy wink. I might not recognize her, but she sure knew me. It was the only explanation. No New York servant would do this to one of Patricia's guests.

"I baked these," Patricia admitted shyly. "If I read too long, I get headaches, and there's only so much music I can bear to hear in a day. When I get bored I go practice baking in the kitchen."

She poured coffee. "Cream, sugar?"

"Double cream, no sugar."

"Did Marion come with you from New York?" I asked politely. I knew I was being nosy, but the wink had made me curious.

"No, Mr. Bennett, our lawyer, hired her and the other help."

"Wade Bennett is also my lawyer and a good friend. I'm surprised that I don't recognize Marion. When you live in a small town, you know everyone. What's her last name?"

"Her name is Marion Padgett. I believe her father raises . . . alligators."

I could hear the disbelief in her voice that a person could make a living raising alligators. We had at least ten alligator farms within Dunston County, and they made good money indeed. Now that gators were off the endangered species list, it was legal. Of course, the same guys were selling them back then, "out the back door," when it was illegal. Now they had legitimate permits and were able to advertise and be listed in the Yellow Pages.

I also knew why I had received the wink from Marion. About three months ago I had walked up on a large moonshine operation that either her brothers or her cousins owned and operated. We had pretended that we didn't see each other and I quickly passed out of view. No one said a word. I trained in the swamp and entered it often. If I reported one still to the authorities I might as well hang up my rescue suit and close the kennel. These ol' boys would retaliate with lightning speed and would be just as deadly as a direct strike.

I hadn't recognized Marion as a Padgett. They're so plentiful in these parts, I doubt if their kin can keep them straight, from first cousins to grandnephews.

I felt like a pig. Only three hours after breakfast, I was scarfing down strawberry scones.

"They taste as good as they smell," I declared. Patricia beamed with pride.

"You should get a job," I suggested between bites. "It sure cures boredom."

"I would love to, but Uncle Bryan won't hear of it!" She laughed. "He says, 'A woman's place is in the home.'"

"A sexist remark if I've ever heard one. Why do you listen to him? You're over twenty-one, footloose, and fancy free."

"Because I always have," she said quietly. "He spent the last thirty years of his life guiding me and protecting me. It would be ungrateful to go against his wishes."

I could see that Uncle Bryan had his claws dug in deep. Total control. Difficult to achieve in these enlightened times. No wonder she had a Victorian aura. Sirmons had raised her as if she were in the nineteenth century, instead of the twentieth.

If he wanted her to be a Southern aristocrat, he was way behind the times. Modern belles went to the University of Georgia, snagged a husband from Georgia or Georgia Tech, became lawyers, executives, and the like. Had their children, a career, and were into their second or third affair by the time they were Patricia's age. I decided to change the subject.

"How do you manage to run this whole house by yourself?" I tried to sound awed at the prospect.

"I've run our household since I was fifteen," she told me with pride. "I didn't attend college but I took culinary courses, flower-arranging, needlepoint. I learned how to train servants and manage money. I've been in charge of my trust fund since I turned twenty-one. I know that an aggressive approach could have doubled my inheritance every seven years, but I'm much too conservative to depend heavily on the stock market. I have increased my trust a comforting amount without taking risks."

"Good for you," I congratulated her warmly.

What do the Catholics say? Give me a child until he's twelve, and he'll always be a Catholic. Sirmons had had control of her since she was eighteen months old. I imagined that one fine day when he found a suitable prospect, he would bring Patricia a husband and he would guide them into the twenty-first century. Not bad for a man who at twenty-seven couldn't afford the down payment on a new truck. If he was the one who had murdered two people—one of them his own daughter—and let another lose thirty years of freedom, the cost was too high.

"I'm so glad that you came to see me. I want to be part of this community. All I can give is money and I'm quite willing to do so. What agency do you represent and how much do you need?" She was sincere in her delivery.

I roared with laughter. "Freelance," I gasped, and emitted more giggles.

Patricia was taken by surprise with my candid answer but didn't seem angry. She was amused by my antics.

"I'm laughing, and I don't know why," she complained. "What is so funny?"

"You're gonna think I'm a nut. I'm sorry, but I came to see you under false colors. I didn't exactly lie, but I didn't level with you. Then you give me the perfect opportunity to present you with my wish list, which I lug around with me every waking hour, and I found it hilarious.

"You see, I too am always trying to solve people's dilemmas. I do what I can, but I can't help those where money is needed because I don't have the funds. Then I meet a nice lady who is willing to open her checkbook for good causes and I start laughing like an idiot. I'm so sorry that I deceived you. I apologize, because I am beginning to like you and would have liked to have you for a friend."

"You're starting to alarm me," she said with a nervous smile, "but I am intrigued by your apology. Why did you come to see me?"

"I'll explain, and then you can toss me out. I own and manage

Bloodhounds, Incorporated. I train bloodhounds for search-and-rescue work, drug raids, arson, and cadaver dogs."

"Marion told me that much about you earlier, when you called. She also mentioned that you work for the local animal shelter. She said you were on the board of directors. I thought you wanted to ask me for a donation."

"The animals are always at the top of my wish list. We sorely need funds, but that wasn't the reason for my visit. It's about the murder and kidnapping that occurred here thirty years ago."

Her pleasant expression turned into a grimace of disgust.

"I should have caught on when you mentioned the word freelance. You want to write a true crime book on the crime? Want me to dig up baby pictures and pose for more pictures, sobbing with despair? Reveal my innermost thoughts? Let me tell you something, Ms. Sidden. My Uncle Bryan has had to live with the memories and fend off vultures like you for thirty years. Until just now, I had never had to meet your type. He kept me safe from your reach. This was the main reason he never wanted us to move back here, which I've wanted to do all of my life. I want you to leave this minute!"

I could have stopped her before she lost her temper, but I wanted to find out how much she knew.

"I will not leave until you know the truth of why I'm here. Please hear me out. It's not to write a sensational book, I couldn't write my way out of a paper bag. Will you please listen to my explanation, and *then* you can toss me out. Please?"

I put everything I had into my voice, trying to convince her. I had remained seated, but she had risen and stood glaring at me. Either she had a hidden service bell under the carpet somewhere near she had stepped on, or Marion had been listening at the door. She appeared as if she had been summoned.

"Can I help you, Miz Patricia?" She was dividing her glance between her employer's red and angry countenance and my calm expression, while I remained on my duff.

"You can show Ms. Sidden out!" Patricia's voice quivered with indignation.

"Marion, will you answer a question for me before you show me the door? Please direct your honest opinion to Patricia. Do you and your family trust me and do I have a good reputation in this town where I've lived my entire life?"

"The answer is yes to both questions, Miz Patricia. Me and my whole family would trust her word on anything. She won't harm you none. She keeps her word, always."

The truth was evident in her emotional statement of support.

Well, that tore it. I got up to leave. If my newest theory was valid, I would harm Patricia greatly. In fact, I would blow her world apart.

26

No Harm, No Foul

January 9, Monday, Noon

On my feet, I really saw Marion for the first time. Before, she had been a uniform and a voice. Now, with hindsight, I saw the Padgett family features and knew she had been somewhere in the background in my few and far between forays to Porky's.

The three of us, Susan, Jasmine, and I, had been there maybe four times in the past two years when we felt the need to kick up our heels. Memories of a large smoke-wreathed dance floor, raucous Western music, and many couples line dancing brought her image into focus. Picturing her in a tight t-shirt and tighter jeans and adding boots completed the package.

Marion's loose black nylon uniform with the white frilly apron cinched 'round her waist had disguised her identity. Her straight nose and thin cheeks with lightly tanned skin even in January, plus her coal-black straight-as-a-ruler hair, gave testimony to her Indian ancestry.

I faced Patricia. "I have no desire to hurt you, and dredge up something that Bryan Sirmons has kept from you all these years. I think it's best that I leave. Thanks for the coffee and your time."

"You didn't even know her a few minutes ago!" Her angry eyes darted between Marion and me. "What's going on here?"

"Marion has a lot of relatives. The uniform threw me off a bit, but I know her and her family." I smiled at both of them and added, "Sorry, Marion."

"I knew you didn't. That's why I winked." A slow drawl appeared in her speech, but she seemed worried. Jobs were hard to find in these parts. I thought that was what she was thinking, but who knew?

"That will be all, Marion. I'll call if I need you."

Her employer's voice sounded cool. Marion left the room in haste.

Patricia indicated the chair that I had just vacated.

"Please sit down, Miz Jo Beth, I think I may have jumped to the wrong conclusion."

"You don't add Miz to my name. Marion does to show respect because I'm older. You and I are equal in age, more or less, so you don't use it with me. Southern colloquialisms," I explained.

"How about Manuel Johnson, my African-American gardener?"

"How old is he?"

"Fifty-four."

"Uncle Manuel, but if you find it difficult to call him Uncle, Mr. Johnson will do just as well. However, if the black man is your age or younger, never use the term uncle. Some of the more progressive thinkers view it as an insult. It isn't meant to be condescending, but that's what they believe. Older black people over fifty know you're showing respect. It sounds difficult, I know, but you'll pick it up in no time."

"Thank you. Will you tell me why you came to see me, now? I'm ready to listen."

"One question first. How much do you know about what happened here thirty years ago?"

"Only what Uncle Bryan has told me, and that was only when I asked. He told me a little at a time, enough to answer my questions and satisfy me. When I was about three, I think, I asked why I didn't call him Daddy and if I had a mommy like the other children. He explained my parents' deaths in simple terms. I was twelve before I found out he wasn't my uncle."

"How did that happen?"

"I saw my name on some papers and his below it, and a place for his signature. It said legal guardian and I asked him what it meant. That's when he told me we weren't related by blood. I was fifteen before I got really curious. We were studying genes in biology. I wanted to know about my family tree and wanted to trace it."

"Did he tell you?"

"Not too much, but he seemed terribly hurt, as if he thought I didn't think he was good enough for me, and that I was dissatisfied with him. I was so sorry that I made him feel inadequate. I swore to myself I would never ask another question and I didn't, until a few months ago."

"What made you ask then?"

"The need to come home. I've always felt like I was dwelling in a foreign land. I had initialed the payments made by the accounting firm for yearly storage fees on the furniture, rugs, and house maintenance since I was fifteen. I longed to live here or just stay a few months out of the year. Uncle Bryan was reluctant, and advised that we could come the next year. Something always came up. It wasn't until a few months ago that my desire to investigate my heritage overcame my reluctance to insist."

"Why?" I questioned as she sat in silence and acted reluctant to continue.

"I met a man. I thought we might marry."

Ah-ha! No wonder she wanted to know her roots. Then I remembered she had said a few months ago. Why hadn't they moved then? Then the answer dawned, clear as crystal.

"Your friend is no longer in the picture, is he?"

My tone was gentle. I bet she was still hurting.

"It didn't work out," she said quietly.

I bet Uncle Bryan played a major role in breaking up the romance.

My cheeks felt as if they were on fire from my indignation on her behalf. I knew I must look flushed, as if I had a fever. All along, I had felt that Samuel Debbs's release and the immediate arrival of Sirmons and Patricia were not coincidental. Sirmons had been notified by the prison of Debbs's release, was my guess.

"I'm so sorry, it must have been awful for you."

"I've had bad luck with the men in my life from the cradle," she replied bravely, "but this was total rejection. I guess I wasn't easy to live with for a while. I was coping with my loss, but I guess Uncle Bryan finally saw I was miserable. He came home from the office one evening less than three weeks ago and announced he couldn't bear to see me unhappy and how would I like to move back to Georgia. So here we are."

"I'm so glad that you're back, I really am," I said from the heart. "If anything that transpires here hurts you, I want you to remember one thing. It will get better with time. Bad times will pass, and I believe you will be strong enough to handle them."

"Why could I be hurt in returning to my home? I don't understand."

"How much do you know about Samuel Debbs?" I asked gently.

"Who?" Her brows drew inward in concentration. "I'm afraid I don't know . . ." She looked startled, and focused her eyes on mine. "He was the kidnapper?" she whispered. She read the answer on my face. "His sentence was life without parole. Has he died?"

"No, he was released on parole because of a heart condition. They say he's dying."

"He's here? He came back here?" Her voice rose with each word.

"Yes, but you have nothing to fear. He's a broken old man and he doesn't have any desire for revenge. He just wants to die in peace."

"Revenge? He doesn't want *revenge?* What are you saying? *He murdered two people!* He kidnapped me, and then left me in a church!"

"I understand your anger, but he's always sworn he did not commit those crimes. I only heard about the case last Tuesday, less than a week ago. I have seen him. He still maintains that he's innocent."

"What's he to you, a relative?" She was trying to find a plausible connection.

"No, I'd never heard of him before last Tuesday. A friend asked me for a favor, so I decided to ask a few questions and poke around."

"So that's why you're here." She nodded. "Well, you can tell him that I'll not forgive him, ever! What he did was despicable, and evil. Wait . . . you mentioned revenge. He was found guilty and convicted of the crime. Why should he want revenge? *Do you believe him?* Do you think he's innocent?"

"I'm beginning to," I admitted.

She sat deep in thought, comparing my information to her stored memories. I know I had hit her with a lot of new facts that she had been unaware of. When she reached a decision, I knew she had gotten it wrong. She seemed to pity me. I bet she thought I was one of those women who wrote murderers in jail and swallowed their proclamations of innocence hook, line, and sinker.

"Ever since I was fifteen, I've really been curious about knowing all the details of what happened. Believe it or not, when I was in town shopping Friday, I wanted to visit the newspaper office and read what the paper had printed all those years ago. I changed my mind. I didn't want to be recognized, I guess. I don't know what happened. Have you talked with anyone other than me?"

"Three, not counting Samuel Debbs," I admitted. "About the newspaper. If you still want the clippings, I can call the editor and get them for you. He's a friend of mine."

"You won't tell them who they are for, will you?"

"Of course not."

"That's very kind of you. I really would like to know the facts. Uncle Bryan thinks that it will just upset me, but I don't think so. I have no memories because I was just eighteen months old when we moved. Would you tell me all about the crime and who you've talked to about it? Do you have the time?"

"Yes, I'll be glad to tell you."

I began with the bare facts, told the newspaper version dispassionately, and kept my tale in chronological order and bent over backward to keep from planting doubt or prejudice in her mind.

Sometime during my recital, Patricia ordered sandwiches and Diet Cokes and Marion delivered them. I don't remember what I ate, just that it was tasty. It became much harder to concentrate and carefully edit my interviews with Alice Trulock, Hanson Aldridge, and Granny Rose Richardson.

I left out all references to her father's obvious lack of interest in her. Patricia didn't have to know that. I told her almost all the rest, except Hanson Aldridge's assertion that he had seen Sirmons near All Souls Church during the approximate time of the kidnapping.

She seemed to enjoy my recital. It took well over an hour and I felt drained.

"Granny Rose Richardson sounds like she's an amazing person. I've met so few people in my sheltered existence. You'll have to tell me about your wish list."

"She's on it," I said, laughing. "Never fear, when my seminar is over and I've done all I can to see if Samuel Debbs is telling the truth, I'll look into what I can do to help her."

"I also want to help. Let me write you a check."

"I didn't come here for money. Don't be hasty. Give me some time and then we'll get together and discuss it. I'll send you the newspaper clips as soon as I get them."

She walked me to the door and admired my van.

"I'd like to see your kennel," she said with enthusiasm. "Can I come to see you?"

"In a few days when I'll have more time. I'll call you," I answered evasively. "Please remember what I said about bad times."

"Why are you worrying about me?"

"If Samuel Debbs is telling the truth, someone else committed the crime."

"And you're worried that it will affect me? I'm strong enough to face the possibility of the wrong man accused. If he's innocent he should be vindicated, even if it means the whole story will become sensational again."

"I hope so," I said sincerely, and bade her good-bye.

27

Odds and Ends

January 13, Friday, 5:00 P.M.

Our January seminar had ended two hours ago, as Jasmine and I had stood and waved as the last car left the courtyard.

I had my feet on the desk and was leaning back in my chair playing telephone tag. Wade Bennett's secretary had put me on hold and, for all I knew, had gone home and left me hanging out to dry.

"Ms. Sidden?"

"Still here," I answered.

"Sorry to keep you waiting, but I can't seem to find him. He may have left without informing me. Could you call back tomorrow? We close the office at five."

Her tactful reminder that I was infringing on her time didn't faze me. She had kept me on hold for over five minutes.

"That's why I called a good five minutes ago," I said sweetly. "I won't take up any more of your valuable time by leaving a message. Oh, hold on a second, will you?"

I gently hung up the receiver.

He had to be dodging me. This was the third time I had tried to reach him since last Friday, when he had promised to get back to me ASAP.

I called his house. His wife, Sheri, answered.

"It's Jo Beth. Is your husband hiding out at home? He's been dodging me for a week!"

"He often does that very thing," she agreed complacently. "It must be bad news and he doesn't want to hear you scream and holler."

"Just remind him that a phone cord has other uses, like a garrote, to name one."

"He doesn't listen to me. After all, I'm just a pregnant housewife."

"Oh my God, Sheri, that's wonderful news! When did you find out?"

"This morning at ten. I tendered my resignation to the library by eleven and pulled Wade out of the courtroom at twelve and told him over cheeseburgers at the Greasy Spoon. He had to go back in after lunch and request a recess for the rest of the afternoon. He was weak-kneed and dizzy."

"No wonder!" I exclaimed. "I feel a little wobbly myself on hearing the good news and I didn't even have a greasy cheeseburger!"

Sheri laughed. "Idiot."

"So when do we find out if it's a she or a he?"

"I'm not sure, but not in the first trimester, I wouldn't think."

"Think female," I urged. "Morning, noon, and night, think female. Maybe we'll get lucky."

"The papa-to-be just got out of the shower. Hold on."

I heard Sheri yelling to Wade to come face the music.

"Sidden, I'm sorry for taking so long to get back to you. He won't budge. I spoke with him again yesterday. He will not agree to see you or try to help in your, and I'm quoting here, amateurish meddling, unquote. Sorry."

Wade didn't sound a bit sorry. He was on such a high, I'm sure he could fly without a ticket or a boarding pass.

"Congratulations, Counselor, on the news of the coming heir! I'm so happy for you both."

"Thanks, Sidden."

"You tell Sheri she's married to a liar, a big wonderful liar, and I love you both. And Counselor? You tell your client Mister Bryan Sirmons that the next time I request an audience, he better grant it, or his ass is grass!"

"You're right, Sidden, I did advise him not to talk to you. He's my client, and he doesn't talk without me present. What's going on? You think he's somehow implicated in those long-ago murders? Are you doing this for Hank?"

"Unofficial nosiness at the present time, and you're right, I'm doing it for Hank. I won't ask you have I ever lied to you—because I have and you know it. But this is the straight dope, Wade. I have a gut feeling about this one. The more I poke, the stronger it gets."

"Are you telling me that we may meet in court over this?" He sounded amused.

"If I find that I can prove it, you'll be the first to know. Remind Sheri for me to think female. 'Bye." I hung up.

Well, so much for my chance to ask Sirmons any questions. He could sit tight and just ignore me.

I phoned Hank at work and the dispatcher said he had gone home. I dialed his number.

"Is the coast clear, can we talk, or do you have a guest?"

"You know I'm saving myself for you, honey."

"Sure you are," I said wryly, "I can smell your cologne over the phone. What's that other smell? I got it. You're cooking your famous spaghetti sauce. You used too much oregano."

"Don't apply for a PI license, Jo Beth. Keep your day job. It's chili."

"I still can't believe that you found that shirt in your evidence room after all these years. You did say it was still sealed?"

"Bagged, tagged, dated, and still sealed. There were only two packages logged into evidence. I've looked high and low for the package with the baby clothes, but it ain't there."

"Wouldn't it be something if there was still enough scent for a bloodhound to pick out a suspect after thirty years?"

"You laughed and laughed when I suggested that just this past Tuesday. Remember?"

"I know. It sounded ridiculous at first. I've been thinking. Remember that case in California we were discussing last month, where the bloodhound was given a gauze pad that had been frozen in the lab for nine months? They used a scent machine?"

"Vaguely. But that wouldn't work on this t-shirt," Hank asserted.

"Why not?"

"A lot of reasons. First, John Fray of the GBI hasn't got the imagination of a turnip. Can you see him giving authorization to have the shirt sent to the state crime lab, where I predict they don't even own such a machine?"

"They are not that expensive. I think they run around five hundred or so."

"Is this an attempt to get me to purchase one?"

"Might be worth it."

"My budget was overspent last October by three thousand and change, which means it comes out of this year's budget. No way. I couldn't buy the gauze pads this year, much less the machine."

"Well, I might spring for one, if my accountant tells me that it won't put me in the red."

"You're dreaming, Jo Beth. Even if you had such a machine and it produced a suspect, the evidence wouldn't be allowed in the courtroom."

"The California case was the first time it was used in a conviction of murder one, so that set a precedent. New York used the machine's evidence several years ago and that was upheld by the appeals court. Georgia may allow it, you never can tell unless we try."

"I'm not sure how it works. You want to explain it to me again?"

"The investigator uses a vacuum device, which is a 'scent machine.' It draws human scent from the fabric, concentrates it, then transfers it to a gauze pad. This allows the investigator to carry the scent to a bloodhound in the field without risking contamination of a key piece of evidence. If we had such a machine your shirt wouldn't have to leave the evidence room. That should keep the prosecutors happy."

"Yeah, well, this case would involve getting permission from Charlene, the 'Barracuda,' who's also your mortal enemy and mine."

"True, true," I replied grumpily. "A sticking point, but not impossible. We could bypass her and go over her head to DA Bobby Don Robbins, her boss. He's had his knife out for her since he found out last year she was plotting behind his back to run against him in the next election."

"Bobby Don hasn't had an original idea in five years," Hank grumbled.

"Well, I guess we'll have to table the idea for a while."

"You haven't even got a suspect for a bloodhound to search for, have you?"

"I've got high hopes for tonight. Keep your fingers crossed."

"You told me Sirmons wouldn't agree to talk to you. Who else do you suspect?"

"Is that your chili sauce I smell burning?" I sniffed loudly.

"Oh, shit," he yelled as he dropped the phone.

"Bye-bye," I said to a silent receiver.

I thought back to Tuesday's phone conversation with Alice Trulock, Calvin Newton's office manager. I had called her basically to thank her for talking with me. During the conversation I asked her casually if she had saved any pictures of Calvin Newton. After a few seconds of silence, she said she hadn't.

"I'm sorry, but when he died I was quite depressed for months afterwards. Since all my dreams were gone, I'm afraid that I threw them away. I regret it now, but it happened in some dark moments."

I assured her that it didn't matter, that I was simply curious. I thought I had another source, but now I wasn't so sure. It was 6:00, and Marion hadn't called, or maybe she had and got a busy signal. I had yakked with Hank for a long time. I called the number. Marion answered.

"Sirmons-Newton residence."

"Hi, it's Jo Beth. Have they left?"

"I'm sorry, ma'am, you have the wrong number."

"I'll call back," I said.

28

Unholy Joy

January 13, Friday, 6:20 P.M.

I didn't trust Marion Padgett to call back. She was a very reluctant ally.

I had called Marion on Tuesday and she had called me back when Patricia wasn't in the house and she could talk.

"How can I help you, Miz Jo Beth?"

"I need a favor, Marion. I hope I can count on you."

"You just name it," was her reply.

"Great. I know Patricia must have a photo album in the house that has pictures of her mother and father, and her as a baby. I'm not interested in any that were taken in New York. I just need to see some snaps of her natural parents."

"That'll be easy, Miz Jo Beth. I'll ask her. She likes you and I'm sure she'll let you look at them."

"Ah, no, Marion. You didn't catch my drift. I want to see them and I don't want Patricia or Sirmons to know that I saw them. Understand?"

If we were face to face, this is where I would give her a broad wink.

"I couldn't do that!" She sounded shocked.

I sighed. I would have expected that a progeny of her vast family's illegal enterprises would be a little more tolerant of some mild skull-duggery than the norm. Who would've guessed?

"Marion, I just want to view them. I won't touch them; they do not leave your hands. I don't want to steal them or photocopy them, just look. Okay?"

"Sorry, Miz Jo Beth, I can't help you."

She hung up on me. Wonder where all the trust and faith that she and her family had in my reputation had gone?

I tried her again on Wednesday. Finally, after a long discussion with a lot of begging from yours truly, she admitted they were having dinner in Waycross on Friday night, leaving about six and returning a little after ten. She said to call, that she would think about it.

I glanced at my watch. 6:20. Time to call her back.

When she answered, I asked when I could come over.

"It's not on the up-and-up, or you would ask Miz Patricia. Why don't you ask her?"

"I'll explain. I like Patricia and I don't want to cause her any pain or heartache. If I asked her and she agreed and later on I can prove that Bryan Sirmons is a double murderer, don't you think that Patricia might imagine she had aided and abetted? Think she had some hand into putting him away? She never need know that I saw the pictures, I promise. That way she will not think she's in any way responsible. Now do you understand?"

"You really think he killed those people?" It was a plea for reassurance.

"Dammed if I know, Marion. But I have to see those pictures! They could give me knowledge that might clear him, or they might not help at all. Look, if you don't want to help, I'll ask Patricia and let the chips fall where they may."

I held my breath.

"Well, if you're sure I won't be breaking any laws . . . "

"I'll be there in thirty minutes."

"Wait!" she said, sounding panicky. "You just can't drive up to the door. What if they came back for some reason?"

She had a point. I remembered standing on top of the van when I had been checking for lights last week. There was a huge oak with sturdy limbs about six feet from the fence.

"I'll park around the corner from the gate and come over the fence. Do you know how to turn off the house alarm?"

"Yes'em."

"I'll come to the back to the patio door that you can see from the pool. I have a question. Why are you working late tonight? You don't usually work this late, do you?"

"No, ma'am. Mr. Sirmons wants someone here when they are both out of the house."

"He told you dinner in Waycross, home about ten?"

"Yes'em. Please hurry, I'm as nervous as a squirrel!"

"Calm down, no cause for alarm. Just be at the back door with the picture album. It won't take five minutes and I'll be out of there. You do know which one I need?"

"Yes'em, she's had it out on her bed for the past two mornings. Soon as you sent over those newspaper stories, she's been looking at it often."

Good for her. The more she learned about it, the less it would shock her if indeed Sirmons was involved.

"He doesn't go into her room, does he? Do you think he's seen it or have you heard her say anything to him about the clippings?"

"I haven't heard her mention anything to him, but I'm not around all the time. I don't know if he goes into her room. I know she leaves her door open all day unless she's dressing to go somewhere."

I hadn't thought of that. I didn't know if Patricia had mentioned my visit or if he had discussed his refusal to see me with her. This was getting complicated. I had to see those pictures. I wondered if he was getting worried because of my insistence on interviewing him. Surely it would occur to him that I might want to talk to her. Oh well, the die was cast.

The niggling question in the back of my mind about what I had heard from Alice Trulock's memory, and Miz Granny Rose's reminiscing, didn't calculate. Something they said didn't make sense, but I couldn't put my finger on it. I thought if I could look at the pictures of Calvin Newton, Bryan Sirmons, and the two little girls, something would explain my uneasiness. I wouldn't know until I tried.

"Right," I said briskly, not wanting to keep her waiting, "I'll be along. Don't sweat it, Marion, okay?"

"Just hurry, Miz Jo Beth."

"You can count on it."

I called Jasmine.

"I have to run out and see someone for a few minutes. Tell Susan I'll be back soon if I'm a few minutes late. Keep the pizza warm."

"Sure," Jasmine said. "It's my time to buy. I'll leave her a note in case I'm not back before she gets here."

"See ya," I said, hanging up.

I went to the garage and checked the storage locker to make sure that Wayne had replaced the rope I had used for Ernestine's search. I needn't have worried, two brand-new packages of pristine rope were there. Wayne was dependable and always on schedule. I stay about three or four days behind in my training exercises, setting a lousy example. He had also put fresh batteries in the five-cell flashlight. I backed out the van and pulled onto the driveway. Approaching the highway, I slowed and scanned the traffic and both sides of the road with my binoculars. No parked cars, either way.

Bubba had been silent too long and I knew damn well he hadn't for a minute forgotten me or given up on the idea of beating me to a pulp. I still got the occasional late-night phone call. He let me hear the jukebox in the background noise and listen to his heavy breathing into the receiver, but he didn't speak. I listened long enough to know it was him and would gently cradle the receiver. It was his way of telling me he was coming to call soon.

I turned and headed for Baker's Mill Road. The night was cool and cloudy, but the low would be high thirties tomorrow morning and wasn't lower than 43 or so at the present time. The moon was gaining now, hardly more than a sliver, and could only be seen now and then when the clouds parted momentarily in their journey from east to west.

When I arrived at the gate I glanced inside. The house was flooded with light, upstairs and down. Marion must not like to be in a dark house alone. The outside nightlights turned on automatically when darkness descended, and turned off with sufficient light. On nights of heavy thunderstorms with lightning, every time the bright strikes lit up the night, every nightlight of mine would suddenly go out and it took approximately ten minutes of darkness before they would come back on. With frequent strikes they can stay off more than two hours at a time.

I drove farther down where the road curved until I saw the oak tree. I pulled off the verge close to the wall. I pocketed my keys, taking only the flashlight, rope, and binoculars.

I climbed up the back of the van on the small attached ladder. I stood on top of the van and scanned the area with the glasses. Sirmons wouldn't travel this part of the road coming back from Waycross, so there was no problem of him spotting my van if they came back early for some reason. I don't know why I was feeling so uptight. It was a piece of cake.

I put on my gloves. The top of the van was about a foot higher than the fence. I wouldn't need the tree. I loosened the twenty-five feet of rope, and tied the two separate ends to the chrome luggage rack that had welded chrome bars for support. I tossed the rope over the wall, which didn't have any obstructions on top like broken glass or barbed wire. I stepped across from the van to the fence, with the flashlight zipped up inside my denim jacket, leaving my binoculars behind.

The open space was a little more than two feet. I stood balanced with my feet placed heel to toe on the top of the fence, then squatted. I wrapped the rope around my left thigh and over my right shoulder, slid one leg down, and pushed off into space. I had planned to rappel down the fence gracefully, lowering myself easily in two or three slides of the rope and landing gently on my feet. The mountain climbers make it look so easy. I must have missed seeing some key handling of their ropes, because when I pushed off, I suddenly slid down the whole friggin' eight feet. I landed with a bone-jarring thud: for an instant on my feet, then my butt, and then flat on my back in the wet grass.

It happened so fast that it took several seconds before I felt my knee screaming in outrage. The flashlight had slipped out of my jacket. All I wanted to do was hold my knee and howl, but I felt around until I found the light. Thank God for small favors, it still worked. I slipped off my glove and trained it on my right knee. What I saw made me start whimpering. It looked as if I had held my knee against an electric sander while it shredded my jeans and sanded the skin from my kneecap.

Obviously, the knee had made contact with the cement wall on my fast trip downwards—two or three times—hell, it could have scraped against it all the way down, for I all knew.

My first aid kit was in my backpack on a bench in the garage. I made a vow never to leave home again without it. I gritted my teeth and forced myself to stand. I stared at my new enemy, the rope. I was gonna have fun getting back up the wall on that sucker.

I took off limping through the grass with the flashlight tucked back into my jacket. The outside lights cast enough light for me to dodge the ornamental flowerbeds and shrubbery. It was a long hike across the vast lawn. After a while, the throbbing eased off somewhat and it only stung and burned with every step.

When I neared the house, I could see all of the front drive. No vehicles in sight. I looked at my watch. It was five after seven. I could read the dial easily from the floods mounted in the ground, and shining upwards to highlight the holly bushes that grew next to the structure, and the floods shining down from the corners of the eaves. I could have read a newspaper if I desired.

I made it up the slight incline to the back patio.

"Miz Jo Beth?"

The whisper was barely audible and came from the shadowed inside corner of the cement patio. I wasn't expecting Marion to be outside. Not prepared to hear anything until I knocked, I jumped a foot high and my heart leapt into my throat.

"With the lights on everywhere else—why is the patio light off?"

I knew I sounded angry, but fear had made me quarrelsome. Persons have been known to suffer heart attacks when they hear their name coming from a leafy bush.

Marion emerged into the open holding a black knitted cardigan together with both arms crossed over her chest. She looked scared.

"What happened to your knee?" she whispered.

"I've found I'm not quite prepared to climb K-Two and I don't have the nerve of a cat burglar. Other than that, everything is peachy!"

I limped to a metal chair, turned the canvas-covered cushion over, and sat down.

"I'm sorry I startled you."

"And I'm sorry I barked at you. My knee's killing me, and you scared the shit out of me with that eerie whisper. Why are you whispering? It's just the two of us, isn't it?"

"Yes'em."

"Good. Is that the album?"

I held out my hand. She had pulled the object from beneath her sweater.

"I'll get something for your knee," she murmured, just slightly raising her voice.

"Never mind, Marion, I don't plan on staying long. Just go turn on the patio light, okay?"

I sat with the book in my lap unopened until the light came on. It was a cheap pink baby book with the words "Our Baby" embossed on the cover in white letters. I was sure before I saw the writing inside that Velma Mae Nichols had been the keeper of record. A small slip of a girl who felt the need to document the memories of a child not cared for by her only living parent.

I slipped off my gloves and turned the pages slowly. The small neat printing was in pencil so she could erase any error. There weren't many pictures. None were taken by a professional photographer. The subject of the snaps was either too close or too far away. In some the baby's head was cut off and in others almost half the child didn't appear.

I stopped at one picture of a man sitting on this patio reading a paper, his back to the camera and a small portable playpen to his right with a sleeping infant inside. Velma Mae had stood behind Calvin Newton and had taken this picture without his knowledge.

The last pictures were labeled "age 4 months." This was two months before the kidnapping. I turned the page and it was blank except for one picture in the upper left-hand corner. It was the picture that had been mentioned by Alice Trulock in telling me her recollections. It had two men, each holding a baby in his arms and smiling for the camera. Alice had taken it in front of the law office of Calvin Newton. I stared at the colored square of film, taken on a sunny November day two months and thirty years ago. Suddenly I knew what had nagged my unconscious about what I had been told by two different women.

I felt the surge of unholy joy spreading through out my system. I knew everything that had happened those many years ago and now knew I could prove it beyond a reasonable doubt.

"What's wrong, Miz Jo Beth? Are you feeling poorly?"

I looked at Marion without seeing her, then closed the book and handed it back.

"I'm feeling poorly, Marion, but not because of my knee. I just had a vision of a dead man."

She looked scared and glanced around her.

"Did he just die? I hate it when I dream of a dead person!"

"No, he's still walking around and breathing, he just doesn't know yet that he's dead," I said with intense satisfaction.

29

A Judge with a Grudge

January 14, Saturday, 10:00 A.M.

I had just made a fresh pot of coffee and poured the fragrant brew into my cup. I had drunk three cups earlier, as I had first greeted and then discussed the morning routine with my faithful crew. Lena, my part-time maid, was cleaning the trainees' rooms, stripping the linens, and readying them for next month's seminar.

Wayne and Donnie were doing the endless chores that came with a kennel that housed sixty-seven dogs at the present time, with twenty-three less than one year old. It was the smallest number of adult dogs on hand for the past two years. We had twelve bitches arriving on the eighteenth of February from a kennel in St. Thomas. The owner was retiring and had given me a deal. They were sound animals, healthy, from good stock, and all nine months old. Most of them had completed their obedience training. I had flown there right after Christmas, checked the dogs, and made the arrangements.

The six full-time trainees worked eight to four Monday through Friday and wouldn't be in today. Jasmine had left a few minutes ago to do our weekly grocery shopping. We usually ate our lunch and dinner together, so I had given her my list and we split the cost.

Jasmine had dressed and gone downtown Thursday to have lunch with Hank. She hadn't discussed with me what Hank had said, but her mood swings had lessened and she now seemed pensive instead of sad.

I sipped coffee, stared out the office window, and longed for a cigarette. I dreaded my next chore and had put it off long enough. Ten in the morning was a reasonable time to call the Chief Justice, Judge Constance Dalby, at her home in Savannah. I didn't look forward to her sharp and sarcastic tongue. She granted my infrequent requests for favors only because I could pull her off her lofty perch and kill her chance of ever being seated on the State Supreme Court. To be blunt—I blackmailed her into reluctant compliance with my wishes.

I dialed her Savannah home number.

"Judge Dalby speaking."

"Good morning, Your Honor, this is Jo Beth Sidden in Balsa City. How's the arthritis?"

"Ms. Sidden, I thought I made it clear that you were to never contact me again. Good day."

"Wait, Judge, don't hang up! I would have to make several boring phone calls on Monday to various agencies of the state and federal government. You know how I hate to deal with bureaucrats."

"No more, Ms. Sidden, I'm adamant. Do your damnedest. I will not cater to your whims any longer."

"Get real, Constance, you're biting off your nose to spite your face. Have I ever asked you to do an illegal deed? I have asked you for legal favors twice. Both times you have come out smelling of roses and heralded as an astute and caring judge. Your daddy didn't make it to the highest bench in Georgia until he was sixty-five. You've got four years yet to beat his record. Be a shame to waste this one, I bet it'll get you an appointment in less than a year."

"Tell me what you want!" she demanded in her imperious manner.

Ah, I had hooked her again. She always went through this charade of reluctance when she knew she would cooperate with me because she didn't dare call my bluff. And it was a bluff. I would never use my knowledge against her. It would also bring down two friends of mine whom I loved.

"Do you remember the trial of Samuel Debbs some thirty years ago, double murder and kidnapping?"

"I'm aware of the case, Ms. Sidden, and I also know that he was recently released on a conditional medical parole."

"Yes, ma'am, he was. I've looked into the case, and I'm convinced he's innocent—"

"Ms. Sidden! You're wasting my time! I couldn't possibly overrule his sentence or order the case reopened without clear, convincing evidence of another person's guilt—"

"If you hadn't interrupted me, Judge, I was just about to tell you that I have a suspect and he will confess to this crime. I just need an attentive audience where you can tell everyone they can leave anytime they want to, that they are not compelled by law to stay as it is an informal hearing, blah-blah-blah. You'll know what legal terms to use."

"What makes you think your suspect will confess after all these years?"

"I'll make you an offer you can't refuse, Judge. You'll love this wager. If my suspect doesn't promptly confess in great detail where he's nailed solid, you'll be off the hook with me. I'll never call you again. If he does confess, you'll be the hero who found justice for the little man. It'll be good timing, Judge. You know Chief Justice Burnside won't live till summer. The governor worshipped your old man and likes you. You'll be a shoo-in."

"I can't issue any subpoenas to force anyone to come to this so-called hearing," she warned.

"None needed. Just get me a courtroom and a date, ASAP. Schedule it for one hour. If any of the people I want there should happen to call you, I hope you will tell them that I have your blessing to ask them to join us."

"Tell me who you're inviting."

God, the woman was seeing if she could accomplish it without sticking her neck out an inch! She fully followed the tenets of CYOA, cover your own ass.

I read her my list and didn't hear an objection.

"I need a date and time," I said, feeling giddy with success.

"I'll have to consult my calendar."

I waited.

"Next Thursday at ten in Judge Thomas's courtroom. I want to warn you, Ms. Sidden, this better go as you promised. I can be a formidable enemy."

"It will, Judge. Trust me."

"In a pig's eye," she pronounced distinctly as she broke the connection.

I chuckled happily as I tackled my list. I'd call Wade first. He would be the most reluctant one. I dialed his office number.

"I wanna talk to Mr. Wade. This is Jansee Tatum."

I loaded my speech with Southern twang. I didn't want to be put on hold all morning.

"Will you hold, please?"

"Yes'em."

"Hello, Miz Jansee, how can I help you?"

"It's Jo Beth, Wade. I didn't relish growing old on hold. I know you're tired of telling me no, so this time you can be different and say yes."

"If you mean a talk with Bryan Sirmons, no way, Sidden."

"Listen carefully, Wade. Judge Constance Dalby and I request the presence of you and your client in Judge Thomas's courtroom next Thursday at nine-thirty. Everyone else will be there at ten. I want thirty minutes alone with Sirmons. Now, before you say you want a subpoena signed by Judge Dalby, I'll give you a message to tell to your client. Call him and tell him that I said, quote, dress rehearsal, unquote. Have you got that?"

"Let's see. Your message is 'dress rehearsal.' What's going on, Sidden?"

"Damn it, Wade, you know my track record. Until I fall on my face, why don't you show a little faith in me?"

"I'll tell you why, you cut too many corners for a respectable attorney of good standing to even be seen talking to you! I could be charged with misconduct if I listened to you! You are the most conniving, irresponsible, scheming . . . "

His voice lost steam and I listened to silence.

"Did Constance really agree to hear this amateur production of yours?"

"You can call and ask her," I replied calmly.

"You think your secret message will get him to appear?"

"Absolutely. Just keep advising him not to show. His appeal fees will keep you in vintage wines till the year two thousand and ten."

"Have I ever told you that you are weird, Sidden?"

"Once or twice."

"See you next Thursday."

"Yeah."

I called Hank, but he wasn't in. I left word for him to call me. I looked up Bobby Don Robbins's home phone number and dialed. A woman answered.

"Is Bobby Don there? This is Jo Beth Sidden."

"He went to the office for a couple of hours. Do you have that number?"

"Yes, I'll try him there, but I'd like to leave a message in case I miss him. Would you tell him to call me?"

I left my number. Before I could punch in his number, the phone rang. It was Susan.

"How's the knee?" she asked.

"Sore as the dickens and stiff, but I'll live. What's happening?"

"I was up at dawn, rode for miles and miles, have eaten an enormous breakfast, and just started a new book. I thought I'd see how folks who have to work on Saturdays are faring."

"Been calling people all morning, and about half of them are unavailable on Saturdays."

"I just wanted you to know that I wasn't fooled by that pitiful story you concocted about your messy knee last night. Jasmine pretended to buy it and I went along, being my natural polite self, but you didn't fall down in the gravel parking lot at the pistol range. Do I get to know what's going on?"

"Maybe next Friday night," I said lamely. She had taken me by surprise. "I thought we had an understanding about my extracurricular activities. You don't like getting dirty and don't care to be slobbered on by a large bloodhound. Most of the nutty things I do involve getting dirty, usually with the dogs and the possibility of being arrested or worse. I love you, Susan. Your parents would skin me alive if you got hurt helping me. By the way, have they forgiven you yet?"

"There you go changing the subject. No, they haven't forgiven me yet, but I'm working on it. Sidden, my life sucks. I sell books during the week and I come out to the ranch and ride horses on weekends. That's it. I feel like you and Jasmine are shutting me out. You have been my best friend all my life and you don't trust me enough to tell me how you hurt your knee. I'm depressed. I'm also thinking about selling the shop and moving somewhere new."

The reason she was depressed wasn't my doing. It was the loss of her credit cards and at least three new outfits she would have purchased this week if she had the means. I really didn't need her feeling sorry for herself this morning, I was busy, but I was also her best friend.

"Don't be silly. You're not selling or moving out, you just need something to plan. You have the winter blues. Why don't we take a trip next month? Just the two of us. Lie on a beach somewhere and soak up some rays by day and stalk some men at night."

"Where?" She had perked up already.

"I'll leave it up to you, but just remember, we take a tour package. No first-class travel or lavish accommodations. Promise!"

"I'll look into it," she replied evasively.

"Susan!"

"Okay, cheap, cheap, cheap. I promise."

"Great. Enjoy your book."

"Yeah, talk to you later."

"'Bye."

It would take my profit from my just-finished seminar, but everyone needs a break now and then, including me.

I heard Jasmine at the door. She came in carrying several small plastic bags from the Piggly Wiggly.

"I don't know why you can't find large paper bags in the grocery stores these days. You can't carry more than three items in these little slippery bags. Loading and unloading is a nightmare!"

"I'll bring in the next load."

"You will not, you have to stay off that knee! I only have one more load, then I start upstairs with mine."

"I feel guilty."

"Nonsense, you're wounded. Besides, you get to cook lunch!"

"Thanks," I murmured.

"You're welcome." She grinned.

The phone rang. It was Hank.

"What do you need, my beauty!" He was chipper today.

"I guess the chili sauce didn't burn last night."

"Oh yeah, I had to toss the pan. Easier than cleaning it. Your telephone nose is only exceeded by your talented bloodhounds."

"I have some good news," I said, ignoring his last remark. "Judge Dalby has graciously consented to an informal hearing next Thursday, where I will unveil the murderer in front of the proper witnesses."

"You're putting me on!"

"Nope, listen well, my lad."

I outlined my plan, telling him I needed him to bring the evidence shirt, unopened, and to wish me luck. I told him most of it, except who had done it and how I had figured it out. He screamed, cajoled, threatened, and coaxed for a very long time. It was quite satisfying.

30

Laying It on the Line

January 19, Thursday, 9:30 A.M.

I was sitting on a marble bench outside Judge Thomas's courtroom. People were passing in front of me, hurrying from one office to another clutching briefcases, files, and assorted items, but I was oblivious. All I sensed was the blur of movement as they passed. I was having opening night jitters.

Bobby Lee was sitting quietly by my right foot. His head would turn at each sound. A sudden cough, a door closing, and the ancient elevator's wheeze when it discharged passengers on the second floor. He was the reason that people were openly staring as they passed, some glancing back over their shoulders to affirm that a large dog was indeed what they had seen.

I was wearing a black knit suit with a white blouse, black hose, and pumps with sensible heels. Bobby Lee was sporting a new harness. While I was giving him the full beauty treatment in the grooming room yesterday I saw on the calendar that today was the birthday of Robert E. Lee, his namesake. I took it for a good omen.

I heard my name and realized I had been focused on two pairs of trousered legs standing in front of me for several seconds. I glanced up and stood.

Wade looked his usual well-groomed self, not a hair out of place. He had just turned thirty-five. He dressed conservatively for his age. Dark suit and a wine-colored tie. I knew the suspenders under his coat would be bright red. Sheri made sure he wore only that color. She declared it made him look "backwoodsy."

"Jo Beth, I'd like you to meet Bryan Sirmons. Bryan, this is Jo Beth Sidden, owner of Bloodhounds, Incorporated."

I gave him a barely civil nod to acknowledge his presence. Age had added maturity to his face and salt-and-pepper hair that wasn't in the thirty-year-old photograph I had recently viewed. His youth had fled and been replaced with conceit and obvious good living. He was carrying a pouch around his middle that told the story of fine dining and too little exercise.

He looked calm and collected, as if he didn't have a care in the world. He was either a very good actor or I had jumped to an erroneous conclusion. I felt a fine line of sweat at my hairline even though the hall was cool and drafty. He gave me a pleasant smile.

I turned to Wade.

"I have permission to use the prisoner holding cell for this conference. Would you watch Bobby Lee for me?"

"Certainly." Wade took the leash.

"Follow me," I said to Sirmons, walking with a confident step. Our heels making contact with the wooden floor in the courtroom was the only sound. I led him back to the holding cell, held the door open, and followed him inside. I felt as if I was entering the lion's den with Daniel.

Iron bars divided the small room, with a cell door in the center. Three metal chairs were bolted to the floor. He and I sat down, leaving a vacant chair between us. I crossed my legs.

"This won't take long. I just want to say that today is the day that justice will be served."

"Really?" he replied in a mild manner. "It was my understanding it was served right outside this door almost thirty years ago."

"No, an innocent man was accused, convicted, and sentenced to life. Only the fact that he is dying got him a few weeks or possibly a few months of freedom. It was a travesty of justice you manipulated by burying the dirty t-shirt directly behind Samuel Debbs's temporary shelter—the child's body further back in the brush—and making the anonymous phone call that placed him under suspicion."

"That is a ridiculous accusation," he said in a mild tone. "I didn't know the man."

"You didn't have to know him. You spent the odd hour or so, on a few occasions, looking for someone to take the fall. Why you chose Debbs is immaterial, but you planted the body and t-shirt and made the call. That I know."

"What makes you so sure, Ms. Sidden? You sound like an expert airing opinions formed after years of research. I understand you only heard about Debbs and his trial just two weeks ago."

"Two weeks and two days," I said. "If you want the exact time it took me to find the solution and to discover that you were the murderer, it was only ten days. I solved the crime last Friday evening."

"And you think I'm the murderer?"

"I know you are and I can prove it."

"Sorry, I'm innocent. All the bravado in the world will not make me guilty or have me say I am. I think you're wasting our time. Shall we join the others that you have called in this morning? I'm curious to hear what they have to say."

"First let me tell you the rules. When I finish telling you my story, we're going back into the courtroom. I will then hold a demonstration using the mantrailing bloodhound that you saw earlier in the hall. The sheriff has sealed evidence from the first trial—the dirty t-shirt. I will see if the bloodhound can pick up your scent and identify you as the person who wore it.

"I want you to know that if the bloodhound identifies you, the evidence can be used in your trial—if there is a trial. If the bloodhound fails to pick up your scent it's not a big deal. You see, I do not need his testimony to convict you. I have a solid case without it.

"To tell the truth, the sheriff and I are curious. No one has ever tried a bloodhound on an article that has been sealed in a paper bag for thirty years and made a positive find."

"All right, we sit through an experiment that doesn't prove my guilt or innocence, and then we all go home. Is that it?"

"The rest of us get to leave, not you. The judge will instruct the sheriff to place you under arrest."

"What would make her do that?"

"Because after the demonstration, I will tell the judge that you wish to make a statement. Then it's up to you. You can confess and be remanded into custody immediately or you can remain silent, but you won't walk out of the courtroom a free man."

"Maybe you ought to enlighten me. Why I would be so stupid and confess at this late date even if I were guilty?"

"I'm getting to that, just give me a minute. When you confess, you can state if you so desire that the death of Velma Mae Nichols and the child was an accident. It might get you a lighter sentence, but I doubt it. Not when you let an innocent man rot in prison for all those years for your crimes. What it might accomplish, Patricia Ann Newton will not think quite so badly of you. She will be horrified and you will lose her love and respect forever, but she might dredge up a little pity if she thought they were accidental killings during a kidnapping attempt. I know that you deliberately killed both of them. It was premeditated and planned for months."

"You will never be able to prove it!" he snapped.

The first chink in his armor had appeared. His composure had slipped. I think it was at that moment that he first began to suspect that I might know what I was talking about. I could have ended the interview with a terse announcement and he would have known that he was doomed. I didn't. I was just thirsty enough for retribution for two lost souls and a man's wasted life to want to see him wriggle on the hook just a few more minutes.

"I can," I replied. "I'll explain. Velma Mae's death was necessary to your plan. You couldn't have disguised yourself so she wouldn't recognize you. She had seen you many times around the estate and the week before the killings she had been up close to you at least twice a day, if not more. When you handed her Loretta Lynn in the morning and picked her up every afternoon. You were close enough for her to smell, to pick up mannerisms, to know your clothes, your walk, and other things that would give you away. She would have known it was you even with a stocking or a croker sack over your head.

"You didn't have an accomplice. I once thought you might have contacted your wife who had run away, but I found she couldn't be located for the funeral. After I began to suspect you, I couldn't believe that you could be so stupid as to kidnap two babies and not have a way planned to take care of them already in place.

"You knew that you would be in the public eye for weeks afterwards. You couldn't possibly have time to slip away and take care of them. But it wasn't a kidnapping for ransom. You knew that you would only have both of them for just a few minutes. One went to the church and one was killed."

"You can't possibly have proof that I killed the maid, Velma Mae Nichols, or my own child, Loretta Lynn. What kind of a father would kill his own child? I loved her! I know you're running a bluff. There is no way you can prove I killed her!"

He still had most of his composure. I was sweating more than he was.

"I don't have to prove that you're guilty of killing her. All I have to prove is that you're *not guilty*. Loretta Lynn Sirmons is alive. You killed Patricia Ann Newton."

31

The Denouement

January 19, Thursday, 9:50 A.M.

The confident businessman who had entered this room some twenty minutes ago had disappeared. The ashen-faced man sitting next to me looked about to faint. He shuddered and placed his elbows on his knees and dropped his head in his hands. I stood and spoke to the back of his neck.

"You didn't know that you were seen turning onto the street leading to All Souls church, did you? Once I heard that you didn't have an ironclad alibi, everything three witnesses told me about you fell into place.

"You were desperate for money. You ingratiated yourself into Calvin Newton's life. You taught him to trust you and conned him into making you Patricia's guardian. You knew he didn't have long to live. Calvin Newton didn't care a fig for Patricia. You knew the authorities wouldn't ask a man with a severe heart condition to identify a dead baby and that they would take your word. After all, she could have been your daughter.

"You knew he wouldn't recognize his daughter, but you had to try a dry run. That was the day that you took both babies to Newton's office and handed him Loretta to hold while posing for pictures. The only one that you were worried about was Alice Trulock. You weren't sure if she could tell them apart, but she didn't spot the switch. That was your dress rehearsal.

"A wonderful woman by the name of Granny Rose Richardson gave me the one fact that finally revealed your scheme. Her mind is still sharp. She remembered that Velma Mae always dressed Patricia in yellow. Alice Trulock remembered they looked enough a like to be twins. Yet in the picture, the baby in your arms had on yellow, and the child in Newton's arms was wearing a green outfit.

"Not court proof, but it convinced me. I hope it isn't necessary to get court proof, but it is available. DNA hadn't been on hand for the first trial, but it will be easy to prove that the woman who calls you uncle is your daughter and the baby in your child's grave is Patricia.

"You were tired of being poor and wanted for your daughter everything that Patricia had. As her guardian, you knew that you could remain close and have the life that you wished for yourself.

"Loretta, your daughter, is an innocent and doesn't deserve to be punished. If you fight this and demand a trial, it will happen. The state will move in and seize the estate and all assets. You've had thirty years of living high off the hog, which is much more than you deserved.

"Go in there and confess. Call both deaths tragic accidents; say you only wanted to collect the ransom. When Velma Mae tried to stop you, you pushed her and she 'accidentally hit her head.' When your child 'accidentally smothered' in her blanket on the trip to the church, you left Patricia in the church and buried your own child behind Debbs's abode. Sweeten it any way you wish. Just be sure to you remove all doubt of Debbs's innocence.

"I will never breathe a word to Loretta. Why should she suffer any more than she has to? Go in there and confess convincingly and maybe she never has to find out that you're her father."

I glanced at my watch. "Do the right thing."

I left him with his head still lowered in his hands.

I walked out and collected Bobby Lee from Wade.

"Is he still in there or did he go home?" Wade whispered.

"He'll be along in a minute."

I crossed to the prosecutor's table where Bobby Don and Hank were seated. I settled Bobby Lee and sat without speaking to anyone. I glanced behind me. It was obvious that no one who was invited here today had issued any invitations of their own or wanted more people in the audience. There were only five men seated behind us.

One was Hanson Aldridge, ex-car lot owner and now a full-time drunk. Another was Samuel Debbs, convicted murderer. Hank had invited the other three to make a respectable lineup of six. The men were all in their late fifties and sixties. Two I knew by name, and the other one looked familiar but I couldn't place him.

"I hope to hell you know what you're doing, little lady, I don't want to look like an asshole today."

The whisper from Bobby Don Robbins, our esteemed DA, sounded as loud as a buzz saw in the silent room.

"Not a bit more than you usually do," I muttered under my breath. I heard Hank suppress a snort.

"What?" Bobby Don asked, not hearing my answer.

"I said, I hope to hell I do too!"

He grunted with dissatisfaction, squirming in the hard-bottomed chair. I had heard the rumor that he suffered from piles. If he didn't, he was sure giving a convincing performance of someone who had trouble in his nether region.

Bryan Sirmons closed the holding cell door softly and walked with purpose to sit beside Wade. Wade's head lowered the nine-inch difference in their height and listened attentively to what Sirmons was telling him. I just had time to see Wade's head twisting from shoulder to shoulder like a metronome when Judge Constance Dalby entered the room without being announced.

We all stood as if we had been simultaneously goosed.

"Be seated." She seemed annoyed.

She sat down briskly, pulled the mike into position, and folded her hands on her desktop. It had been two years since I had last seen her and she still looked indestructible. She was short and sat ramrod-straight, with her back not touching her chair. Her hair was a thin cover of tightly rolled curls in various shades of gray. Her wrinkled face was gaunt, her thin lips were drawn together, and she didn't look happy to be here.

"This informal discussion is taking place in this courtroom at the request of a concerned citizen, Ms. Jo Beth Sidden. I want to inform all of you that this meeting is not going to be a matter of public record. As you can see, no bailiff or court reporter is present.

"Any of you can leave at any time. It is not at the request of the court that you are here. If you wish to speak, Ms. Sidden, do so."

I stood and moved Bobby Lee around the table until I stood before her.

"This bloodhound is fully qualified to present evidence in a court of law. This short experiment will follow the prescribed outlines of official testimony, but I understand that the findings, either positive or negative, aren't binding on anyone and can't be used against them in any court.

"Sheriff Cribbs has a sealed package of a sweat-stained t-shirt that has been held in the Sheriff's Department evidence room for almost thirty years. The shirt was buried for several days prior to discovery.

"Sheriff Cribbs, would you position the six men who have volunteered to stand in a lineup in front of the jury box?"

Hank stood and the men moved forward and formed a ragged line. Bryan Sirmons placed himself as the third man in the row. He certainly didn't look like a man who knew his goose was cooked. I started to sweat again.

Hank opened the package, being careful not to touch the garment, while I pulled on thin surgical gloves. I lifted the shirt from the paper. I leaned over and placed it under Bobby Lee's nose.

"Find your man! Where's your man? Where is he? Find your man!" I chanted in an animated voice.

He sniffed the shirt, lowered his head, and started with Bobby Don. He smelled his shoes and trouser legs, then moved to Hank. He took a few breaths and circled back to me. I lowered the shirt and repeated my litany.

He paused and sniffed the spot where Bryan had been seated. I held my breath. He let out a small whine and gave a couple of shakes of his tail. Bobby Lee glanced back at me and seemed to be saying, I can't be sure. He left the area reluctantly and moved on to Wade.

I let out my breath slowly. It was the first second that I realized that this crazy, chancy mantrail experiment was going to be successful. Bobby Lee didn't waste much time on Wade's shoes or pants. He moved over to the lineup and quickly passed the first two men and fell on Bryan Sirmons, whining and baying and nudging him with his nose.

He literally jumped for joy and for a second his paws were on Sirmons's shoulders as if he was hugging him. Sirmons swayed from the onslaught but stood his ground. It always effects the perp the dogs pick out; they act like they're frozen in disbelief.

I moved forward and pulled Bobby Lee back out of Sirmons's range. I knelt and hugged him, burying my face in his thick fur. I finally got him to calm down and mute his celebration. He was softly whining as I led him back to stand in front of the bench.

Judge Dalby's penetrating eyes were speculative as she waited for my next move.

"Your Honor, I believe Mr. Bryan Sirmons wishes to address the court."

"Do you think you can quiet your animal, Ms. Sidden? His emanations are annoying."

"Yes, Your Honor." I shortened Bobby Lee's lead and walked him over to my chair with my face burning. The bitch. She had to rain on my parade. She had seen my pride in Bobby Lee's success and the gleam of satisfaction on my face.

I glanced over to Wade and Sirmons. They were having a whispered debate. Sirmons suddenly lurched out of his chair and approached the bench with Wade hot on his heels.

"Your Honor—" Sirmons began, but Wade's voice rose to override his.

"I object, Your Honor! My client is going against his counsel's advice. May we have a fifteen-minute recess so I can confer with him?"

"Your objection is not being noted," she said with wry overtones, spreading her hands in a gesture of indifference.

"You can see we are not on the record here. As far as I'm concerned, we can *all* go home."

She was enjoying herself. However, her voice had softened as she was speaking. She and Wade had become friends these past few years. After Wade's mother died, Constance Dalby and Wade's father had been an item and Wade had resented her. When Wade's father died they had buried the hatchet. Now they were tight. I had to fight the urge to scream. So close.

"I want to confess to a double murder and kidnapping!"

Sirmons voice was both loud and demanding.

"My advice is to listen to your attorney, as he is acting in your best interest." She gave him a parsimonious smile. "If you still insist on unburdening your soul, I suggest you tell it to the proper authority, who would be Sheriff Cribbs. He is seated behind you."

She stood and left the room.

Sirmons turned, shrugging off Wade's attempt to restrain him, and marched over to Hank, who stood as he approached.

"I want to confess!"

"All right. Follow me. We'll talk in my office."

"He's not saying a word unless I'm present!" Wade said firmly. He glanced at me and rolled his eyes upward.

I slumped with relief. It didn't have the proper ending that I had envisioned. Sirmons being led off in handcuffs after his dramatic confession, the onlookers cheering, me blushing at all the accolades heaped at my feet. It finished not with a bang, but a whimper. I would take what I could get.

"Gal, I better tag along with those fellers if I want to get my name in the papers. See ya." Bobby Don gave me a solid whack between my shoulder blades as he departed.

As I started out of the courtroom, I saw Samuel Debbs waiting at the door.

He stuck out his hand. "Thanks."

"You're welcome, Mr. Debbs." I shook his outstretched hand.

I received a shy smile for restoring his respectability and by addressing him as Mister. It was enough.

32

Armageddon

January 25, Wednesday, 5:00 P.M.

I was tooling along in the van doing fifty, listening to WAAC country ballads and thinking of chicken and dumplings. Bobby Lee was leaning against the door with his head out the window enjoying the cold air whipping his elongated ears in a straight line behind him. The interior of the cab was cold with the windows down. The temperature was dropping quickly without the sun's warmth. I was in my rescue suit and warm enough, so I was letting him enjoy pointing his nose into the wind.

It was that time between daylight and total darkness when the headlights hindered more than helped, but I was on a deserted narrow blacktop road and being prudent. Locals drove like maniacs away from radar guns and seldom-seen deputies.

We were both happy as clams. We had just spent two hours at Gilsford County Nursing Home. Bobby Lee had been petted, hugged, and fondled to his heart's content, while I basked in the warm glow of doing a good deed and seeing the happiness that we had brought to the aged residents. We were ten miles from home.

Bright lights rapidly approached, coming toward us at great speed. When the vehicle swished past, I caught a glimpse of a truck's profile in fire engine red, reflected from the glow of my low head beams. My heart dropped into my gut and I sucked in air.

I stomped the gas pedal, trying to shove it into the floorboards. I reached for Bobby Lee's harness, pulling him straight in his seat, and latched the shoulder brace. He was already connected to the center bolt, but I wanted him tightly confined for high speed. I kept my vision divided between the rearview mirror showing the receding truck's taillights and the road ahead.

The truck's rear lights suddenly flared a brighter red. The driver had applied his brakes. I swallowed and realized Bobby Lee and I were in a whole heap of trouble. No way could I outrun a truck with my van. It took forever to reach eighty. Above that speed the van was unstable. The road ahead and behind showed no traffic. The driver was turning around and coming back. Mile after mile of planted pines. No one lived out here. I was on my own. I had dreaded this moment for the past eight years. So be it. I would be forced to shoot the son of a bitch. I reached under my seat and felt for the .32. The holster was empty.

My mind snapped back to early afternoon. I had showered, dressed in jeans and pullover, socks and joggers. The gun was lying on the bed. I reached for it—the phone rang. My back was to the bed while I talked. I hung up and left the room. The phone call had distracted—What was I doing? I had a murderous ex-husband turning around to come after me, and I was checking into my failure to bring the gun. I had to concentrate on survival.

I couldn't outrun him; I didn't have maneuverability, so I had to outthink him. Not if but when he caught me, he would kill Bobby Lee first. My heart was pounding, sending adrenaline surging through my arteries. I had to drop Bobby Lee and trust he would stay in place until I could return for him, but where?

The indicator was hovering on seventy-five. Bubba would be tailgating me in the next two or three minutes. I glanced at the small green mile marker as I blew past. I was a mile from the Tarver crossing. Tarver was dirt and clay and would be a mess. It had rained for the past three days. A steady, unrelenting downpour.

In mud I had low-range 1 and 2, and four-wheel drive. He had the same gears but my van was heavier and the tires were positive-traction, whatever that meant. Another plus would be the curves. Tarver twisted like a snake. If I could stay far enough ahead the van would be out of his sight long enough for me to drop Bobby Lee.

Oh, God, what if he tried to follow me! Bobby Lee had no defense against Bubba. He wouldn't know to run, or to dodge an oncoming truck! I had to drop him and get his location to Jasmine, in case—the cellular phone! She wouldn't have the base CB on because I wasn't in the field, but if I was within range of the signal, just maybe I could reach her. I fumbled with my right hand and retrieved it from beneath the seat.

With the case wedged between my legs, I worked the zipper open. I grabbed the cord, hooking it under my left hand on the wheel, and ran my right fingers down the length, straightening it out and feeling for the plug-in. I was about seven miles west of Balsa City and the tower was halfway between Balsa City and Waycross, which was thirty miles. Say forty total, and the maximum range was fifty. Should work if it was my lucky day. With Bubba breathing down my neck, I kinda doubted it.

The turn onto Tarver was coming up fast. I took my foot off the gas to slow my speed. On a straight road you can see lights from a good distance, but he wouldn't see my turn if I didn't hit my brakes, which would give me away. It seemed I was merely crawling along but I was doing sixty, and the turn was getting closer. I didn't want to try any fancy downshifting because I wouldn't know what I was doing. I saw the rearview mirror was still dark, so I took a chance on the brakes. Even using them I almost lost control taking the turn at forty onto a clay-slick quagmire. I steered my heart out trying to gauge the slide. A rain-filled ditch loomed alarmingly close to my right wheels. The mud had slowed my speed to twenty-five. I eased off the gas and made it back to the center ruts.

Large splats of raindrops began to hit the windshield, mixing with the mud I had kicked up with my gut-wrenching turn. I would drop Bobby Lee around the next curve. Steering is chancy in mud with both hands. Using just my left was suicide. I slowed even more. I could hear the comforting sound of the motor whining in four-wheel drive.

I reached over and began releasing Bobby Lee's restraints. First his seat belt, then the safety chain, then his leash. I didn't want it trailing behind him with him loose.

I made the turn and started easing over to the right. The trees grew close to the ditch and were about five years old. I was thankful because there were thick pine limbs closer to the ground for concealment. Now if I could just get Bobby Lee to run into cover. I stopped and reached over and threw open the door.

"Unload! Unload!" I yelled excitedly. "Out! Out! Unload!"

Bobby Lee stood, turning awkwardly in the seat, and dropped his head to sniff out the void he was supposed to jump into. There wasn't time for his newly found slow and deliberate descent. I had my lap belt and shoulder restraints in place. I flipped open the latch in my lap, swiveled to the right, placed my foot on his tailbone, and gave a hard shove. He fell out of my sight as I scrambled for the five-cell flashlight under the passenger seat. I took a quick peek at the rearview mirror. No headlights yet.

I trained the flashlight on Bobby Lee as he regained his feet. He was facing the woods.

"Go! Go! Go!" I screeched. "Go! Go! Go!"

I attached my lap belt, then fumbled with the cord and plugged in the phone without looking.

I still had the light on Bobby Lee. He had charged forward, hit the water in the ditch, and was struggling to pull himself out of the water. He stopped and turned around, waiting for further commands. Damn! He was now facing me, and I couldn't say go, or he would come across the ditch towards me.

"Retreat! Retreat! Retreat!"

I saw him back up a couple of backward steps, then stop.

Bright lights appeared for a second in the side mirror, then disappeared. Bubba had turned the curve. I had just run out of time.

I yelled "Retreat!" over and over again out the open door as I pulled forward. I pressed down hard on the gas pedal, twisting the wheel sharply to the left, trying to gain momentum. I careened sideways, slipping and sliding in the mud. I suddenly twisted the wheel back to the right and heard the door slam shut. I fought the wheel and slid all over the road.

Getting control of the wheel and trying to stay in the middle of the slippery surface was taking all the skill I could muster. Bubba's lights in my mirrors were a constant reminder of who was behind me and closing fast.

If I could stay ahead of him for most of a mile, I was going to bail out of the van. But before I did, I had to reach Jasmine. I had to slow for the second curve. I listened to the phone and heard the wonderful sound of a dial tone.

I ran my fingers lightly over the tiny buttons and started picking out my number. I pushed each choice very carefully. Now was not the time to misdial . . . It was ringing! I had a death grip on the steering wheel with my left hand. Hitting a soft spot, the mud would jerk the wheel and I would find myself in a skid without traction heading for a ditch. If I overcorrected, I was heading in the opposite direction.

I was subconsciously counting the rings. After five, the answering machine would activate.

Four. Five. "I am unable to answer the—Hello."

"I'm on Tarver Road going east, after turning off Highway Ninety-four. I dropped Bobby Lee about a hundred yards after making the first turn. He's on the right side of the road without a lead. Bubba is behind me. Notify Hank and bring Gulliver. Find Bobby Lee *first*, Jasmine, and don't let Wayne or Donnie Ray leave the kennel. If I can make it past Tom's Creek Bridge, I'll ditch the van and hide in the woods on the right side. Be sure and bring your gun, I don't have mine."

"Oh, God, anything else?"

"Prayer would be nice." I dropped the phone.

Bubba was directly behind me. I was guessing that he would try to pass so he could draw even, bump me, and send me into a ditch. The road was wide enough. I would have to anticipate his moves and stay in front of him. If he couldn't get around me, he would ram me from behind, which would produce the same result.

There was no question about it, I was going in a ditch. If I could reach the bridge, I would have a better chance of eluding him in the swamp. The creek bank on the town side of Tom's Creek was lower. I could hide from him knowing I would have the water, where I could retreat if he was close to nabbing me. On this side there was a long slope down to the creek and the bank had an eight-foot drop to the water.

The rain was coming down harder. The wipers were on the highest speed and I still was straining to see the road. I knew that Bubba was the better "mudder." He'd had enough practice from his early teens till he turned twenty-one and started a new life of sitting in a prison cell.

"Mudding" was the main sport when the guys weren't hunting. They would take new trucks, add on all the accessories available, and take their valuable and usually only asset out where rain had made a muddy field on the soft shoulders of deserted roads. Then they would try to see how deep they could bury them in mud. Mature women could see the utter stupidity of this action, but I have to admit that when I was a teen, I was out there sitting on a hood or standing on a flatbed truck cheering on the winners.

The swamp had been my milieu for the past few years. I didn't know if that gave me an edge. It had been his playground from the time he was eight until he was grown. I had been told that he pumped iron in prison and that his body bulged with muscles. I hadn't had a good look at him in the past eleven years.

I wondered if he had changed his irresponsible habit of never being prepared. A cold night would catch him in short sleeves. If he had a flat, he would put on the spare and throw the damaged tire in the back and never think of it again until he had another flat. He never carried water for the radiator, a tow rope, or the basic necessities like a flashlight or accident flares.

I was dressed for a cold wet night in the woods. I had on my rescue suit. I had a flashlight with fresh batteries. I wondered if he had on warm clothing and could put his hands on a flashlight that worked. It just might make the difference of who survived the night.

He rammed the van. The impact sent me sliding sideways towards the ditch. I managed to fight the skid and remain upright, but I knew that the next one, or the one after, would do the job.

I speeded up and saw the fluorescent painted metal reflectors glowing for Tom's Creek Bridge. I had made it. Another few seconds and I would be on the narrow wooden bridge. Just at that moment I felt the truck strike the van a glancing blow. I saw the right corner of the bridge rushing towards me and knew that I had lost the race.

I felt the wheels leave the suction of the mud as the van tilted. I only had time to lift my hands to protect my face from the sudden inflation of the airbag before I hit the bridge rail. The impact didn't halt my forward progress. I was sailing free in unoccupied space and it seemed to take forever before I reached the water.

33

Misery Loves Company

January 26, Thursday, 1:30 A.M.

I was having a miserable dream. I was cold, wet, and confused. My head was pounding and something was gnawing on my left leg. Its sharp teeth were biting clear to the bone in a relentless crunch that kept pace with my throbbing temples. I was so tired. I didn't feel like getting up just to take aspirin. I decided to turn on my right side. Maybe that would ease my pain.

Sharp teeth? Whoa. I forced myself to concentrate on waking up. I lay there with my eyes closed debating the merits of resting awhile longer, versus opening my eyes to confront the owner of the teeth. My hands were so cold. I had them folded across my chest and tucked under my armpits.

Discomfort forced me to make a decision. I felt cold rain pelting my face. Had I left a window open or had the roof sprung a leak? I was out in the rain and I wasn't in bed. Memory was returning. I had a confused vision of falling. The van had turned over. I saw a bridge fly past. I shook my head to clear it and regretted it mightily.

I groaned aloud. I should sit up. No, I was already sitting up and slumped back on something. I moved a cold hand to my forehead and felt water running down my arm inside my rescue suit. I lowered my right arm into water up to my chest. I opened my eyes and forced myself to look around. I couldn't see much, it was dark and the rain kept coming down. I brought my other arm up and felt more water draining down into my suit.

Okay. Let's take stock here. There was a bridge and I fell and now I'm in water up to my armpits. It had soaked into my suit from the elastic cuffs on my wrist and ankles. Every new discovery jarred my senses. I could smell the sweet rotten stench of mud. I held both hands out and let the rain clean the mud. I rubbed them together to warm them.

I ran my hands over my wet curls and didn't feel any gaping wounds, just a lump over my right ear. I had fallen and hit my head. The area was sore and tender, but I couldn't feel an opening that might be leaking blood. I pressed my fingers over the bump and held them close to my eyes. I could only see a faint blur lighter than the surrounding darkness.

I continued my examination. I was leaving my left leg for last, I knew damn well that it was hurt. My stomach felt bruised and my left shoulder ached. Finally I gritted my teeth and tentatively moved my left leg. The pain overwhelmed me. I closed my eyes and took deep calming breaths. When the worst was past, I welcomed the familiar deep throb. Basically I was whole except for a bump on the head and a bum leg. I hated to admit it was broken.

With my eyes closed, I leaned my head back and let the rain pelt my face. Licking my lips, I drank until I wasn't thirsty. I decided it wouldn't be a good idea to fall asleep. I didn't know where I was and how I came to wake up in the muddy water. Probing my mind, I encountered a bewildering void, a dark hole type of thing. A gray wispy mist veiled my reasoning mind where you go when you want to recall a memory. The more I tried, the more my head ached, so I said to hell with it.

I sat there in the water and existed. I remembered yesterday. The wonderful feeling of being right and piecing together Sirmons's scheme to get rich and the tragedy he had caused. The shy smile on Debbs's face as I called him mister and shook hands with him. When I returned home I'd received some of the laurels that I had fantasized about. We sat down and had an appreciative audience of one. Jasmine had applauded in all the right places. Of course, the ending had been a little anticlimactic because I couldn't mention my brilliant reasoning about Patricia's death and that Loretta was still alive.

Jasmine had given me a puzzled look.

"Maybe I missed something. It seems strange that he confessed after all these years. Really all you had was an eyewitness who saw him near the church but hadn't told anyone. Since that witness is now a drunk, he certainly wouldn't be credible at this late date. And Bobby Lee's performance was fantastic but you know the law, Jo Beth. A bloodhound's evidence to convict must have other collaborating proof. You had none."

"Yes, well, I made him see that a jury would find him guilty." It sounded lame even to me.

"He is an intelligent man and has done very well in real estate," she insisted. "If I can see you didn't have positive proof, Sirmons should have realized it. Why didn't he take the chance and fight it? The sentence would be about the same even if he was convicted."

We were eating lunch at Jasmine's kitchen table. Healthy Choice soup and diet crackers. I was gonna indulge in a candy bar when I went downstairs. Eating healthy wasn't very satisfying at this moment. My urge to brag was so strong it was all I could do to keep quiet. I knew that if I told Jasmine the secret it would be safe with her, but if I caved in now, then who would be next? Susan? No, a secret shared is a secret no longer. I spooned some soup into my mouth and shrugged. Jasmine must have seen something in my expression.

"You're not telling me everything." She made it a statement of fact, not a question.

I gave her another shrug.

"You can't tell it ever?"

"Never."

"Just tell me this, is this one of those big warm-feeling secrets that makes you feel good all over? Answer this and I'll never mention it again."

"Yes!"

"Damn!" She looked wistful.

I placed my hands together under the water. They would feel warmer out of the wind. That memory of yesterday was clear as a bell. No gray mists. I'd just have to rest awhile and maybe I could remember what happened to me.

The word *amnesia* floated into focus and reared its ugly head. No, that was not true. I knew who I was and could remember with clarity all the way back into childhood. I tried to sit straighter to ease my leg and had quite a few bad moments. My groans mixed with the noise of wind and rain, then finally faded away. I gave myself a strong lecture on survival. It only helped to pass the time.

Time. I begin to wonder why I wasn't worried about the time slipping by. I was not a fanatic about time, but my days were very full. Some people watch the clock like a hawk. Having my own business gave me some slack except for court appearances and planned appointments. I didn't know if I had been here an hour or a week. I wasn't sure if the yesterday I was remembering had really been yesterday.

I drifted through the mist for awhile, hurting but not alarmed. I decided to go back to yesterday and see how far I could remember before I lifted my arm out of the water, pulled back the elastic cuff, and checked my watch. It not only would give me the time; it had small squares that would let me know the month and day.

After lunch yesterday, I had gone to the weighing room to catch up on my charts. My puppy training class of six clowning bundles of wrinkles was over a week behind schedule. Running late and missing several days only made more work for me. By now they would have forgotten what I taught them last week. Hank called several minutes later.

"Hey there, Miracle Worker, what did you give Sirmons, truth serum?"

"He confessed, huh?"

"Wade couldn't shut him up. If it had been possible he would have clubbed him over the head and dragged him from the interrogation room. Sirmons was a motor mouth for over three hours. First for Bobby Don and me, then for the videographer. Why it took so damn long was Bobby Don's doing. He thinks this trial is going to clean his tarnished image and help him beat the Barracuda in next election. I didn't have the heart to tell him that Sirmons told me he was going to waive a jury trial, but he still might change his tune."

"He won't."

"'Fess up, how did you get him so willing to hang himself out to dry?"

"Just by being my usual charming self," I said demurely.

"Bull. You've got more stuffin' than a Christmas turkey. Why does everything you touch have to be so devious and sneaky?"

"Just lucky, I guess."

"Well, before I lose it and want to wring your lily-white neck, I thank you. I didn't expect such a quick and surprising solution. In fact, I didn't expect you to find anything."

"I didn't either," I admitted.

I sat in the mud and ruminated. I couldn't believe I had only said those words yesterday. It seemed so long ago. I suddenly saw myself driving to the dentist's office for the appointment I had dreaded for weeks. The sun was shining on my left car windows and I was worried about one of my molars. But that had to be wrong, the appointment was for the twenty-fourth, next Tuesday. Yesterday was Thursday the nineteenth. I assumed it was after midnight by now, that was what my internal clock was hinting, so today was Friday, the twentieth.

I decided it was time to look at my watch. It had a luminous dial, so I should be able to see the hands. It was supposed to be waterproof and it had better be because I had paid dearly for the sucker. I lifted my arm out of the water, pulled the elastic cuff back over my watch, and wiped my palm over the glass face. I brought it close to eye level.

I saw the greenish glow of hands and the surrounding numbers. I concentrated on the big hand and saw the dial slip sideways, and for a second I was looking at two dials. They merged long enough for me to see the big hand on four and the small hand on three. I rested for a minute holding my arm above the water. It was twenty after three in the morning. The wind on my hands felt icy. I made an effort to merge the two images of the watch face into one and with concentration saw that one small square had a one, and the other had twenty-five. I pulled the cuff back tight around my wrist and lowered my hands to my lap.

My head was throbbing and I now knew what was causing it. A lump on the head—I had been unconscious and I now had double vision. I had a concussion or at least all the signs of one. Now how in the world did I get concussed? Of course I was pushing away the larger worry. I hadn't lost just a few hours; I had lost five days. The last thing I could remember happened in the early afternoon on Thursday, the nineteenth. My watch was showing me that it was Thursday, early in the morning of the twenty-sixth.

What about the earlier flashes of a bridge and thinking I was falling and the van rolling over? I quit trying to piece together the fragments of memory. It was too taxing and I felt too rotten to care. The water seemed closer to my chin since I first opened my eyes. Was the water rising?

Almost like an answer to my question, the rain slackened. The last few drops raced across my face and the rain and the wind were gone. It was quiet for a few seconds; then the croaking of bullfrogs and the occasional screech of a hoot owl filled the silence. I thought I heard something above the normal sounds of the swamp. I listened. It was the baying of an excited bloodhound. I'd know that sound in my sleep. Help was on its way.

34

It Ain't Over Till it's Over

January 26, Thursday, 3:35 A.M.

There was a glow of light. I heard splashing noises, felt loose mud sliding into the water, and then got a glimpse of two wonderful faces of Bobby Lee. The double image slid back into one, and I saw he was poised to dive.

"Stay! Stay!" I yelled.

His shape disappeared as I heard Jasmine giving him the same command. I could dimly see she had pulled him back from the edge. She hurriedly gave him the command for silence. His victorious baying made it impossible for us to hear each other. I waited.

Four heads appeared at the edge. It seemed they were at least four feet above me. They merged into Jasmine and Bobby Lee. She was clutching his harness. Her flashlight's strong beam blinded me. I closed my eyes and raised a hand to protect them.

"Sorry, oh Lord, it's good to see you alive and breathing!" Jasmine voice cracked with emotion.

"Doctor Livingstone, I presume?" I croaked.

"That's my line." She choked. "Are . . . are you hurt?"

"What's the date!" I demanded.

"It . . . it's almost four in the morning."

"Not the time, the date!"

"It's Thursday, the twenty-sixth," she said. "I've been searching for you since last night at seven. Don't you remem—" She remained silent for too long.

"Remember what? The last thing I remember is talking to Hank over the phone on Thursday afternoon after we finished lunch of soup and crackers! What happened?"

"That can wait for later." She was acting too cheerful. "First we have to get you out of this hole. Are you standing up?"

"Hole?" I was totally bewildered. "Shine the light around and let me see!"

There was nothing wrong with my hearing. She whispered, "Oh my God," while she complied. She sounded scared.

I saw the four walls of mud for the first time. It was about eight feet wide, twelve feet long, and ten feet deep.

"Where am I?" My voice rose with each syllable.

"I don't know," she admitted. "Listen, I'm gonna move the light for just a minute, I have to look around. I'll be right back!"

"No!" I said quickly, "Don't leave me!" After seeing I was in a hole, I couldn't bear her leaving me in the dark.

"I'm only gonna stand," she soothed. "You'll still be able to see the light. I'll shine it around to see if a house is close by."

I could see her silhouette as she shone the light in a circle. I closed my eyes as she passed it over my head.

"I don't see anything," she reported a few seconds later. "A small area has been cleared. Someone must be planning on building a cabin or pulling a trailer out here. Maybe for a hunting camp."

"Start from where I can't remember and give me a capsule version of the past five days," I said, feeling hollow in my gut. Just hunger. It could wait. I wanted some answers.

She knelt, still holding onto Bobby Lee, and kept the light pointed down at the water and shining on the wall of mud on my right. I looked that way so the glare wouldn't blind me.

"Everything was normal until yesterday afternoon when you and Bobby Lee went to the nursing home in Gilsford County. You were coming home on Highway Ninety-four when you called me on the cellular phone." She stopped.

"What did I say?"

"Nothing is ringing a bell?" she asked with anxiety deepening her voice.

"I hit my head somehow. I have a slight concussion. Nothing serious, I guess, I've just got a rotten headache and a lump as big as a grape on my head. Go on."

"You told me over the phone that you had turned off the highway onto Tarver Road and you were gonna release Bobby Lee on the side of the road because Bubba was chasing you—"

"Oh God," I groaned. "Bubba put me here and left me?"

"Yes. I came down Highway Ninety-four from town and turned onto Tarver, coming in behind you. I found Bobby Lee right where you said he'd be."

"Was he still on the edge of the woods?"

"Yes, I slowed down and used the bullhorn to call him. He came out when he heard me calling."

"Wonderful. What happened next?"

"Hank cut into the other end of Tarver from Highway Twenty-seven and found your van at, ah, Tom's Creek Bridge."

"Did I have a wreck?"

"Yes, do you remember it?" She was relieved.

"No. I had a blurred fragment of a memory earlier of falling and turning over and glimpsing the edge of a bridge. I didn't know where it was. I still don't remember."

"When Hank arrived at the bridge you weren't in the van."

"Bubba didn't pass him?"

"No one passed him until he reached me. I was scent-tracking using one of your dirty socks."

"Bubba didn't come back your way?"

"No. I tracked you on the road until he turned off about a mile back from here. The track was overgrown and with the heavy rain the ruts washed out quickly."

"So Bubba hasn't been caught?" It suddenly dawned on me that he was still out there somewhere and still capable of coming back.

"As of thirty minutes ago he hadn't." Jasmine confirmed my fears. "I've got to call Hank and give him directions. He left to search the crossroads for tire tracks turning off Tarver. I'll call him right now!"

"No," I replied sharply, "that can wait. First, did you bring a gun?"

"Don't worry. You told me that you had forgotten yours. I brought mine and yours."

"Great," I whispered. "Now before you get out the phone to call, give me my gun. Did you bring two flashlights?"

"Let me call first, Jo Beth, so Hank can get here faster to help get you out. I don't—"

"Listen." I yelled, "Pay attention! It hurts my head to yell. Bubba must have put me here. He came upon me unexpectedly. This was not planned. He dropped me here because it's his land or he knew about it. He'll be back soon. He knows this is the last chance he'll have for a long, long time to finish me off if he's caught. He'll come back while it's still dark. I want my gun this minute and a flashlight!"

"Don't you think—"

"Dammit, Jasmine, move it, because I can't! I'm sorry I'm yelling but can't you see I'm terrified? It's gonna take some doing to get me out of here, my leg's broken. I feel helpless and need my gun!"

"Sorry, can you catch it?" She was taking off her pack and bending over. She had put the flashlight on the ground, shining my way.

"No, come over behind me on this side. Do you have some rope with you?"

"Full pack," she panted as she ran around to my side of the hole, carrying her pack and leading Bobby Lee.

"Good. Cut off about twelve feet and loop it through the trigger guard. Lower it in front of me. When I have a firm grip, turn loose one end of the rope and pull the other end back to you."

I continued talking while she was preparing the rope. I wanted a plan in place if Bubba walked up or drove up while we were talking.

"If we hear anything, a car motor or if Bubba jumps out from behind a bush, I want you to know instantly what to do so you can act immediately. Run into the woods. If he doesn't see you, fine. If he does, keep on going until you lose him."

"I'll shoot him. I won't leave you and let him hurt you."

"You have to listen, Jasmine. You don't know if you're capable of pulling the trigger. You haven't been tested. Don't risk your life trying to bluff him. He'll keep on coming. I want you to run at the first sign of him! What do you think I'll be doing? I'll have my gun, and I've shot a man before. I know I can pull the trigger. Anyway, you can't shoot him; he's my responsibility. Do you understand me?"

"I won't leave you." She was being stubborn.

"Don't do this to me!" I wailed. "I'm helpless in this damn hole. Do you think I want to sit here and hear him beat you and Bobby Lee to death with a baseball bat? Promise me you'll leave! You're making me feel worse!"

"All right. Calm down. Don't cry. I promise."

All of it wasn't acting. I felt frustrated and a tear eased down one cheek. I was close to tears. Very close.

"I'm lowering the rope. Get ready."

I saw the rope in front of me with the dangling gun. I clutched it with my wet cold hands to my bosom and carefully checked the safety before I unzipped my rescue suit a few inches and placed it tenderly over my left breast inside the suit. I moved one hand so she could slide the rope out.

"Now the flashlight," I called to her.

"You want me to give you the five-cell?"

"No, I want the small one. It has to go inside my suit."

She lowered it tied onto the rope. I picked at knots with one hand while I cradled it with the other. When the rope was loose I pushed the switch and it lit up the area around me. I turned it off and slipped it inside next to the gun. My sweatshirt was bulky and the suit was tight enough that they wouldn't slip. I lowered my hands back in the water to warm them.

"Now get back into the woods with Bobby Lee where you're out of sight and call Hank. I'll breathe easier when you're not standing here."

"As soon as he's on his way, I'm coming back to you."

"Jasmine," I said, starting to cry for real this time, "you're doing it again. Please, please, get the hell out of here so I can rest easy!"

"I'm going right now," she vowed. I heard her trying to get Bobby Lee to leave the edge. Obviously he didn't want to go either.

"Go! Go! Go!" I yelled until I heard Jasmine's voice floating back to me.

"We'll be back soon!"

Suddenly it was quiet and dark again and I was alone. I eased my head back against the wet mud to rest my neck. God, I was tired. With the stress of convincing Jasmine to leave, my headache had been pushed back and almost forgotten. With nothing to do but wait, it came back with a vengeance, along with the agony in my left leg.

I sat there and tuned in to the night sounds. I wanted the earliest warning possible if the bastard really did come back for me. I'd been exaggerating when I was trying to get Jasmine to leave me. At least I hoped to hell I was. Bubba had acted on impulse when he chased me. He pulled me from the van and brought me here because he was hoping to get away from the scene without being spotted. I hoped he was with one of his buddies right now trying to concoct an alibi.

I didn't know if I had crashed on my own. I hadn't had time to hear all the details. If I had, he was home free. It would be my word against his with no witnesses. I couldn't have Jasmine testify in court about my phoning her. It would only be hearsay and Bubba's high-priced lawyer, bought with his father's money, would rip her apart on the stand. He would discredit her testimony by reminding the court of her past. Nineteen arrests for prostitution. They were misdemeanors, not felonies, but that wouldn't help. She also worked for me. The jury would look at her with a jaundiced eye. I couldn't put her through that ordeal, even if it meant letting him walk on this last assault.

If he had hit my van to make me leave the road, and this thought made me feel better, he would be holed up somewhere getting new parts installed. I had a vision of him hovering over some mechanic's shoulder urging him to hurry before Hank found him. I felt safer just knowing that Hank was out there somewhere looking for me. By now, he should be on his way. I began to breathe easier.

I fantasized about a long needle filled with morphine being slipped into my hip. They'd wait ten minutes or so, then gently lift me out of here and I would wake up in a clean dry bed with white sheets. In the morning I would have a nice breakfast. It was the one meal that the hospital didn't mess up too much. There'd be bacon, scrambled eggs, toast, juice, and coffee. I licked my chapped, dry lips. I could almost smell the coffee.

A vehicle door slamming brought me alert and shivering with dread in a heartbeat. I strained to hear. I left the gun and flashlight where they were. If it were Bubba, he would want to taunt me first, give me a vocal preview of what he was going to do to me.

Oh, God, please let it be Hank that leans over the side and puts a light on me. I strained my eyes in the darkness looking for the first hint of light. A few seconds passed. Then I could see a faint glow coming from my right. It got steadily brighter. A dark shape was behind the light. I couldn't see even his feet.

"Who is it?" I called. I couldn't wait another second in suspense.

After an eternity, he answered.

"Hello, bitch. Been thinking about me and my handy bat?"

My heart hammered in my chest.

I put my left hand up to shield my eyes. The light had robbed me of my night vision.

"Who's there?" I said weakly. "I don't know you."

He did what I was praying for. He turned the flashlight on himself so I could see who to expect. With him temporarily blinded by his own light, I reached shakily for my gun, thumbed off the safety, and waited until the two images I was seeing merged into one. I raised the gun and fired.

Epilogue

A few days after my walking cast was removed, I had a visitor. Patricia Ann Newton drove in the courtyard and waited by her car until I went out to her.

"In days of yore they killed the messenger that brought them bad news." She seemed to have it all together.

"I can understand why," I replied politely. "Bad news can be traumatic."

"That's how I felt for the first day or two. Then I realized that you really cared and had tried to warn me. I came for two reasons."

"Which are?" I prompted.

"I want a tour of your kennel and a copy of your wish list."

I gave her both. That is why I was able to tell Granny Rose Richardson, with her perpetual pot of soup, that her larder would always be full, and Miz Cora Pendleton, caretaker of her gentlemen borders, that her table for conversation would always have ample meat for every meal.

Patricia wanted to remain anonymous, so I got to inform them of the trust fund that would deposit a check each and every week as long as they had need of it.

All of us involved still have trouble believing that Bubba gets to walk on this latest assault on me. Hank made the mistake of coming to our pizza party last Friday night. Jasmine and Susan wouldn't let it rest.

"Bubba ran her off a bridge, for God's sake," Susan said with exasperation.

"Jo Beth never saw him. Only caught a glimpse of a red truck as it passed." Hank was patient.

"Surely he pushed her over," Jasmine chided. "Wouldn't there be paint scrapings you could compare?"

"If we had the old parts that had traces of paint from her van we could do that very thing, but when we ran Bubba's truck to the ground over in a garage in Summerville three weeks later the whole front end had been replaced with new factory panels, radiator, chrome bumper, the works. The old parts are probably building an artificial reef out in the Atlantic. Buford Sidden Senior owns some fishing boats that work out of Jacksonville."

"I still don't understand about the bullet. Didn't you ever find it?" Susan asked.

"Jo Beth shot him in the left knee and it shattered his kneecap. When he came in by ambulance to the hospital in Waycross some twenty hours later, there wasn't a bullet in the wound. The doctor won't testify with certainty but he told me confidentially that he believes it was taken out by a doctor or skilled medic before his arrival, but he couldn't medically prove it. My men don't even want to hear the word bullet. They shoveled tons of mud against a screen backdrop for days looking for it out there. They still have the blisters to prove it."

"How he dragged himself to the truck and got clear of the area without being seen still amazes me," Jasmine said.

"Jo Beth couldn't move her leg, and hers was only broken!" Susan said, eyeing me.

"I'm just a weak helpless female," I said, aiming a pillow in her direction.

"Jo Beth wasn't facing another twenty years in the slammer if she got caught out there," Hank said. "It's amazing what you can do with the right incentive. Anyway, she accomplished one good thing. He'll walk again, but it will be with a bad limp and a cane, according to his surgeon. That ought to slow him down some."

"I read in a book once about a prosecutor using 'preponderance of circumstantial evidence' to convict. You know how it goes, how can you explain you just happened to get hurt at the same time after she claims she shot you, how you just happened to replace half your truck because of an unreported accident, how you just happened . . . you see what I mean?" Susan inquired. "Why wouldn't that work?"

Hank sighed. "In a perfect world, and some other county, maybe. But not here and not now. Bobby Don couldn't get a conviction with three ministers and Walter Cronkite as eyewitnesses and the Barracuda isn't interested. Sidden Senior has too much political pull and too much of a say-so about who gets called for jury selection."

"If you believe that, you should do something about it," I told him.

"That's a good idea, this can be your next project to tackle, you prove Bubba's old man is tampering with the jury pool."

"Thanks but no thanks!" I replied with spirit.

Hank threw up his hands. "I rest my case."

"Can't Judge Dalby help you, Jo Beth?" Jasmine asked. "She has before."

I gave a realistic shudder. "It's not healthy to get near Judge Dalby right now. I understand she was expecting to be named to the State Supreme Court by the governor when Chief Justice Burnside died, but a judge from the Third District got the nod. I hear she's really a terror these days."

"If Jo Beth gets her five days of lost memory back and if she remembers seeing Bubba pull her out of the van, then will they prosecute him?" Susan asked Hank.

"If I can get Bobby Don to indict, you bet!" Hank assured her.

I didn't comment. I had regained my memory weeks ago. The reason I hadn't told the others was it was a long shot if we could even get him into court, much less get a conviction. Hank's name was linked too closely with Jasmine's and mine. A win would cost him votes and a loss might keep him from winning his next election.

Also, I had a personal reason. My ego. If we tried and failed, Bubba and his pals would give me the horselaugh. I'd much rather think about Bubba sweating the fact that I might remember than knowing I had remembered and lost. I'd rather be a victim than hurt Hank and Jasmine. He who fights and runs away, lives to fight another day.

After Susan and Hank said good night and departed, I sat Jasmine down for a heart-to-heart talk.

"Have you given some thought to how you feel about continuing on rescue work? Have you had enough time . . . ?"

"I've given it a lot of thought. You and Hank seem to think that I'm doing the job reasonably well, and I've known all along there was nothing I could have done to keep Tom alive, I just needed time to think it through. I took part in finding you when you needed me, and was able to function even though I was terrified. I took pride in that. If you still want me . . ."

"Oh, yes, I want you." I let out a pent-up sigh of relief.

On the second day of April, I was sitting on my back porch having a second cup of coffee. It was Sunday morning and promised to be a beautiful day. It was early and the grass glistened with dew. I could hear the titwits and mockingbirds and songbirds as they warbled and flew among the roses.

In the stillness I heard the fast pitpats of sneakers on Jasmine's apartment stairs. I turned and watched amazed as she came flying around the corner, took the porch steps with one bounce, and came to a screeching halt. Her binoculars were around her neck and her hair wasn't combed. Her eyes were stretched wide and I couldn't read their expression.

"Come quick! You have to see this! Hurry!" She was breathless from running so hard.

I was slow to react. It seemed that all movement had ceased and I was frozen in apathy.

She turned and ran down the porch steps and veered to the left, tossing words over her shoulder.

"It's Bobby Lee. Hurry!"

She said the magic words that unlocked my stupor. I sprang into action, hitting the steps and turning on the speed. She was already past the rose garden and the resident quarters for trainees. I picked them up and put them down, but she ran down a path leading to a small meadow and was quickly out of sight.

When I made the turn and could see the old oak tree that could almost shade an acre, I saw Jasmine leaning against it with her binoculars at her eyes and holding her side and trying to get her breath.

She turned when I raced up to her.

"What is it? Where is he?" I croaked out in short gasps.

"Look!" She pointed to the meadow.

I didn't see them at first. My eyes swept across the meadow. The wild grass was a foot tall and would have to be cut soon. We left it because of the small wildflowers that grew there. Blooms of all color and sizes covered the field. On my second scan I saw Rudy sitting on an old stump washing his face and tidying his shining coat, covered with dew and looking bored.

Then I saw Bobby Lee. He was leaping clear of the ground, turning and twisting in odd dance-like positions. His ears were flapping around his face. He wasn't in distress. He seemed to be playing in the wet grass. I slumped against the ancient oak with relief.

"Jasmine, you just scared the hell out of me, and I bet it took a year off my life! I thought he was hurt."

I took a breath and looked at the pastoral tableau of the flowers, the cat, and the running and jumping dog. We were about a hundred yards away. I turned to Jasmine.

"I'm glad he's feeling better, I've been worried about his strange behavior. Whatever it was—he must be feeling better."

Jasmine gave me the oddest look. "What do you think he's doing?"

"Practicing for dancing around the maypole?" I joked. I looked again and took another guess. "Maybe he's celebrating spring."

"Can't you see?" She spoke with a terrible intensity.

I stared back at Bobby Lee.

"You saw him from your kitchen window with the binoculars. What made you notice?"

"I was looking at the flowers and saw movement, but I couldn't see what he was doing. With the binoculars I could. That's when I came to get you!"

"If I didn't know better, I would swear he was chasing butterflies. Only he can't see them and even if he could there are none around him," I said softly.

"I couldn't see them either until I got the glasses," she said in a small voice.

I turned to look at her. "What?"

Tears of joy were streaming down her face.

"Use the binoculars," she whispered.

I jerked the glasses from her and focused on Bobby Lee. Then I saw the butterflies.